Ice Moon

Jan Costin Wagner

Ice Moon

TRANSLATED
FROM THE GERMAN
BY

John Brownjohn

HARCOURT, INC.
ORLANDO   AUSTIN   NEW YORK
SAN DIEGO   TORONTO   LONDON

www.HarcourtBooks.com

This is a translation of *Eismond*

First published in English in Great Britain by Harvill Secker in 2006

Library of Congress Cataloging-in-Publication Data
Wagner, Jan Costin, 1972–
[Eismond. English]
Ice moon/Jan Costin Wagner; translated from the German
by John Brownjohn.—1st U.S. ed.
p. cm.
1. Serial murderers—Fiction. 2. Police—Fiction.
3. Detective and mystery stories. I. Brownjohn, John. II. Title.
PT2685.A44442E5713 2007
833'.92—dc22 2006033110
ISBN 978-0-15-101269-5

Text set in Berkeley Oldstyle

Printed in the United States of America
First U.S. edition

A C E G I K J H F D B

My special thanks for their valuable assistance go to Niina, Georg Simader, Wolfgang Hörner, Esther Kormann, Renate, and Dietrich.

For Kaisa and Kerttu

PART ONE

I

Kimmo Joentaa was alone with her when she went to sleep. He sat beside her bed in the darkened room, held her hand, and tried to feel her pulse. When he lost it—when he also ceased to hear her breathing softly in and out—he held his own breath and bent over her without moving, so as to regain contact. He relaxed, slumping a little in his chair, when his fingers once more detected the faint throbbing beneath her skin.

He kept looking at the clock because he thought it was over. Without wondering why, he had resolved to note the time of her death. The idea had occurred to him some days ago, while he was sitting on the bench outside her room, staring at the snow-white door beyond which she lay. Rintanen, the physician in charge, had taken him aside before going in to see her, armed with some powerful medication and an encouraging smile, and told him it could be over very soon. Any time now.

He no longer left her. He took his meals beside her bed and spent the nights in a restless doze from which he awoke with a start every minute, afraid of not being with her during the final seconds of her life.

His sleep was an entanglement of gray dreams.

In the days preceding her death she began to tell stories he didn't understand. She told him about images she could see, about a red horse she was riding, and about her travels in the realms of her imagination. Speaking more to herself than to him, she gazed through his eyes into nothingness. Once she asked who he was and what she should call him. "Kimmo," he said, and her lips mouthed the name.

He stroked her hand, listened to her, smiled whenever she smiled, and forbade himself to weep in her presence. Once or twice she asked if he could see her riding the red horse, and he nodded.

In response to his inquiry, Rintanen had explained that these hallucinations were side effects of the medication.

She was in no pain, he said.

Her death occurred at night, three days after Rintanen told him her condition had worsened. The room was dark. He could feel her hand and sense rather than see her eyes and lips. On the point of dozing off, he was jolted awake by a sudden fear that the interval between her breaths would never end. He did what he had often done: held his own breath, bent over her, and remained quite still. He waited for her faint, shallow breathing, for the throb of her feeble pulse against his fingers, but this time there was nothing.

He began to stroke her arm, bending down still further until his cheek brushed her lips. Slowly, he caressed her chill face and rested his head on her lap. Then he sat up and looked at the clock.

It was fourteen minutes past three, and she had gone to sleep.

The thought of the moment of her death and of the minutes thereafter had often exercised his mind and haunted him, and he had striven to shake it off. Half consciously, he had believed, hoped, that her final breath would bring his own life to a standstill. He had sometimes envisioned that he would weep as he had never wept before. That was a comforting thought, for in his mind's eye the tears had overlaid his grief and might even have slowly consumed it.

Now that the moment had come he gave no thought to his preconceived ideas of how it would be. He stroked her hand without being aware of it. His life hadn't come to a standstill and he wasn't weeping. His eyes, his mouth, his lips—all were dry. Later, he couldn't recall having thought of anything at all during the minutes that elapsed before the night nurse came in and he told her that Sanna was dead.

The night nurse turned on the light, went over to Sanna's bed, felt her pulse, and gave him a practiced look of commiseration. He evaded it and saw Sanna, whose face he had earlier sensed in the darkness, glaringly illuminated.

For a moment he thought she was only sleeping.

The nurse went out without speaking to him and returned a few minutes later with Rintanen, whose sympathy seemed genuine. It was Rintanen who had enabled him, in defiance of hospital regulations, to remain with Sanna day and night. He made a mental note to thank him sometime.

Rintanen, too, verified what had already been ascertained. He gave an almost imperceptible nod and stood there for a moment, then gently brushed Sanna's shoulder with his fingertips—a gesture that lodged in Joentaa's memory.

"She really has gone to sleep," he said, and Joentaa knew what he meant. Her face betrayed no pain.

"Would you like to stay with her for a while?" Rintanen asked. Joentaa nodded, although he wasn't sure he wanted to. He tried to analyze his thoughts while the doctor went out into the corridor with the night nurse. He felt he was skating on thin ice. Rintanen and the night nurse were talking in the corridor. He couldn't catch what they said, but he knew it was about Sanna and what was to be done with her. With her dead body.

Sanna doesn't belong to me anymore, he thought.

Looking at her, he felt he could easily have withstood the gaze of her closed eyes. He tried to absorb the fact that she would never look at him again, that he was losing her altogether. He tried to breathe in the lines of her face. After a while, when he sensed that it was no use, he turned away.

His relief at feeling nothing gave way to a fear of being unable to weep, a vague fear that grief would erode him from within before he knew it.

Abruptly, on impulse, he stood up. He lifted her body and clasped it to him, kissed her lips, her neck, gently bit her throat, her shoulders. Then he laid her down and covered her over.

He turned out the light, left the room without looking back, and strode swiftly along the corridor. Once in the car he started to think. He sensed that something lay ahead and knew it would be something beyond his ken. He dreaded it, but was waiting for it, yearning for it. He wanted to be at home when it burst upon him.

He drove in the direction of Angelniemi, parked in the driveway, and walked down to the lake that glittered among the dark trees. The rickety dock gave under his weight, and he felt as if he were being dragged down into the black water.

He had planned to install a new dock in the summer, but she'd said she liked everything the way it was. He recalled her words and the warmth in her voice. She had been sitting where he was standing now. He saw again her smile, her pale face, and felt the fear that had taken his breath away when he looked at her.

He had reached his destination, he knew. Removing his shoes, he immersed his feet in the water. He inhaled the cool breeze and noted with relief that the chill of the water was spreading upward from his legs. He waited for the freezing sensation to permeate his body. Then he sank down, lay flat on his back, and closed his eyes. He saw her astride a red horse with her long, fair hair streaming out behind. He waited for the horse to break into a gallop, waited for her to laugh and shout something to him, waited until she rode swiftly toward him, happy, calling out . . . Then, at last, he stretched out his arms to her and embraced the pain, the deep, stabbing pain, that would never leave him again.

2

The piano tuner waited until he felt that all was quiet, then struck a note and inhaled the harsh, discordant sound. Shutting his eyes, he saw it stand out bright yellow against the black background of his thoughts. A yellow circle, a dazzling full moon that dwindled and disappeared as the note receded into the womb of silence.

He opened his eyes and looked up into the face of Mrs. Ojaranta, who had brought him a coffee and asked if he was getting on all right. He nodded and did his best to smile.

Floating in the cup she handed him was a dazzling yellow moon.

He hoped that Mrs. Ojaranta would leave him alone, but she sat down and started talking. She asked what he thought of the piano, told him it was a quarter of a century old and inherited from her parents.

She had told him the same thing the day before.

He saw her words trickle slowly to the floor.

It was a good piano, he said, a very good one, and she nodded and smiled, content with his answer. She herself wasn't musical, she said, but her sister played extremely well and would be pleased the next time she came to stay.

He sipped his coffee, enjoying the heat, the pain, on his tongue. He took a big mouthful, hoping to choke on the full moon, but he gulped it down.

The sun was shining through the French windows that led to the terrace; he could see specks of dust swirling above the keyboard. He forbore to tell Mrs. Ojaranta that her instrument was past tuning. What a glorious summer it was, she said. Looking into her eyes, he thought he detected a yearning for perpetual sunlight.

Outside, the pale blue sky overlooked a green lawn.

Mrs. Ojaranta smiled, rose, and wished him success. He watched her until she disappeared from his field of vision, then struck the note again, gently this time, and waited for the vibrations of the discordant sound to fade away to nothing.

He tried to imagine what it was like, submerging oneself in no-man's-land, but it was no use. He sat there for some minutes, then got up and went over to the French windows, which were open. Mrs. Ojaranta was watering some flowers in the garden. Her practiced movements had a fluid, casual quality.

He felt sure she wasn't thinking.

She bent down and pulled some weeds from the damp soil. He

watched her working for a while. She was wearing a white bikini over her pale skin. He inhaled the image, shut his eyes, opened them, and saw her die.

He saw a rapid succession of images in which she burned to death in crisp chiaroscuro and glaring colors.

The sun was red and orange and very hot.

He turned and retreated to the shadowy part of the room, which he found agreeably cool. Then he started walking. He drifted slowly down the long passage into the big, bright bedroom with its wide wooden bed, white sheets, white blankets and pillows, soft and cold. Gingerly, he ran his hands over them.

Hanging on the wall in the passage was a painting he liked, an ill-defined landscape in which everything merged: a lake with a mountain, the sky with the moon.

He looked at the picture for a long time.

Then he went downstairs to the cellar. He distinctly felt the onset of cold and darkness. The washing machine was working in the laundry and some clothes were hanging on the line. Water was dripping on the floor.

He drew the moist, muggy air into his lungs.

The sauna, which was scrupulously clean, smelled of damp wood and shower gel. It was still warm in there, and a red towel was lying on the upper bench. He pictured Mrs. Ojaranta stretched out on it a few minutes earlier.

Beside the sauna he found a large wine cellar. He resisted the impulse to smash a bottle and swallow it—wine, broken glass, and all.

He went back upstairs. His tread became heavy and the moon that was devouring his thoughts grew bigger and more sculptural.

Some keys were hanging on a board in the hall. He removed several of them and looked without haste for the one to the front door. He soon found the key and put it in his pocket.

He inhaled the scent of power.

Running his fingers over the backs of the books in the elegantly furnished living room, he came across a shiny, new, almost mint edition of the *Kalevala* epic. He saw Mrs. Ojaranta through the open French windows. She was standing in the sunshine with her back to him.

He took the book from the shelf, leafed deliberately through the 49th Song, and read how Ilmarinen, the divine smith, had forged a golden moon and a silver sun . . .

He replaced the book on the shelf, looked outside, and caught Mrs. Ojaranta's eye. She was smiling at him. "You're welcome," she called. She came back into the shadowy room, mopping her brow.

He saw the beads of sweat on her cheeks.

"I've finished," he said mechanically, and her face brightened further. She went over to the piano and struck a note. It sounded much better, much clearer, she said. He nodded, happy in the knowledge that the note was just as out of tune as ever. She said he'd done a good job and he thanked her.

He felt the shadow over them sink lower, unable to see more than the outlines of her face.

The fear was imminent now.

Mrs. Ojaranta gave him some money. He said goodbye and reluctantly made his way outside. The road ahead was melting before his eyes, but beside him it was gray and hard. He trod carefully until he was sure he wouldn't sink. He walked over to his car in the lukewarm breeze and put the purloined key in the glove compartment. The key felt cold and small, and he was afraid its magic had already been extinguished. He resolved to forget it until tonight—to forget it as completely as if it didn't exist.

It turned cool while he was driving. The sun looked pale red, wine red, the color he liked least, his signal that the tide of fear was nearing its zenith.

He pulled up in a parking area. Seated at a wooden table were some vacationers, a young couple with two small children. They were talking in a language he didn't understand. They were eating and drinking and he saw them die. The wine red image turned blue and gray and cold as ice. He concentrated hard, though he strove not to watch the children's short-lived death throes.

The image faded after a minute or two. The children kicked a plastic ball around, the couple packed up the remains of their meal.

He sat back and closed his eyes. He wanted to sleep for a long time and hoped that his wish would be fulfilled.

He knew now that he wasn't himself, and the thought soothed him. He started to gain a clear mental picture of the next few hours and sensed that the knowledge of the key in the glove compartment was lending him strength.

Confident now, he felt that all was normal, all was right and inevitable.

Just before he fell asleep he was relieved to note the advent of the unconsciousness that would deaden his fear before he conquered it during the night.

3

Kimmo Joentaa was lying on the dock. He stretched out his arms and legs and tried not to move, tried to do nothing and be nothing.

Dawn broke at some point. He observed its changing colors for the first time in his life. Black became gray and gray became pale gray, dark blue and pale blue in turn. It grew lighter, quickly and seamlessly, and although he felt a compulsion to watch closely, he missed the moment when the threshold between dark and light was crossed.

It was a fine, cold morning.

When the spectacle ended he thought how much Sanna would have enjoyed lying here beside him. Some children in a red rowboat were paddling out across the lake from the neighboring property on his right. He gazed after them until the image became blurred and their exuberant cries faded.

He shut his eyes and saw Sanna sitting, laughing, aboard a gray rowboat on gray water. He tried to picture the boat as red and the water as blue, but it was no use. The more he tried, the paler the image grew. After a while it vanished altogether and he fell asleep just as he was thinking he would never be able to sleep again.

He slept badly, forever hovering near the surface, and was awakened by something cold on his face. He sat up with a start and let out an instinctive cry. The three boys in the red rowboat were sitting nearby, staring at him wide-eyed. Was everything all right, one of them asked. Joentaa nodded and apologized.

"I must have fallen asleep," he said.

"We thought something might be wrong," said Roope, the son of the young woman who lived in the house next door. "The way you were lying . . . It looked funny somehow."

"I'm fine," said Joentaa. He got to his feet. "Still, thanks for checking on me." He took off his jacket, which was creased and dusty. "School vacation?" he asked for something to say.

"Another two weeks," one of the boys replied.

Joentaa nodded, turned away, and climbed the slope to his car. The key was in the ignition. He took it out and stumbled up the three steps to his front door. He noticed while unlocking it that the day was very hot. He had obviously slept for quite a while. In the kitchen he looked at the clock. It was a quarter past eleven. The plates in the sink were green with mold because he'd spent the past week almost entirely at the hospital, returning home only to change his clothes.

On one occasion Sanna had asked him to bring her some old snapshots. Photos of Lahti, where they'd met six years ago while watching a cross-country ski race. He'd hardly recognized himself in them, and she'd laughed when he got worked up over his shoulder-length hair and blue peaked cap. He looked absurd, he said, but she told him she'd particularly liked his hair that way. "Who knows, maybe I wouldn't have taken you on without that hair, not to mention the cap."

He remembered how she'd smiled and squeezed his hand. The next day she started to hallucinate, more and more often asking who he was and where she was.

He filled the sink with hot water, dunked the plates in it, and proceeded to open every window in the house. Lying on the glass-topped table in the living room was the fashion magazine Sanna had been reading that last day. Their bed was unmade. The bedclothes were trailing on the floor.

He recalled the night she'd woken him and said she thought she ought to go to the hospital because the pain had become unbearable. She was on the verge of tears, he could tell, but she didn't weep, just forced herself to smile, and he suddenly knew for sure that she would die before long—that the doctors were right and her case was hope-less. During the drive to the hospital she'd sat quietly beside him, choking back the pain.

He'd felt he was driving into a total void.

In the living room he opened the doors to the terrace, perched on the arm of the sofa, and reflected that the void was really there now, final and all-embracing. He sat for a while, then went to the kitchen and ran himself a glass of water. As he raised it to his lips he noticed that his hands were trembling. He put the glass down, laid his hands flat on the table, and braced the muscles and tendons to suppress the tremor.

Through the kitchen window he caught sight of Pasi and Liisa Laaksonen, the elderly couple who lived nearby. They were walking down to the lake, as they did every day at this hour. Pasi was carrying his fishing rod over his shoulder, Liisa the pale brown basket for the fish her husband regularly yanked from the water with astonishing ease. They saw him standing at the window and waved. He didn't respond.

He looked down and watched the beads of air bursting in the tumbler. His stomach was slowly pervaded by a numb sensation that expanded until his entire body felt anesthetized.

After a while he went to the telephone in the living room and dialed the number of Merja and Jussi Sihvonen, Sanna's parents. He stopped short before keying in the final digit, put the receiver down, and drew a deep breath.

Sanna's parents had visited her the day before her death, promising to return the following weekend. He recalled Merja's loving, weary expression as she looked at her daughter and Jussi's futile attempts to be cheerful. They lived near Helsinki, some two hours' drive from Turku. It had puzzled Joentaa at first, their failure to take time off in recent weeks and spend it all with their daughter. Then it gradually dawned on him that they were either unable or unwilling to grasp how ill Sanna was.

Jussi Sihvonen, in particular, had refused from the outset to accept that his daughter's illness was an established fact. At first he persisted in speaking of a faulty diagnosis, criticizing the doctors and the whole public health system in turn. It was inconceivable that Sanna had Hodgkin's disease—indeed, he said, it was a statistical impossibility. Only men developed that disease, he'd made inquiries. Later, when Sanna's condition deteriorated and the effects of chemotherapy rendered the disease visible, he was all enforced jollity, whereas Merja held Sanna's hand and talked to her encouragingly with a lethargic smile. Joentaa had more than once been annoyed with Sanna's father, but now, when he thought of Merja and Jussi, of their horror and their hopeless attempts to cope with the disaster, all he felt was profound sadness.

He paused for a moment, then dialed again. His stomach contracted when he heard Merja's hoarse, tired voice at the other end of the line.

"Kimmo here," he said.

"Kimmo, I'm glad you called," she said quietly. "How is she?"

"Merja . . . It's over . . . She fell asleep last night." He had meant to utter the words calmly and distinctly, but his voice broke halfway through. Several seconds went by. Merja said nothing, and the words he'd just spoken resonated in his head.

"She wasn't in any pain," he said when the silence dragged on.

"But we meant to come this weekend, you know we did," cried Merja. And, while he was groping for something anodyne and

– 13 –

comforting to say, she let out a wail and burst into tears. Joentaa heard Jussi's voice, faint at first, then right in his ear.

"What's wrong, Kimmo?" he demanded feverishly, and Joentaa repeated what he'd said to Merja. Again his voice broke, and again the unreal-sounding words echoed like waves breaking in his head. Jussi remained silent, but Joentaa seemed to sense his dismay even at that distance.

Sanna's mother was sobbing convulsively in the background. "You must see to Merja now," Joentaa said, but Jussi's silence persisted.

"Last night . . ." he said after a while, very slowly. "Last night, you said . . ."

"Just after three o'clock last night," Joentaa replied.

"This is bad news," Jussi said, more to himself than to Joentaa. "Very bad news . . ."

"You must see to Merja now," Joentaa repeated. "I'll call you again this evening."

"Please do, Kimmo," said Jussi, but Joentaa still felt his father-in-law wasn't taking anything in and didn't seem to have grasped what had happened.

"Till tonight, Jussi," he said. Sanna's father made no reply, so he cautiously hung up. Gazing through the open French windows, he heard children's distant shouts and laughter and the sound of splashing.

Perhaps it was the three boys in the rowboat, who would long since have forgotten their morning encounter with him and his curious behavior. He tried to imagine how Merja and Jussi Sihvonen would cope with the shock and hoped that Jussi would have the presence of mind to summon a doctor for Merja. He briefly considered calling them again, but dismissed the idea. It relieved him to have got the call over so quickly.

He went out onto the terrace and leaned against the chaise longue on which Sanna had for months spent her afternoons cocooned in woolen blankets. She had insisted on her right to sit outside, even in April, and indignantly brushed aside his objection that it was too cold by simply proclaiming it springtime. It had remained cold, one of the coldest summers he could remember, and she'd died during the night that preceded the first really warm summer's day.

He recalled the moment when the nurse turned on the light and he saw Sanna's face. She'd looked just as she had on the many nights he'd watched her while she slept.

Despite himself, he began to imagine that she really had been asleep, that she'd awakened long ago and wondered where he was. He knew it was a mistaken idea—sensed that it was dangerous and tried to shake it off, but he failed. The notion tormented him, yet it simultaneously alleviated the dull ache.

He straightened up, went to get his car key, and drove to the hospital.

During the drive he had a vision of Sanna smiling at him when he opened the door to her room. The image had almost faded by the time he reached the hospital and got out of the car, but he strove to preserve it as he entered the massive white building and took the elevator to the second floor. He made swiftly for the room in which Sanna had lain, but her bed was now occupied by an old woman who looked at him inquiringly when he burst in. He turned and walked back along the corridor, asked a helpful young male nurse for Rintanen, and was informed that the doctor had a day off.

"I'm looking for my wife," he said. "Sanna Joentaa. She was in Room 21 until yesterday."

The nurse looked disconcerted. "I was, er, under the impression that she died during the night," he said.

"I'm aware of that," Joentaa replied curtly. "I want to know where she is. I'd like to see her."

"I don't know if . . . if that's possible," said the young man, looking around helplessly. "I'll ask. Just a moment." He turned and walked off in the direction of the nurses' room. Joentaa watched him go. Before long he was approached by a sturdy-looking nurse not unlike the one who had shown no emotion as she stood beside Sanna's bed during the night. She looked him straight in the eye.

"Your wife's in cold storage," she said bluntly. "It isn't customary, but you may see her if you wish."

"I'd like to," he said.

She gave him a searching look, then with a jerk of the head signaled to him to follow. They took the elevator to the basement. Joentaa stared at the wall as they glided downward. The nurse strode briskly on ahead. She conducted him into a room that was smaller than he'd expected.

Sanna was lying on a gurney against the wall, her body covered with a pale green sheet. The nurse went over to the gurney and glanced at him before she lifted the sheet.

He endured the sight for only a moment. Sanna's face looked bloated and discolored. It wasn't her face, but he recognized her nonetheless.

He instinctively turned away and heard himself utter a cry, felt himself sinking to the floor. Out of the corner of his eye he saw the nurse give a start and hurry over to him. "It's all right," he said as she tried to help him up. Shaking her off, he walked unsteadily to the door, then hurried along the corridor and up the stairs. She called after him, but he wouldn't listen.

Once outside in the big forecourt, he stood there taking deep breaths. He was sweating. Two young women sitting on a bench eyed him covertly and giggled.

While driving home he tried to convince himself that Sanna was dead, and that this fact would govern his life from now on.

Pasi and Liisa Laaksonen waved to him in the distance when he got out of the car. He pretended not to see them and hurried into the house. He leaned back against the door and closed his eyes, striving to think of nothing and feel nothing.

He gave a start when the doorbell rang. Through the kitchen window he saw Pasi and Liisa standing on the steps, Liisa expectantly swinging her wooden basket.

He went to the door and opened it.

"Surprise, surprise!" Liisa called, holding up the basketful of dead fish.

"They were biting very well today," Pasi said, and Joentaa saw the pride in his eyes. "We thought we'd pass by and bring you some more . . . Your wife is always so—"

"Many thanks," said Joentaa.

Pasi handed him two trout on a carefully folded sheet of silver foil. Joentaa said, "Sanna died last night."

They stared at him, and he could see the news slowly percolating their consciousness. A long silence ensued.

"But Kimmo, that's . . . terrible," Liisa said eventually. Pasi nodded with his mouth open.

Joentaa felt he ought to say something, but he didn't know what. He turned away. "See you soon," he said before shutting the door.

4

L ate that afternoon Joentaa drove to Lenganiemi.

The nurse had called from the hospital to remind him that he must make arrangements for the burial. When he heard her deep, unyielding voice he involuntarily saw the gurney on which Sanna had been lying, and her bluish, discolored face. "If you'd like us to," the nurse said, "we can engage an undertaker."

Joentaa hastily replied that he would fix everything himself. He thanked her for calling and terminated the conversation.

An undertaker . . . He hadn't thought of that, even though it had all been arranged. Sanna had planned her own funeral at a time when he was still incapable of contemplating her death.

She had broached the subject several months ago, on a cool day in early spring. Seated on the dock with her feet dangling in the water, she told him she wanted to be buried at Lenganiemi, in the little seaside graveyard near the red wooden church. She said she could picture the spot exactly in her mind's eye—she'd memorized it.

He didn't understand at first. They had paid only one visit to the peninsula on the outskirts of Turku, and that was years ago. "I picked the spot when I was still in good health," she explained when she saw his puzzled expression.

With bewilderment and mounting annoyance, he asked why she hadn't told him at the time. Why was she thinking about death instead of concentrating on beating the disease?

He got no answer. The glint in her eye told him that she disapproved of his reaction, and he promptly regretted his anger. He came up behind her and clasped her to him. She resisted briefly, then returned his embrace and proceeded to talk about their trip to Lenganiemi, which he had almost forgotten. All he could remember was that it had been enjoyable—too enjoyable to merit a place in the present, depressing situation. He had privately refused to listen and felt relieved when Sanna's flow of words gradually subsided.

She hadn't made any further reference to her death for a long time after that. As for him, he'd avoided the subject, partly out of fear and partly because—to the very end, and even when he knew it was self-deceptive—he'd persuaded himself that there *was* still hope, and that she could win the battle if only she shook off the thought of death.

Some weeks ago, not long before her condition worsened so obviously that Joentaa requested long-term compassionate leave, she'd told him that it was all arranged. Her words took a moment to sink in.

It wasn't quite the place she'd wanted, she said, but it lay between the church and the sea.

Slowly recovering from his surprise, he asked why she hadn't told him earlier. She smiled, gave him a hug, and left the question in the air. Later she said she'd spoken to the pastor, and she told Joentaa to get in touch with him when she died.

He started to say something, but she sealed his lips with a forefinger.

He drove to Lenganiemi after receiving the phone call from the hospital. While taking the ferry he had a vague recollection of the day he'd spent there with Sanna. It had been far colder then, a day in autumn or winter.

As he drove up the lane he was surprised to find that he knew exactly which direction to take. After a while he sighted the church, its bright-red paintwork silhouetted against the pale-blue sky. He parked on the sandy forecourt and made slowly for the rows of graves in the shade of the trees.

Two women, one elderly and one middle-aged, were coming toward him. The older woman was leaning on the younger and talking wildly, the younger woman trying to calm her. He said good afternoon as they passed, but they didn't acknowledge him.

He accosted a sexton who was watering some flowers on a grave and asked him the way to the parsonage. "Right beside the church," the man told him, pointing in the direction he meant. Joentaa thanked him and had already taken a few steps when the man called after him. "If you're looking for the pastor, he's in church. Choir practice . . ."

Joentaa thanked him again. When he opened the church door he heard some children singing softly. He sat down in a pew at the back and tried to listen. After a few minutes he began to feel very cold. He got up and was about to go outside when the pastor brought choir practice to an end.

"Many thanks, that'll do for today," he said with a smile, collecting the hymn books. The children scampered past Joentaa and out into the open air. Slowly, he made his way up the aisle. The pastor was stacking the hymnals with care and blowing out the candles.

"Excuse me," Joentaa said. The pastor turned and looked him in the face. Joentaa was struck by the mischievous light in his eyes, which darted restlessly to and fro.

"Yes?" said the pastor.

"My name is Joentaa. My wife . . . Sanna Joentaa—"

"Of course, I remember," the pastor broke in, then paused for a moment. "Has she passed on?"

Joentaa nodded.

"I'm very sorry. Your wife spoke with me on two occasions. She said she liked Lenganiemi very much. She thought it nice that the graveyard was beside the sea." He inserted another pause. "Come with me," he said, leading the way outside with short little steps. "Your wife impressed me," he called over his shoulder as they emerged into the brilliant sunlight, "she had to clear a number of bureaucratic hurdles in order to obtain the two plots. It's a very small graveyard."

He halted in front of a rectangular patch of grass.

Two plots . . . Sanna had thought of everything—she always did, once she'd made up her mind about something. Joentaa stared at the place she'd fought for. He felt dizzy. The pastor was speaking to him, but all he heard were echoing sounds. "Mr. Joentaa . . ."

"I'm sorry," he said.

"When did she die?"

"Last night."

The pastor nodded. "I liked your wife. She was . . . a very strong person. I think she had truly accepted her death. I've known many people who were dying, but I've seldom encountered that." He seemed to deliberate. "Are you a believer?" he asked.

Joentaa was thrown by the question.

"Sorry, I didn't mean to embarrass you. Your wife told me she wasn't a believer—at least, she didn't subscribe to any formal religion. That surprised me . . ." He fell silent for a while. Then he squared his shoulders and gripped Joentaa's hand. "I wish you the strength your wife possessed," he said. Joentaa looked up to see that the pastor was smiling, which intrigued him.

The pastor gave him a nod and walked off. Joentaa watched him until he disappeared into the church. After standing there for a moment or two, he made slowly for the slope overlooking the sea and sat down on a rickety wooden bench at the edge of the cliff.

A motorboat was cleaving the calm surface. The noise of its engine gradually faded. The car ferry made its leisurely way toward the opposite shore.

Thinking back on the pastor's smile, he construed it as the expression of a faith in God which he himself had never been able to comprehend. A faith in God that cushioned grief because it refused to acknowledge the horrific nature of death: because it denied its finality.

But Sanna's death was final.

He strove to accept the fact that she'd planned her death without involving him, but it was hard. Against his will, he persuaded himself that she'd deceived him while simultaneously trying to grasp that her behavior had betrayed sympathy and affection. Sanna had presented him with an accomplished fact because she'd known, ever since their conversation early that year, how unbearably great his fear of her death had been.

At the thought that she, who was seriously ill, had wanted to spare him, who was in good health, the pain dissolved. He began to weep and talk to himself aloud. He accused himself of having failed her— of having left her alone with her own fear of death because he'd desperately, obstinately, clung to the mistaken hope that she might survive.

Then his mood changed, and he told himself that Sanna had deliberately plunged him into this inner conflict—that she'd wanted to torment him from beyond the grave.

That thought disappeared as quickly as it had come. He failed to understand how he could have entertained it, but the fear that he would never entirely fathom what she'd done persisted.

He tried to imagine what would happen tomorrow, but tomorrow was a blank.

As he was walking back to his car along the narrow gravel path, the sexton looked up at the sun and called out what a glorious day it was.

5

His wish had been fulfilled: he'd had a good long sleep. It was still light when he awoke, but the sun was already low in the sky. He started the car and drove down to the sea to watch the sun set.

The beach was still crowded. He sat down on a secluded bench and saw the red fireball hovering just above the trees on the island opposite.

He tried to visualize what Mrs. Ojaranta was doing at this moment, but his mental picture frame remained empty. The sun slowly disappeared behind the trees. He bowed his head, shut his eyes, and heard it sink, hissing and bubbling, into the water. When he looked up again the sea was already aflame and the people had disappeared.

He walked slowly to the water's edge. When he got there he took off his clothes.

The cold red sparks pricked his skin.

There was a huge moon on the horizon.

He leapt high in the air and dived into the searing, freezing fire. When he surfaced he knew he would live forever.

He swam to the shore, which lay in shadow, and got dressed. Then he walked back to his car. Black abysses yawned behind and beside him, but he made his way like a sleepwalker along the narrow path that lay beyond the darkness.

He got into the car and drove toward the moon, which was sinking down on him. Having parked in a side street, he took the key from the glove compartment and made his way to the house. He approached it from the rear and climbed over the wall into the garden. Going nearer, he saw Mrs. Ojaranta sitting on the sofa in her living room. The television was flickering. She was obviously alone.

He enjoyed watching her unobserved, and was relieved to feel no impatience. The living room was bathed in a warm glow. The thought that he would soon leave the cold darkness and enter that glow excited and reassured him. He bowed his head and concentrated on the frisson that was slowly traveling down his back.

When he looked up, Mrs. Ojaranta was coming toward him. He had a momentary fear that she'd spotted him. He gasped with fright and was about to run off when she went to the telephone and picked up the receiver. He saw her lips shape the sound of her name.

She was right beside the French windows, leaning against the glass only a few yards away. He took a step back. Her face brightened and she uttered an exclamation, evidently pleased that someone had called her. She listened awhile and laughed. Her absent gaze was directed straight at his eyes, but she couldn't see him in the darkness.

He took another step back, annoyed at his fear and his stupid urge to run away.

He was invisible and invulnerable. It was important—no, essential—to grasp that.

Mrs. Ojaranta shook her head, rolled her eyes, giggled, said something. The conversation went on for a long time. His idea, his desire, became crystallized into utter certainty as he watched her. When she smilingly replaced the receiver and went back to the sofa, he knew he would cross the frontier this time. He now felt quite sure that it would be simple—simpler than anything he'd ever done before.

Mrs. Ojaranta turned off the television and the living-room lights. He gave a start, the onset of darkness was so abrupt. Deprived of the golden glow, the building of which he intended to take possession looked forbidding and insignificant. He gripped the key in his jacket pocket tightly, but his self-assurance proved hard to regain.

He left the terrace and walked back into the garden until he could survey the whole house. He stared at the window behind which the bedroom must lie. He had memorized clearly the layout of the rooms.

Moments later the bedroom light came on. Going closer, he saw Mrs. Ojaranta silhouetted against the curtains, which were drawn. He saw her remove her clothes and put on a nightdress. Then the light went out. He gasped, feeling his excitement mount, but his fear returned too. His fear of failing to accomplish the great task ahead.

His fear of failing to gain release.

He waited for a while, but the darkness persisted. He seemed to sense that she was asleep.

He circled the house at a safe distance to satisfy himself that no one could see him from the road or the neighboring properties. Then, with head erect, he slowly made for the front of the house. While doing so he put on a pair of gloves. His self-confidence was returning—he was beginning to feel weightless and could sense a smile on his face. By the time he inserted the key in the lock and started to turn it, he had at last become all that he wanted and needed to be to accomplish his task.

Quietly opening the door, he saw the outlines of his face in the large hall mirror. His smile startled and reassured him.

He didn't recognize himself.

He could sense the glare of the moonlight on his back. Quickly, he shut the door and stood there in the gloom. Inhaling the stillness, he made his way along the passage and into the living room. He resisted a strong desire to flood it with golden light. He groped his way along the wall to the piano, removed the red cloth, and ran his fingers lightly over the keys. It seemed years since he'd sat there and spoken with Mrs. Ojaranta.

His eyes were becoming used to the darkness. He walked slowly along the passage and down the stairs to the wine cellar. The door was locked, but the key was there. His stomach churned with pleasurable pain to think that Mrs. Ojaranta had intended to guard against any burglars who tried to enter her home through the wine-cellar window.

He took a bottle from one of the racks and went back upstairs. He paused briefly outside the bedroom door. It was ajar. Going closer, he thought he could very faintly hear her regular breathing.

In the kitchen he opened the bottle and took a glass from one of the cupboards. Then he sat on the sofa in the living room and concentrated on the bitter, felty flavor of the wine, trying to breathe as evenly as Mrs. Ojaranta.

It was good to know that everything belonged to him—everything he wanted.

It was good to be a part of the darkness.

He waited until he stopped thinking.

Then he got up and made for the bedroom, taking long strides. Outside the door he paused and drew several deep breaths. He sensed that he must act fast, so fast that he wouldn't realize what was happening. If he acted fast it would be simple.

Cautiously, he pushed the door open and entered the room. When he reached the bed he stood looking down at her. She was lying in a slightly contorted position, hugging the pillow and breathing shallowly. He wondered what she was dreaming of and tried to inhale the power of it, but he failed because his fear had returned and was holding him tight.

He couldn't afford to be afraid. If he was afraid it would all be pointless.

To accomplish his task he would have to be as quick and unerring as a puff of wind extinguishing a candle flame.

He bent down and picked up the pillow that lay beside her. He felt her gentle breathing fan his neck and dug his fingers into the pillow. He thought of running away, of forgetting the whole thing, of diving into the darkness undetected, but that was impossible.

He shut his eyes and clamped the pillow to her face. He was relieved to encounter so little resistance, just a slight tensing of the body and some smothered cries of no significance. When he was sure it was over he let go. He was trembling.

He avoided looking at her again.

In the living room he turned on the golden light. He removed his gloves, sat down at the piano, and played the tune he liked best, a simple melody that always cleared his head.

He floated across the gentle notes into no-man's-land.

After a while he stood up, wiped off his fingerprints, and turned out the light. In the passage he removed the ill-defined landscape from the wall.

Then he went outside. It was very cold. He stood at the foot of the hill he had to climb in order to be nothing anymore—nothing and everything. He groaned softly at the thought that beyond the hill death ended and his life began.

He climbed, slowly at first, then faster. When he neared the summit he vented his elation in a cry.

And then he was in the void.

When he saw the color nobody knew, he began to weep. He was safe for evermore.

6

It was half past seven when Kimmo Joentaa entered the big police building in central Turku. He took the elevator to the third floor. Two uniformed colleagues, who had been on night duty, were leaving just as he walked into his office. They said a casual hello, obviously too tired to notice that he shouldn't have been there at all. He nodded to them and proceeded to skim through the neat stack of files on Ketola's desk.

He was tired too, and no wonder, after failing to get to sleep all night. He had lain on the living-room sofa and stared into the darkness. In the early hours he'd briefly lapsed into a kind of doze. When he awoke from it he'd turned over and reached for Sanna's arm.

It had taken him a second or two to grasp that she wasn't there.

He had got dressed and driven into Turku without debating whether or not it was the right thing to do.

The files on Ketola's desk contained some clumsily worded reports of an attempt on the life of a senior local politician who had been shot in Turku's marketplace the week before. Joentaa had registered this with indifference because Sanna was then his sole concern.

The incident had been much discussed in the hospital canteen. The would-be assassin was still unidentified. Witnesses claimed to have seen a nondescript little man armed with a pistol board a bus which drove off unimpeded. Although the bullet had only grazed Sami Järvi, the politician in question, attempts to assassinate public figures were so rare in Finland that even this scratch had become a nationwide topic of conversation.

Joentaa surmised that Ketola was snowed under with work and even tetchier than usual. He looked at his watch. Ketola would enter the office precisely six minutes from now, on the dot of eight. He would be in a foul mood but a model of self-discipline. Although he might beef about his life and the people he had to contend with, he made every effort to do a good job.

Joentaa had always respected Ketola but never liked him. For a time he'd even considered putting in for a transfer, but Sanna had dissuaded him. His addiction to harmonious personal relations was almost unbearable, she said with a wry smile, but she couldn't believe that anyone who had fought so hard to get into the CID would throw in the towel after a few harsh words from his boss. Although annoyed with her, Joentaa had known she was right.

He wondered, as he flicked idly through the files, why he had joined the police force in the first place. Why had he completed his training as quickly as the most ambitious careerist and done his utmost to obtain an immediate appointment to the CID?

When friends asked him, sometimes with amusement, what underlay his choice of profession, he usually replied offhand that he didn't know himself. It was better to say nothing at all than admit what he now considered to be the embarrassing truth: that he'd chosen his profession in the vague hope of combating evil on the side of the good guys.

He was examining a portrait photograph of the politician who had been shot when Ketola walked in, punctual to the minute and firmly convinced, no doubt, that he would be the first to arrive and the last to leave.

Ketola paused in the doorway and stared at Joentaa inquiringly. "What are you doing here, Kimmo?" he said after a moment, and Joentaa seemed to sense more annoyance than interest in his tone. "You're on leave."

It was only now, when he was confronted with the situation, that

Joentaa guessed how many similar-sounding questions he would be asked and how difficult it would be to answer them all.

He forced himself to speak calmly. "I'm back now. Sanna . . . died yesterday."

Ketola stood there without moving. He was wearing one of his smart, uniformlike jackets, a dark green one. For a moment Joentaa thought he detected genuine dismay in his eyes, but Ketola quickly recovered himself. "I'm sorry, Kimmo," he said. He came to life with a jerk and went over to his desk without looking at Joentaa. He put down his briefcase, leaned on the desktop with both hands, and seemed to be debating what to say next.

"I'm not sure you'll be much help to us in your present state," he said eventually, and Joentaa winced under the impact of the words. "Don't get me wrong, Kimmo, but I know how you must be feeling, and I consider it advisable for you to prolong your leave."

Joentaa was too taken aback to reply at once. He tried to resist the impulse, but just as he had the day before, with Pasi and Liisa Laaksonen, he was beginning to assess people's reactions to the news of Sanna's death. He was shocked by his departmental chief's detached manner and the way in which he had acknowledged Sanna's death in one brief sentence. As for his advice to go home, it surprised and puzzled him.

"I don't think you can know how I'm feeling," he said after a while, "and I'd like to get back to work right away." He was disconcerted by his own blunt tone and thought he glimpsed a momentary flash of anger in Ketola's eyes. Then the craggy face stiffened and he gave a curt nod.

"As you wish. It isn't as if we don't have any work for you."

Ketola rose and strode briskly out of the office, leaving Joentaa alone with the question of how to interpret his reaction. Ketola had been an enigma to him ever since his first day at work, when the CID chief had barely noticed him. It wasn't until that afternoon, after they'd evaluated a crime scene, that it had occurred to him to greet his new subordinate with a casual "Welcome aboard."

Joentaa had no idea what to make of Ketola even now. Ought he to construe the man's meager, chilly words and offer of extended leave as clumsy gestures of sympathy and compassion, or had they betokened indifference and disdain for his work?

He was still turning this over in his mind when Ketola returned with two folders. "I'm sure you heard about the incident in the marketplace," he said as he came in. He didn't wait for an answer. "We're under pressure from all sides, and all because some idiot has testified that the would-be assassin boarded a bus and got clean away, just like that." Ketola smacked the desktop. "It's nonsense, of course, but who cares?" Hard though Joentaa usually found it to fathom Ketola, he could tell that some general expression of displeasure was coming.

"It's enough to make you puke," Ketola said, more to himself than to Joentaa, and applied himself to the folders.

At nine o'clock Heinonen came in to report that a woman had been murdered in Naantali.

"It seems the husband began by calling a doctor, who concluded from a preliminary examination that the woman had been suffocated," he said. "Then the husband called us. Grönholm took the call. The man sounded pretty bemused and agitated, apparently."

"That figures," Ketola said drily, pulling on his jacket with a disgruntled air. Looking at his face, Joentaa thought he saw fear in his eyes. Fear of being overwhelmed with work, he assumed.

"Come with me, Kimmo," called Ketola, already out in the corridor.

"Is your leave over?" Heinonen asked as Joentaa squeezed past him. He didn't reply, just ran to catch up with the chief.

7

The first thing Joentaa noticed was that the house was a very handsome, dark blue clapboard villa in an exclusive residential district unfamiliar to him. Outside were a patrol car, an ambulance, and a dozen inquisitive bystanders craning their necks in the hope of seeing something through the front door, which was open.

"What happened?" a young woman asked as they got out of the car.

"Nothing," said Ketola brusquely. She opened her mouth to pursue the matter but was too flummoxed to react with sufficient speed.

A uniformed policeman intercepted them in the hall and presented a brief report: "Laura Ojaranta, age thirty-three. Her husband returned from a business trip this morning and found her dead in the bedroom. I think he's pretty cut up."

"Where is he?" Ketola asked. The policeman gestured to the left. Joentaa saw a well-dressed, middle-aged man seated at a table in the living room. He was staring apathetically into space and slightly but incessantly shaking his head. As Joentaa turned and looked back into the policeman's face, he thought of Sanna and the fact that she was dead. Ketola said something, but he didn't hear.

"I'm talking to you, Kimmo," Ketola snapped.

Joentaa came to with a start.

Ketola gave him a searching stare and led the way into the bedroom, which was in brilliant sunlight.

It's going to be even hotter than yesterday, Joentaa told himself.

Laukkanen, the police surgeon and pathologist, came over to them. "She was very probably suffocated with a pillow during the night." Kari Niemi from forensics was crawling around on the floor. He jumped up when he saw them and hurried over, smiling broadly.

Cheerful as ever, thought Joentaa. He liked Niemi and had discovered over the years that his mischievous smile did not denote any indifference to death or injury. It was simply that nothing could shake Kari Niemi's almost incomprehensibly optimistic attitude to life.

"I've only just started," Niemi said as he shook Ketola's hand. "There's a lot going on at the moment—just for a change." Ketola made a face.

Niemi turned to Joentaa.

"Hello, Kimmo, I thought you were still on leave."

"Not anymore," said Joentaa.

Niemi shook his hand and smiled.

"How's your wife?"

Joentaa drew a deep breath. "She died on Monday night."

He detected a change in Niemi's expression without being able to interpret it precisely. He could still see the mischievous smile, but it lay in shadow, so to speak, and slowly congealed. Niemi's hand detached itself from his. "I'm sorry, Kimmo," he said, and did something that utterly disconcerted Joentaa: he gave him a hug. "I'm very sorry," he added.

Ketola cleared his throat, looking embarrassed. "Anything yet?" he asked, clearly endeavoring to change the subject.

"We've only just started, as I say. Give me half an hour and I'll be able to tell you more."

Ketola nodded and Niemi turned away. Joentaa walked over to the king-size bed on which the dead woman lay. A police photographer he didn't recognize was taking pictures from various angles.

The woman might almost have been asleep, like Sanna.

Ketola nudged him aside and bent over the corpse. He didn't seem to find anything of interest. "I'd like a word with the husband," he said, turning to Joentaa. He set off for the living room ahead of him. In the passage a policeman came to meet them looking worried. "The man seems to be getting a bit, er, worked up," he said.

"Meaning what?" asked Ketola.

The policeman started to reply, then confined himself to a helpless shrug. Ketola left him standing there and walked on faster.

The smartly dressed man who had been staring apathetically into space when they arrived was now pacing restlessly up and down and giving a tongue-lashing to a uniformed constable who was standing in the doorway, clearly out of his depth. Ketola brushed past him and went up to the man.

"Mr. Ojaranta?" he began, extending his hand.

"Are you in charge here?" Ojaranta demanded in a tremulous voice. He was very tall, Joentaa noticed.

"I'm the chief investigating officer, yes. Mr. Ojaranta, allow me to express—"

"You can dispense with the soft soap. What the hell happened here, that's what I'd like to know!"

Ketola stood there with his mouth open. He started to speak, but Ojaranta exploded again.

"I want to know what happened here!" He was going red in the face. "I walk in and find my wife dead, get the picture? No, you don't get it because the whole thing defies explanation!"

Ketola took a step back and asked Joentaa if Laukkanen was still there. "Afraid not," Joentaa told him. Ketola nodded but went to check all the same. Meantime, Ojaranta had flopped down on the sofa and was whimpering softly to himself.

Joentaa was involuntarily fascinated by the situation. It surprised him how easy he found it to interpret the behavior of a man who had grasped that his wife was dead, but who was nevertheless incapable of digesting the fact.

"The doc's gone already. It's the usual thing—they're never there when you need them," said Ketola, who had suddenly reappeared at Joentaa's side. Joentaa flinched, conscious that he'd begun to relish Ojaranta's despair in the hope of dulling his own.

Ketola sat down in an armchair facing the sofa. Joentaa remained standing to one side.

"Mr. Ojaranta," Ketola said quietly in a voice that didn't belong to him. "I understand your grief, but we need your help—"

"You don't understand a thing," said Ojaranta. Joentaa remembered having said much the same when Ketola expressed his sympathy that morning.

While Ketola was trying, with mounting impatience, to get through to Ojaranta, Joentaa endeavored to form an idea of him. This giant of a man, who looked so strong, had subsided after his furious outburst. He isn't used to being overwhelmed by situations, he thought.

"You returned from a trip this morning . . ." Ketola prompted.

"I'd been away on business for a week, in Stockholm," Ojaranta mumbled without looking up. "I got here around half past eight—I thought my wife was still asleep . . ." He sat up and looked Ketola straight in the eye. "Everything was fine, we spoke on the phone only yesterday afternoon . . ."

Joentaa seemed to discern, in Ojaranta's eyes, the crazy notion that had occurred to him too: that he could turn the clock back and return to normality if only it were possible to obliterate the moment when disaster struck.

"I thought she was asleep even when I saw her lying there in bed," Ojaranta said dully, slumping again. "The pillow . . . it was as if she'd buried her head in the pillow, but I thought . . . I went into the kitchen, had a cup of coffee, and read the paper. I'd seen her lying dead in bed, and I read the paper because I thought she was only asleep, you see . . ."

Ketola nodded vaguely. "What happened then?" he asked when Ojaranta seemed to be relapsing into a torpor.

"After a while I went back to the bedroom, intending to wake her. It was a week since we'd seen each other, after all . . . Well, I soon saw something was wrong, because she looked somehow . . ."

"Mr. Ojaranta?"

"I just don't understand it all . . ."

Ketola was about to resume, but his cell phone started to chirp a merry tune that suited neither him nor the current situation. He jumped up and clumsily fished the phone from his jacket pocket. "Excuse me for a moment." He went over to the French windows, which led out onto the terrace and a colorful, neatly tended garden.

Joentaa heard him swearing in the background. He was just devoting his attention to Ojaranta when Niemi tapped him on the shoulder from behind. "Can you spare a minute?" he asked.

Joentaa followed him into the kitchen. Niemi proceeded to report his preliminary findings in hurried, disjointed sentences. After a moment or two he broke off. "Kimmo, this news about your wife, if I can help in any way, don't hesitate to ask. Any time . . ."

Joentaa wanted to respond but he couldn't get a word out. You could say it isn't true and bring her back, he thought.

Aloud, he said: "Have you found anything—anything unusual?" He was uncomfortably aware how halfheartedly he'd asked the question and how uninterested he was in an answer.

"There is something, actually," Niemi began in a hesitant voice.

Joentaa looked at him inquiringly.

"We've examined every door and window in the house. There's no sign of a forced entry."

Joentaa nodded absently.

"It's very likely there are no usable fingerprints either, but I'll be checking the wineglass and bottle in any case."

"What do you mean?" asked Joentaa.

"The first things I found on entering the living room were a half-empty bottle of red wine and an empty glass from which the wine had obviously been drunk."

"Presumably by Mrs. Ojaranta."

"Or by the killer, if we find no prints on the glass."

"What makes you say that?"

"There was another glass in the kitchen sink and another bottle of wine on the drain board, white wine, also half-empty, as though two people had been drinking, but not together and at different times. I asked the husband, but he didn't have a clue. When I got here he was still sitting in the bedroom, staring at his wife. He said he hadn't been in the living room at all before my arrival."

"Mrs. Ojaranta may have sampled both bottles."

"Maybe, we'll see. I don't have anything else. I'm off now. I'll call as soon as I know more."

Joentaa nodded.

"You can give me a lift, Kari." Ketola was coming toward them brandishing his cell phone. "Nurmela has set up a press conference on the Järvi shooting—without informing me, needless to say." He looked at his watch. "I have to be there in half an hour. No idea what I'm supposed to tell them. It's bull, the whole thing." He mopped his brow with a handkerchief. "You carry on here, Kimmo. We'll talk this afternoon."

Before Joentaa could say anything, Ketola had marched smartly out of the house and disappeared from view.

"Catch you later," said Niemi. He went off to inform his colleagues, clearly reluctant to be hassled by Ketola.

"Where's he gone to?" Ketola called from outside.

Joentaa returned to the living room, where Ojaranta was sitting limply on the sofa, looking as if he hadn't moved in the last few minutes. Joentaa sat down in the armchair facing him. He was about to speak when Ojaranta got in first.

"I was unfaithful to my wife, you know." He gave Joentaa a piercing stare. "I cheated on her unmercifully, left, right and center, again and again." Joentaa saw a smile on his face, a daft, despairing smile. He avoided Ojaranta's eye, wondering if the man was having a nervous breakdown and, if so, what he ought to do.

I don't know how you recognize a nervous breakdown, he thought confusedly.

"I *was* in Stockholm on business, of course. No, no, that's not the issue, it was nearly all business, pure and simple," said Ojaranta. "But the business could wait, know what I mean?"

"Mr. Ojaranta . . ." Joentaa began.

"Attractive, twenty-seven, blonde, younger than my wife . . ." Ojaranta was rambling on like a drunk. "Prettier too, of course, very attractive, a marketing secretary or something of the kind, no idea what that entails." He drew a deep breath. "Know when I met my wife? Twelve years ago. Know how long I've been cheating on her?" He looked at Joentaa expectantly, his eyes wide in his pale face.

"Twelve years, sheer habit." He sank back against the sofa's yielding upholstery.

Joentaa said, "I'd like you to help me, Mr. Ojaranta."

The big, muscular man eyed him lethargically. It was clear that he'd talked himself out. "I'd like you to come with me," said Joentaa, standing up. Ojaranta got clumsily to his feet. Joentaa saw he was even taller than he'd thought, a good head taller than himself, a regular giant.

"What is it now?" asked Ojaranta, who seemed to have pulled himself together again. Joentaa got the impression that he was already regretting his outburst.

"I'd like you to tell me if anything in the house is different. Is there anything that wasn't here before, anything missing, anything that's been moved?"

He led the way. Ojaranta followed him with reluctance. "Everything's the way it always was," he said, and uttered a faint groan, probably because the absurdity of that statement had just struck him.

They went from room to room. Ojaranta merely shook his head each time. Joentaa steered him past the bedroom on the pretext that forensics were still at work in there. In the study, a large, ostentatiously furnished room, Ojaranta seemed to have a sudden flash of inspiration. He made straight for a picture with a wall safe behind it. "Nothing," he said. "Untouched."

"Your wife appears to have let the killer into the house herself," said Joentaa. "It wasn't a break-in."

Ojaranta stared at him. Joentaa had the feeling that, over and above the fact that his wife was dead, the question of who had murdered her was penetrating his consciousness for the first time. "Not a break-in?" he said softly. Joentaa shook his head.

"So what really happened here?" Ojaranta whispered. For a moment Joentaa thought he perceived, in the man's despair and perplexity, the key to the solution of the scenario in this house, which struck him as more and more peculiar and unreal.

Something here isn't as it should be, he thought, and swiftly condemned the idea. Nothing could be as it should be in a place where someone had just been murdered.

Until now he felt he'd taken an outsider's view of the crime scene. The whole setup, the dead woman lying in the sunlight, her big, bewildered husband, forensics working in their practiced way—all were merely a superficial, temporary distraction from what really preoccupied him. He wondered how he could bring himself to talk to a stranger about his dead wife when Sanna was dead and his own life had come apart at the seams.

"What's the matter?" Ojaranta demanded, eyeing him suspiciously. Joentaa felt a momentary urge to tell him about Sanna, her illness and death, but he promptly dismissed the idea.

They went downstairs to the basement. Two of Niemi's people were busy examining the sauna and wine cellar.

"What could have happened here, Mr. Ojaranta?" asked Joentaa.

He got no answer. Ojaranta gave an almost imperceptible shrug, but that was all.

"Your wife let someone in. Who could it have been?" Even as he asked the question, Joentaa spotted an inconsistency in the scenario, a logical flaw of which he'd been only subconsciously aware until now. The woman had let someone in and then gone to bed. Or had the murderer only put her there after her death? Had he dressed her in her nightgown? He knew too little and was feeling completely at sea.

Ojaranta didn't seem to have heard what he'd said. He gave Joentaa a blank stare and walked off—abruptly, as if he now knew what had to be done. He climbed the cellar stairs without a backward glance. Joentaa followed, but Ojaranta's spirit of initiative seemed to wane when he reached the ground floor.

"I must lie down, I feel sick," he said, making for the living room. Suddenly he paused and turned. "There is something missing," he said.

Following his gaze, Joentaa saw a nail protruding from the wall in the shadow cast by a cupboard.

"There was a picture here," said Ojaranta.

"What sort of picture?"

Ojaranta seemed to have to think this over. "Some painting or other. A landscape, I think."

"It was hanging here in this passage and you don't know what it depicted?" Joentaa promptly regretted his aggressive tone.

"It was just a landscape," said Ojaranta. "I was only too glad when Laura hung it behind the cupboard. One of her girlfriends painted it at some art course or adult education class—don't ask me . . ." Now I'm seeing him as he really is, or as he is most of the time, thought Joentaa. A man with a high opinion of himself and a low opinion of other people.

"Are you sure it was there when you went away?" he asked.

"Of course it was. It's been there for years."

"Could your wife have taken it down?"

"I can't think why she would." Ojaranta seemed to have lost interest in the picture and its disappearance. He turned away. Joentaa was feeling less and less enlightened instead of more and more.

"For you!" One of the forensics people came up and handed him a cell phone.

It was Niemi. "Your phone's turned off," he said.

Joentaa instinctively felt in his breast pocket. At the same time he remembered having left his cell phone at the hospital. He had last seen it on the table beside Sanna's bed—the bed in which Sanna had lain, now occupied by an elderly stranger.

I must make the funeral arrangements, he thought.

"It's as I suspected: no prints on the wineglass."

"Huh?"

"The wineglass we found in the living room. It's clean, and so is the bottle."

"Which means . . ."

"Which means that the killer sat and drank wine in the living room without leaving any prints behind."

Joentaa said nothing.

"I thought I'd let you know right away."

Joentaa nodded, said goodbye, and returned the cell phone to Niemi's sidekick. "Anything important?" asked the latter.

"I don't know yet," Joentaa said.

I must get out of here, he thought. At once.

An ambulance man accosted him at the front door. "Okay to take the body away now?" he asked in a bored voice.

"Just a minute," said Joentaa. Some of Niemi's men were still at work in the bedroom. He went over to the bed and looked down at the dead woman. "Has she been moved?" he asked. One of the forensics people shook his head. "Of course not," he said without looking up.

Joentaa surveyed the body. Laura Ojaranta was lying half on her back and half on her side. Her eyes were closed. Only the unnatural rigidity of her features betrayed that she was dead.

He was moved by the picture she presented, although he still felt he was seeing everything with a detachment that was alien to him.

She was taken by surprise and died in her sleep, like Sanna, he thought, simultaneously aware that this was mere conjecture. He would have to wait and see what Laukkanen could tell him. The right-hand half of the bed looked unslept-in. The sheet had been neatly turned down.

The murderer could have arranged that too, like everything he'd seen so far.

The second pillow was missing. This puzzled Joentaa for a moment. Then he remembered Laukkanen's preliminary verdict and realized that it had probably been used to suffocate the woman. Forensics would naturally have bagged and removed it.

He went outside. Nausea overcame him when he emerged into the sweltering sunshine, and for an instant he was afraid he would be sick. The ambulance men were leaning against their vehicle, laughing at something. Joentaa choked back his nausea and told them to remove the body.

"Okay, boss," one of them said. Without exactly knowing why, Joentaa itched to bawl him out. He was just going back inside when his path was barred by one of the curious onlookers, whose numbers had swelled considerably. She was a stout woman in a tracksuit.

"Are you a policeman?" she asked diffidently.

He nodded and made to walk on.

"I'd like to tell you something."

"Very well."

"My husband and I live over there," the woman said, pointing to a big white clapboard bungalow situated in a luxuriant garden at right angles to the Ojarantas' blue villa. "We're next-door neighbors, or almost. Terrible, what's happened. Is it true that Mrs. Ojaranta—"

"What was it you wanted to tell me?"

"Last night, very late . . ."

"Go on."

"The light went on."

"The light?"

"Yes. I was awake—I'd taken a pill. I oughtn't to, really, but I couldn't sleep for the pain. I've been sleeping very badly since my thrombosis, and—"

"You said the light went on. Where?"

"In the Ojarantas' living room."

"When was this? What time, exactly?"

"Half past two, I think." She thought for a moment. "Yes, I'm sure it was just after half past two, I looked at the clock when I got out of bed. I was surprised, naturally. All the lights are usually out by then. I often stand at the window around that time of night."

"So the light went on. Was it turned off again?"

"Yes, but not for a while. It was definitely on for half an hour."

"Did you see anyone? Mrs. Ojaranta, perhaps, or some other person?"

"No, how could I? There are trees in the way," the woman said, indicating the Ojarantas' garden. "All I could see was the light."

Joentaa nodded. "And you're quite positive about the time?"

"Of course," she said peevishly. "I'm only trying to be helpful, believe me."

"Many thanks. Today, or tomorrow at the latest, we'll come and take a formal statement from you."

He shook her hand and walked quickly back into the house before she could ask him any more questions.

Ojaranta was lying on the sofa in the living room with his eyes shut. His eyelids were twitching. Joentaa was about to speak to him when he realized that the man had lapsed into a restless sleep. Although the big room was flooded with sunlight, he felt cold.

You shouldn't be here, he told himself.

The ambulance men were carrying the dead woman along the passage. One of them was chewing gum.

I must go now, he thought.

"Where are they taking my wife?" cried Ojaranta, who had suddenly appeared at his side. He stood there swaying, bleary-eyed but wide awake.

"To the pathology lab," Joentaa told him. "There'll have to be an autopsy."

Ojaranta nodded. He seemed about to say something, but after a few moments he shuffled slowly back to the sofa.

Joentaa left without saying goodbye.

Glancing in the rearview mirror as he drove down the hill toward the city center, he saw the blue house grow smaller and finally disappear from view. He was often compelled to slow down and wait because the whole of Naantali seemed to be heading for the beach: men in swimming trunks, women in bikinis, all clearly delighted by the belated arrival of a summer in which they'd ceased to believe.

Joentaa waited, forcing himself to smile whenever someone happened to catch his eye.

The image of the dead woman in the blue clapboard villa had already faded, and with it the question of the story behind the painting. He thought of Sanna and how fond she'd been of the beach at Naantali.

He would never, he thought, set foot on it again.

He drove to a funeral parlor in Turku. The window was discreetly adorned with flowers and black drapery. He had passed it innumerable times over the years, but it had never occurred to him to go inside. The man he spoke with informed him of the cost and made no effort to feign sympathy.

When he left the man shook his hand and promised to see to everything.

Driving home, Joentaa felt he'd lost Sanna a second time.

8

He awoke to reality.

The images were gone.

He pretended they'd never existed.

He got up, washed, made himself some coffee, and drank it. He sat in the little kitchen and stared out of the open window. Children were soaring to and fro on the swings in the playground between the gray blocks of flats.

He could hear their laughter and the ominous creak of the ring-bolts.

The day struck him as pale and bright, paler and brighter than its predecessors. He had no recollection of them. He knew only that they lay in darkness.

It's a nice day, he thought.

He pretended it was the first day of his life.

He set off at half past nine although he knew it wasn't necessary. He would be too early for work, but he would sit in the car and wait until ten, as usual.

He got there at nine fifty-two, parked on the verge, and settled down to wait.

He counted the cars that drove past and tried to catch a glimpse of the drivers' faces.

He remembered doing something he shouldn't have done. He experienced a faint tingle of excitement at the thought, an excitement as indeterminate as the thought itself.

Perhaps he was imagining the whole thing.

If it had happened at all, it had done so in the other world. The one he disliked.

Sometimes, when he sat waiting in the car, he felt a desire to think everything over—to get to the bottom of himself.

Although he knew it was impossible.

At one minute to ten he got out and made his way across the street to the Handicrafts Museum. Mara, who was already ensconced in her little ticket office, smiled at him when he walked in. "Punctual as ever," she said. She often said that.

Looking at the little timber buildings in the sunshine and the pale-blue sky beyond them, he reflected that they might all be an illusion, a beautiful illusion that posed no threat to him.

"There's a group of tourists coming at ten-fifteen," Mara called.

He nodded without taking his eyes off the houses that had survived the great fire. He sometimes imagined that the old buildings might disclose some of their secrets if only he were capable of listening.

9

In the evening Kimmo Joentaa suffered the collapse he'd seen coming at the Ojaranta house that afternoon.

He was standing under the shower. When the hot water came pattering down on his back, his weary body relaxed so abruptly that everything went black before his eyes and his knees buckled. He felt he was watching himself as he fell.

When he opened his eyes he was lying doubled up on the floor with the water pounding away at him. It took him a while to grasp where he was.

Getting slowly to his feet, he dried his smarting body and pulled on a bathrobe. Then he emerged from the hot, steamy atmosphere and went out into the passage.

Although he could hear himself sobbing loudly, he felt no pain.

I won't be able to live here anymore, he thought when he was sitting in the living room.

His paroxysm of weeping gradually subsided.

He remembered that he'd meant to give Merja and Jussi Sihvonen another call the day before. He wondered how they were doing and was surprised they hadn't called back. Something disastrous may have happened, he thought. Merja may have succumbed to the sudden shock and died. He pictured Jussi sitting beside her deathbed.

It was a vivid but spurious vision, and it vanished at once.

His thoughts turned to his own mother, who knew absolutely nothing. Nothing about Sanna's death and very little about her illness.

He hadn't forgotten to tell her. He had postponed the call, in fact he'd even considered avoiding it altogether and lulling her into the belief that all was well with Sanna and himself.

Whenever he thought of his mother he saw her in a carefully constructed idyll, a cramped but harmonious environment. Secretly, he realized that this idyll might not exist at all. It was years since he'd talked with her at any length, and his replies to her voluminous letters had been friendly but uncommunicative. He had neither mentioned his own problems nor inquired about hers.

When he informed her, soon after leaving school, of his intention to join the police force in Turku, she had more than once tried to convince him that it was too soon to decide.

Did it have to be Turku? she asked.

It was the only place that had a vacancy for a probationer, he told her. He said nothing about his wish to move south, away from her and Kittee, the little east Finnish town in which he'd grown up.

He had no recollection of his father, who had died in a car crash when he was three years old. In his estimation, his mother had never truly recovered from that catastrophic bolt from the blue, even though she was comfortably settled in her modest existence and had made her son the object of her overpowering love.

It was wrong to think of not telling her, of course, but he felt sure she would catch the next train to Turku.

He would have to dissuade her.

He pulled the phone toward him and slowly, after a moment's hesitation, began to dial the number. He hoped she would be out.

Just before she answered he felt an urge to hang up and think—to rehearse what he was going to say first.

"Anita Joentaa." Her voice was low and tremulous.

She's aged, he thought.

"Hello, Anita, Kimmo here."

"Kimmo, how nice, it's a while since we . . ." She broke off. He could sense how pleased she was that he'd called.

"I've got something to tell you . . ."

She waited in silence.

"Sanna's dead."

"What?!"

"I wrote and told you she was ill."

"You said she had a benign tumor, and that it was being treated for safety's sake."

Had he really written that?

"The last time you wrote you said she was much better." Her voice broke.

"It wasn't true. Sanna was seriously ill—the disease killed her."

Silence fell. He tried to visualize his mother at the other end of the line, but all he saw was a blank.

"Why didn't you . . . ?"

"I don't know."

"You should have told me the truth."

"Please, let's just forget that now. I'm sorry, I can't explain it to you and I've no wish to do so."

"But I could have helped you . . . helped you both, I mean."

"No, you couldn't!" He winced, surprised by the vehemence with which he'd uttered the words. "Believe me," he said more quietly, "you couldn't have done anything to help."

Nobody could, he thought.

He already regretted having called her.

"I'm coming to Turku," she said. "I'll leave tomorrow morning."

"Please don't."

"Why not?"

"I feel I need to be alone just now. For the moment, I'm the only one who can help myself."

It was true, Joentaa realized that the moment he said it. He dreaded the sympathy of others, dreaded having to bare his emotions, emotions he couldn't really understand himself.

He would find it impossible to discuss Sanna's death with anyone, least of all with Anita, whose stifling affection would miss the mark and only bring more problems in its train.

Anita didn't speak, either taken aback by what he'd said or simply overwhelmed by the news and by concern for her son.

Joentaa said: "I'd like you to give me a little time."

"Of course," she replied.

"And I'd like to apologize for having written so seldom and for leaving you in the dark. I can't explain that either . . . Maybe I simply didn't want you to suffer again." That was at least partly true. Once again, he was surprised by his own words.

She preserved a long silence. "All the same," she said eventually, "it was wrong of you."

He made no comment, aware that she was right.

"I'll call again tomorrow," he said, ". . . and, of course, I'll let you know when . . . when the date of the funeral has been fixed."

There was another silence, but he sensed that she was longing to say something, that she had a thousand questions—too many to be able to ask even one. "I'm so sorry," she said.

He hung up. While on the phone he'd become conscious of having forgotten something else, something important: he would have to inform Sanna's friends and colleagues and all the people she'd been fond of. She had received regular visits from many of her women friends, especially Elisa, who was employed by the firm of architects for which Sanna had worked with such success before her illness.

He jibbed at the thought of drafting an obituary notice. How could he encompass the fact of Sanna's death in a few words?

To shake off the idea he reached for the phone again and dialed Merja and Jussi Sihvonen's number. When it had rung four times he hastily hung up, relieved not to have to speak to them. At the same time, his concern for them intensified.

He wondered if his father could have helped him to cope with the situation. He doubted it. Joentaa pondered the question until he felt quite sure that his father would have been just as powerless to help as his mother.

He turned on the television in the hope of not having to think anymore. The late news dealt in detail with Sami Järvi, the politician who had been shot. The length of the report belied the obvious absence of any new developments.

Petri Nurmela, Turku's police chief, delivered a few unconvincing remarks. Ketola, seated beside him in the electric storm from the photographers' flash bulbs, made an uneasy impression despite his efforts to sit up ramrod straight and look self-assured.

Sami Järvi himself was interviewed, and Joentaa was astonished to see him sitting in a lush, colorful garden in the best of health. The only sign that something had happened to him was the sling round his neck and arm, which he presented to the camera with studied nonchalance. He was feeling much better, he declared, and would not, of course, revoke his intention to stand for a seat in the parliamentary elections. Looking at his masterful, politico's smile, Joentaa suddenly wondered if Järvi had staged the incident himself as a vote-winner. He banished the thought at once and warned himself not to draw any false conclusions from the mere fact that a politician had not only survived an attempt on his life but was obviously handling it well.

Joentaa watched the foreign news reports, the sports round-up, and the weather forecast without taking anything in. His muddled thoughts alternated between Sanna, the smiling politician, and the woman lying dead in bed.

The latter recollection pricked his conscience. Not having given a thought to the Naantali murder all afternoon, he couldn't help wondering if Ketola had been right. Was he really in a fit state to work?

He spent several minutes trying to reassess what he'd seen at the blue villa and the confusing items of information he'd gleaned there, but he was too tired. For the first time, he felt the full force of the pent-up exhaustion of the last few weeks. He'd scarcely slept since driving Sanna to the hospital.

He hoped he'd be able to sleep now.

And not have to think anymore.

He had a bath and put on the pajamas Sanna had given him for his birthday two years ago. He almost took them off when he remembered this, but he forced himself to wear them.

He lay down on his side of the bed and turned out the light. After a few minutes he got up because he felt unable to remain in the room.

He went into the living room. His legs were aching, and he was trembling.

As he lay on the sofa in the dark, he was struck by the thought that he had to find the person who had murdered the woman in the blue villa. He didn't know where the thought had come from and couldn't account for it.

He thought of the picture that had disappeared, and of Ojaranta's ignorance of what it looked like.

He tried to imagine the landscape in the picture.

Sleep bore down on him like a towering wave.

He dreamed of Sanna. Nothing happened in the dream, and he never saw her. She was just an invisible presence, but that didn't matter. The dream was a pleasant one. He felt himself laughing in his sleep, felt tears on his face.

He hoped he would never wake up.

He felt relieved, infinitely relieved, that she was alive.

10

Joentaa awoke early in the morning. The first thing that occurred to him was that Sanna was dead, and that he had been dreaming. He got up because he knew he wouldn't be able to go back to sleep. He forced himself to eat and drink something, although he was not hungry or thirsty. He sat on his makeshift bed in the living room for a long time, looking out through the picture windows at the placid, pale-blue surface of the lake.

He recalled the afternoon on which they had viewed the house two winters ago. He had found it hard to drive there through the deep snow without coming to grief. Annoyed that the only access to the little house was a narrow forest track, he got out of the car with the firm intention of remaining in their cramped Turku flat rather than moving to such a remote spot.

The estate agent, a hunched figure muffled up against the cold, had been waiting for them on site. He greeted them with a barrage of sales talk and persisted in plying Sanna with compliments.

The house was empty, the previous occupants having taken their furniture with them. Joentaa's first thought was that it would need redecorating.

He remembered how Sanna had lingered at the living-room window, gazing out at the frozen lake. After a while she turned to him with a broad grin that told him the die was cast. He read the unspoken question in her eyes and nodded. Sanna promptly interrupted the estate agent's spiel and informed him that he'd made a sale. Surprised and delighted, the man rewarded her for her shrewd decision by kissing her hand.

Joentaa could remember the episode in every detail, yet he felt it had never taken place. He wondered why this was so and came to a conclusion that shocked him.

The past seemed unreal because Sanna was still alive there.

He forced himself to get up and drive to Turku, where he got stuck in a lengthy traffic jam. The local radio DJ kept trying to make a joke of it.

Ketola was seated at his desk when Joentaa entered the office, in the act of raising a glass to his lips and knocking it back. The bottle in front of him was filled with amber-colored liquid.

He caught sight of Joentaa. "Get out!" he said, deftly concealing the bottle and glass in his bottom drawer.

Joentaa stood there, transfixed.

"Get out," he repeated in a quieter but more incisive tone. On his face Joentaa detected a look of boundless fury directed at himself. He shook off his inertia, shut the door in a hurry, and stood waiting in the corridor outside.

He drew a deep breath and debated what to do next. It occurred to him how absurd it was to be unable to enter his office because his boss wanted to drink hard liquor undisturbed.

Just as he was turning away, a victim of indecision, he saw Nurmela striding purposefully toward him. "Hello there, Kimmo," he called from a way down the corridor.

Joentaa took a moment to collect his wits. He hesitated for a moment, then opened the office door. Ketola looked startled. The bottle and glass were back on the desk in front of him.

"Nurmela's coming," Joentaa hissed, and shut the door again.

He turned to face the police commissioner, who was still some ten feet away. "I want a word with Ketola," said Nurmela, giving Joentaa's hand a vigorous shake. "Is he in?"

Joentaa nodded. He wondered whether to engage him in conversation, but before he could make up his mind Nurmela knocked on the door and opened it without waiting for an answer. Looking over his shoulder, Joentaa saw Ketola sitting at his desk, seemingly engrossed in some file or other. The bottle and glass had vanished.

"Any developments?" asked Nurmela.

"No," said Ketola. "I'm going to have another word with Järvi later this afternoon."

"What good will that do?" Nurmela demanded sharply, dispensing with the eloquent charm and affability that characterized his public appearances. "The man didn't see who it was, and that's that."

"I was hoping to—"

"Don't hope, just produce some results. Incidentally, what about that other case, the woman murdered at Naantali?"

"Kimmo took charge of that yesterday," said Ketola, who was sitting bolt upright and clearly hoping that Nurmela would cut his visit short.

Nurmela nodded and turned to Joentaa. "The same thing applies there. I want some results in double-quick time."

"Do you think I don't?" snapped Ketola. "I can't understand why the whole of Finland should be in uproar just because someone took a potshot at a politician. The man's as good as new and in the best of health!"

"He could be dead, though."

Nurmela obviously felt that said it all. He gave them both another nod and strode out.

Joentaa removed his jacket and sat down at his desk, wondering how to break the awkward silence. He was annoyed with himself for letting it bother him. It shouldn't have mattered in the least.

He was about to make some trivial remark when Ketola forestalled him. "Thanks," he said.

Joentaa, who had been avoiding his eyes, turned to look at him, but Ketola had reimmersed himself in his papers. Joentaa was going to say something, but he restrained himself and merely nodded.

After a while Ketola pushed the file aside. "How did things go yesterday?" he asked.

"I interviewed Ojaranta and went round the house with him. I thought he might have noticed something."

"Well?"

"There are a couple of curious features."

Ketola looked at him inquiringly. Joentaa thought he detected a recurrence of the apprehension he'd noticed the day before, when Heinonen had informed them of the murder at Naantali.

He thought of the bottle and glass in the bottom drawer of Ketola's desk and wondered how long they'd been there.

"Seems a picture is missing."

"What sort of picture?"

"Ojaranta said a woman friend of his wife's painted it at an adult education course."

"A what?"

"Which suggests that the picture is worthless. Ojaranta said it was an ugly piece of work."

"You mean the murderer took an ugly, worthless picture away with him?"

Joentaa gave a hesitant nod.

Ketola seemed about to say something but merely shook his head. "That's crazy. What else?"

"Forensics found no evidence of a break-in. Niemi has tested a glass and a wine bottle found in the living room." Joentaa broke off, reminded of the bottle and glass in his boss's drawer, and thought he saw Ketola stiffen. "Neither the glass nor the bottle yielded any prints," he went on quickly. "Which implies that the killer wiped them clean after use."

Ketola nodded and thought this over for a while. He looked confident and relieved when next he spoke. "So Laura Ojaranta let the murderer in and split a bottle of wine with him. An acquaintance, a lover . . . Very convenient, the husband being away. It's all far simpler than I feared."

"But there was only one glass in the living room."

"Then only her visitor had a drink."

"It looks as if the woman went to bed on her own. The other half of the bed appeared to be untouched."

Ketola thought some more. "Perhaps the murderer arranged that. Or perhaps it wasn't a lover, just a friend, of either sex—someone known to her."

"But why would she have gone to bed while her visitor was still there?"

Ketola seemed unable to come up with a convincing answer.

"And why did that picture disappear?" Joentaa went on.

"My guess is, the picture is completely irrelevant. Laura Ojaranta may have taken it down herself."

"Her husband is certain it was still there when he left."

Ketola shrugged. "If you're so obsessed with the picture, what's your theory?"

"I don't have one. I'm puzzled, that's all."

"I see."

"And there's another odd thing," said Joentaa.

"Like what?" Ketola seemed to be regretting that he'd asked about the dead woman at all.

"According to a neighbor, the light in the Ojarantas' living room went on around half past two in the morning. It was turned off half an hour later. If Laura Ojaranta was already dead at that time, it must have been the murderer."

Ketola stared at Joentaa. He seemed to be waiting for him to continue.

"It would be strange if the murderer had remained in the house with the lights blazing for half an hour after the crime."

"We still don't know the time of death," said Ketola. "The woman may still have been alive at half past two."

Joentaa nodded, but he remained unconvinced.

"Know what worries me, Kimmo?" Ketola went on, and Joentaa registered the edge in his voice. "I get the feeling you're obsessed with this woman's death and trying to make a big mystery out of it. That worries me because God knows I've got enough on my plate with this hysterical fuss over Järvi." He paused, and his tone became even more scathing. "It's enough that the woman was murdered, understand? I can do without any bizarre theories about ugly pictures and empty wineglasses. They're the last thing I need right now, get it?" His voice had steadily risen and he'd begun to sweat. He dabbed his brow with a handkerchief before continuing on a quieter note, controlling himself with an effort. "I want you to carry on at Naantali today. Take a closer look at the husband. Check whether he really was in Sweden until yesterday morning."

Joentaa nodded again, although the idea that Ojaranta might have killed his wife struck him as wholly improbable.

"And let me know when the pathology and forensic reports become available—if they ever do." Ketola rose abruptly. "I'm off to see Järvi now. Politicians mustn't be kept waiting."

"Are there any more clues to who shot him?" Joentaa asked. Ketola paused for a moment, apparently wondering if he was obliged to answer the question. "Nothing definite as yet," he said at length. "I'll be able to tell you more in due course. For the time being, concentrate on the killing at Naantali."

He draped his jacket over his shoulder. "Heinonen and Grönholm are still interviewing the marketplace residents. Nobody saw a thing, of course, but it pays to be thorough. You'll have to go there on your own."

Joentaa nodded, secretly relieved that the two of them would not be plying him with sympathy and distressing questions.

He found time, when Ketola had gone, to be surprised by Nurmela's behavior. He wondered whether the police commissioner knew of Sanna's death, or whether he'd simply ignored this momentous event in Joentaa's existence. Having turned the question over in his mind for some time, he came to the conclusion that Nurmela knew nothing.

Ketola had probably been too busy the day before to mention it.

Joentaa stifled the thought and pulled the telephone directory toward him, meaning to call Ojaranta and ask him for the address of the woman who had painted the missing picture. He looked for the Ojarantas' number in the directory.

There it was, under "Ojaranta, Arto and Laura."

Sanna's name was in the directory too: "Joentaa, Kimmo and Sanna," together with a number at which Sanna could no longer be reached.

He was just about to hang up, Ojaranta took so long to answer. His voice sounded very calm and remote.

Joentaa asked how he was.

Ojaranta didn't reply. "What do you want?" he asked.

"I'd like a word with your wife's friend, the one that painted the picture. Can you give me her address and phone number?"

"One moment," said Ojaranta. Joentaa heard him rummaging in a drawer. It took him a while to find the relevant particulars.

Joentaa wondered whether to say something consoling, but dismissed the idea.

He said goodbye and hung up.

He got through to Jonna Koivuniemi, the painter of the picture, and was relieved to learn that she had already been informed of her friend's death.

He fixed an appointment with her.

While driving to Naantali he wondered whether Ketola was right— whether he really was reading something nonexistent into the woman's murder so as to take his mind off Sanna's death.

I I

T he fear was returning, together with an awareness that it wasn't over.

That it had only just begun.

He inhaled the fear.

He was being slowly drawn down into the world known to him alone, and he offered no resistance.

He allowed himself to drift and he saw himself laugh. He was enjoying his renewed transformation into the Other, whom he hated.

He tried to imagine that fear was the beginning of redemption.

He was telling a group of young Swedish tourists that Turku had been almost entirely consumed by fire in 1827.

While speaking he sought eye contact with his listeners.

He told them that only the little group of buildings on the

Klosterberg had been spared. A small boy asked why. No one really knew, he replied. The Vardberg might have acted as a windbreak.

He savored the tourists' interest as he conducted them through the various craftsmen's workshops. The Klosterberg museum had opened in the summer of 1940, he informed them. He demonstrated with the aid of some old instruments how clockmakers had made time-pieces in years gone by and how saddlers had processed leather.

Gratified by his listeners' admiring gaze, he took only a few minutes to make a brown leather dice cup for the little boy, who delightedly showed it to a young man, evidently his father.

The young man smiled, came over, and thanked him for the gift.

He returned the smile and crossed the frontier between the worlds.

Patiently, he conducted the group round the little buildings, joining in the laughter when grown-ups hit their heads on the door frames.

He heard voices deriding the lousy food the youth hostel provided.

He tried to catch the eye of the little boy, who now sat perched on his father's shoulders and had ceased to pay any attention to him.

The dice cup was dangling, forgotten, from his hand.

When they emerged into the open, the sun looked wine-red.

12

While Jonna Koivuniemi was making coffee, Joentaa wondered whether he had any right to pass judgment on the extent of her grief.

She had ushered him into a small, comfortably furnished living room.

She hadn't slept a wink all night, she said. It troubled him to hear her say that and made him doubt that it was really true.

She returned with the coffee and asked him with a smile if he took milk and sugar. He shook his head, warning himself not to try to form a picture of a woman he didn't know at all.

She was surprised when he broached the subject of the painting and could offer no explanation for its disappearance. "I think Laura liked it," she said. "Arto thought it was awful." She gave a little laugh, but smothered it when she realized how inappropriate it sounded.

"I'm not a real painter, by the way, it's just a hobby," she explained. "That's how Laura and I got to know each other, painting at the adult education college."

"What's the painting of?" Joentaa asked.

"A landscape at night. A lake and a mountain."

"How is it painted, I mean . . ." He broke off. "I don't know much about these things. Is it . . . true to nature, or more abstract?"

"Abstract," she said. "All my paintings are abstract. It might be best if I showed you another of mine. Come with me."

The picture Mrs. Koivuniemi wanted to show him was hanging in the basement. She turned on the light. Joentaa had an uneasy feeling that the sun had set outside.

"I don't really like hanging my own pictures," she said. "But my husband liked this one so much, we made an exception. After all, nobody else sees it down here next to the sauna." She smiled.

Joentaa nodded.

The picture surprised him.

So did the fact that it had been painted by the insignificant little woman at his side, but he knew how nonsensical his astonishment was.

The picture showed a pale green field and a gray sky.

He knew nothing about painting, but this picture appealed to him.

"It's very good," he said.

"Thanks," she replied. "I doubt if many people would agree with you. The teacher at the adult education college thought my pictures were, well, bloodless."

"Do you always paint like this—in these pale colors, I mean?"

She nodded. "I think that's what my teacher was getting at."

When they went back upstairs he asked if she could think of any reason why her friend had been murdered.

"It must have been a burglar," she said, looking puzzled.

"That's possible, but not certain," Joentaa said after a moment or two. "Let's assume it wasn't a burglar. Can you suggest some other explanation?"

She stared at him uncomprehendingly.

"No," she said.

Joentaa stood up.

"Is it conceivable that it *wasn't* a burglar?" she asked.

"It's early yet," he told her.

"But the picture's gone. It must have been a burglar. There have been several burglaries here recently; I heard the police had questioned some foreigners, immigrants from Russia, I believe . . ."

Joentaa looked at her, wondering why a woman who painted such interesting pictures should have such a one-track mind.

He nodded and took his leave.

13

Joentaa drove not to police headquarters, but to the hospital.

Rintanen took the time to say hello and ask how he was, although he was obviously under pressure.

"I'm sorry, I have to go," he said after a few minutes. "An operation."

"Of course," Joentaa said. He wanted to thank him for devoting so much time to Sanna, but he couldn't get the words out. Rintanen gave him a firm handshake, said goodbye, and hurried off. Joentaa stared after him until he disappeared down the stairwell.

In answer to his inquiry, a young nurse handed him a transparent plastic bag containing the things from Sanna's room.

She gave him a look of commiseration.

He couldn't get out of the hospital fast enough. In the car he put the plastic bag on the passenger seat, where Sanna had always sat.

He wanted to weep but couldn't.

He opened the bag and spread out its contents on the seat.

The cell phone's voice mail included a message from Elisa, Sanna's colleague at the architects'. She said a meeting had run over and announced in a cheerful voice that she would be paying Sanna a visit.

See you soon, she said.

Joentaa resolved to call Elisa that evening. Her and Sanna's parents too.

He flicked through a book that had been in the bag. He remembered Sanna telling him several times how amusing it was and how much she was enjoying it. Although she hadn't read much of it at the hospital, it had seldom been out of her hands during her last week at home.

She had often laughed aloud and told him what was happening in the story.

He had laughed too and pretended to be listening, unable to think of anything but his fear of her death.

A bookmark showed where Sanna had got to.

He resolved to read the book and tell her how it ended.

14

He returned to police headquarters and called Laukkanen. The pathologist wore his usual harassed expression, as if he were on his way to an important meeting. Joentaa had learned to ignore this. What mattered was that the man was a fast worker and a good one. Not for the first time, he had some surprising information.

"I haven't completed the autopsy," he said, "but I'm assuming that the woman was killed in her sleep. It seems she had little or no chance to defend herself."

Joentaa thought awhile, trying to square what he'd heard with what he already knew.

"What exactly happened, in your opinion?" he asked. He had found that, unlike most of his colleagues, the pathologist could easily be prevailed upon to make detailed observations of a speculative but often helpful nature.

"I'm still assuming she was suffocated," said Laukkanen. "Judging by what I've seen and, more especially, not seen, the killer appears to have been very determined, but extremely circumspect as well."

"Circumspect?"

"Yes, strange as it may sound."

Joentaa said nothing.

"Of course, those are only my initial impressions."

"Of course," said Joentaa. "Thanks."

He hung up.

He tried to classify the new information but failed. In seeking to get closer to the dead woman in the blue villa, he was becoming more remote from her.

He thought of the little painter and her look of horror when he'd asked her to suggest some possible motives. The notion that her friend might have been killed deliberately had struck her as quite absurd.

He himself had felt just the same.

The woman's death had impressed him as unnatural from the first, as if something wasn't the way it ought to be.

He wondered why this was so, and came to the conclusion that it probably had to do with the seeming unreality of his own circumstances.

What if all that was happening was unreal, he thought. What if he was dreaming a very long and startlingly lifelike dream?

He yearned to wake up.

When the idea became too much for him he rose and went to see if Petri Grönholm and Tuomas Heinonen had returned from questioning the marketplace residents.

After a long search he found them in the canteen. They had finished their meal and were laughing at something over their coffee.

Heinonen's smile froze when he caught sight of Joentaa, but Grönholm noticed nothing.

"It seems more and more likely that Sami Järvi was shot by a fat young man," he called to Joentaa. "Mind you, he may also have been very old and thin—or possibly a woman. Dead drunk, in any event. Having done the deed, he or she calmly boarded a bus that was just leaving." Grönholm guffawed and waited in vain for Heinonen to join in.

"What's wrong?" he asked.

Joentaa said nothing.

"I never got around to telling you . . ." Heinonen began.

"My wife died," said Joentaa.

Grönholm stared at him.

"Petri was off duty yesterday, that's why I hadn't told him yet," Heinonen pursued as if he needed to justify himself. In fact, Joentaa was grateful that he hadn't immediately broadcast the news of Sanna's death to all and sundry.

"I'm sorry," Grönholm mumbled. He seemed about to say more, but stopped short.

Joentaa nodded, reflecting that neither he nor Heinonen had known Sanna well. They'd met her only a couple of times. He himself had very seldom spent any time with them outside working hours in recent years, although he liked them both, gruff Grönholm and quiet, rather self-effacing Heinonen.

Obsessively harmonious people get on well with everyone, Sanna had sometimes told him with a meaningful smile.

"Isn't it conceivable that the man who shot Järvi really did board a bus?" Joentaa asked after a while.

Grönholm opened his mouth to reply, but stopped short again and groped for words, clearly thrown by the change of subject.

"I've been wondering that myself," Heinonen said hesitantly. "It's a statement that's been around from the outset."

"Has it been checked?" asked Joentaa. "Have inquiries been made at the municipal bus depot?"

"Ketola has that in hand," Heinonen replied. "He thought the story was absurd at first, but several witnesses now claim to have seen the same thing."

"Probably publicity seekers who've read in the newspapers how easy it is to attract the attention of the police," said Grönholm.

"Perhaps," said Joentaa.

Silence fell.

Joentaa sensed that their thoughts had reverted to Sanna's death, and that they didn't know what to say. He got the impression that they found the silence discomfiting and was struck by how little it bothered him.

Personally, he could have kept it up for hours.

"By the way," said Heinonen, clearly relieved to be able to break the spell, "a woman was asking for you."

Joentaa looked at him inquiringly.

"The sister of the woman who was murdered at Naantali," Heinonen went on. "She says she phoned her the night she was killed."

"When, exactly?" Joentaa asked.

"I don't know, sometime that evening. I told her you'd call because I wasn't too familiar with the case. I don't even know the victim's name."

"Laura Ojaranta," said Joentaa. "Can you give me her number?"

"I jotted it down. It's on a slip of paper in my office."

Joentaa nodded. "I'll call her right away. Where did you put the note?"

"Beside the phone on my desk," said Heinonen, puzzled by his haste.

Joentaa thanked him and hurried off. Heinonen always kept his desk scrupulously tidy, so he wouldn't have any difficulty finding the number. He ran upstairs, found the slip of paper, and called the woman from Heinonen's phone.

For no reason he could identify, he suddenly felt tense.

While waiting he was haunted once more by the thought that he had to find the killer of the woman in the blue house. He couldn't account for the thought, but it was there.

The voice that answered was low and husky, but sounded very young. "Kerttu Toivonen," it said.

"My name is Kimmo Joentaa. I'm with the CID. A colleague told me you called."

"Yes, about Laura . . ."

Joentaa waited, heard her draw a deep breath.

"She was your sister?"

"Yes."

"You told my colleague you phoned her."

"Yes, that's right. The night she . . . it happened."

"When exactly did you speak to her?"

"Around ten, I think . . . I can't say for sure."

"Did your sister have a visitor?"

"No. She wasn't expecting anyone either." Silence. Joentaa waited. "She was glad I'd called and complained of feeling lonely. She didn't make a big deal of it, of course, but Arto often goes away. She said he'd be back the next day, which she was happy about."

"What else did she say?"

"Very little—I hardly let her get a word in. I'd had a very good exam result on Tuesday. I'm studying sociology and history."

"So she said nothing at all about expecting a visitor?" Joentaa asked.

"No, she was just about to go to bed. She said she'd been working hard in the garden and it was very hot . . . Oh yes, and she said something about a surprise."

"What sort of surprise?"

"I don't know. She said I'd find out the next time I came. I often visit her."

"Any idea what she could have meant?"

"No. It was something amusing, I think, because she laughed. But we didn't pursue the matter because I started telling her about my exam."

"Did your sister have a job of some kind?"

"No—at least, not at the moment. She's unemployed. I don't think Arto wants her to work. She's a qualified nurse, but Arto's earning so much as a computer programmer these days, she doesn't need to work anyway." She'd begun to speak about her sister in the present tense, Joentaa noticed.

He promised to call again before long and said goodbye. He lingered awhile at Heinonen's desk, wondering what Kerttu Toivonen was doing at that moment, what sort of life she led, and how well she was coping with her sister's death.

For a moment he had the nonsensical notion that nurses didn't deserve to be murdered.

He went to his office, where it took him a good half hour to ascertain that Arto Ojaranta really had been in Sweden, and that he'd boarded an SAS plane which had landed at Turku's small airport early on Wednesday morning.

It gave him a vague sense of satisfaction to be able to present Ketola with this alibi as soon as he got back from his interview with Järvi.

15

That evening, while he was having supper, he pondered on what he'd done.

He now knew that it had been something monstrous, and he relished the knowledge.

He had done wrong.

But he would eradicate that wrong by repeating it.

He would eradicate it by returning to the world known only to himself—the other world, where what he had done was not wrong.

He enjoyed being a commuter between the two worlds.

He enjoyed not being the person that other people thought he was.

He enjoyed the fear that slowly grew until it engulfed him altogether.

For a while he looked at the picture he'd hung above his bed. He waited until he lost himself in the magical landscape.

Then he went out onto the balcony and looked down at the playground, which was bathed in dark red evening sunlight.

He breathed the balmy air.

Two drunks were standing on the edge of the playground, having an argument. He heard their vituperations grow steadily louder and more ferocious. A window was flung open in the block of flats opposite. At the top of her voice, a young woman told the antagonists to go to hell.

She threatened to call the police if they didn't pipe down.

The drunks shouted something at the window, which had already been closed. After a while they set off for the bar from which they'd probably come.

He watched them go. They were laughing and exchanging conciliatory hugs. Just before they left his field of vision, he saw them die.

He waited until the light slowly faded and the air became colder.

16

When Joentaa got home that evening, Merja and Jussi Sihvonen were standing in the shade of the apple tree that almost entirely filled his small front garden.

As he drove slowly up to Sanna's parents, he seemed to see them standing in a picture like lifeless figures in a softly delineated Arcadia.

He felt a strong desire to paint this scene.

He parked the car alongside and nodded and smiled at them through the windshield, but they didn't respond. They hardly seemed to register his presence.

Beside Merja stood two brown suitcases, one large and one small. He got out and went over to the couple. He stared at them and waited for them to come to life, but they didn't move. He went right up to them, smiling and sensing the warmth of the sun on his neck.

He had a feeling that they were dead—that they would crumble away to dust if he touched them. Uncertain what to do, he awkwardly extended his hand.

"I'm glad you came," he said.

Jussi Sihvonen looked up and shook his hand.

"I meant to call you yesterday," Joentaa said. "Sorry, I'm afraid it slipped my mind."

"It might be better if we went to a hotel," said Jussi, as if he hadn't heard.

"Nonsense, you're welcome to stay here." Joentaa picked up the suitcases. Halfway up the steps he turned and saw them slowly detach themselves from the shade of the tree.

He ushered them into the living room, where he removed the pillow and blanket from his makeshift sofa bed and invited them to sit down. While making tea for himself and coffee for Merja and Jussi, he had a sudden recurrence of the nausea he'd felt under the shower the day before.

Just before he'd plummeted into the dark abyss.

He concentrated on pouring tea and coffee into white cups. His dizziness gradually subsided.

He put the cups and the coffeepot on a tray and carried it into the living room.

He heard the tinkle of china, heard sugar lumps falling into coffee, heard Merja's hoarse, desperate breathing, and realized that she still hadn't uttered a word.

"The doctor forbade Merja to travel, actually," said Jussi, catching Joentaa's eye. He raised the cup to his lips. His hands were trembling, and some of the coffee trickled down his neck into the collar of his pale-blue summer shirt. "He prescribed a very strong sedative."

Merja was sitting huddled beside him on the sofa, staring straight into Joentaa's eyes. He turned away when he intercepted her gaze.

He cast around for something to say, but without success.

Merja's voice sounded strange when she broke the silence.

"I always hoped she would live on," she said.

Joentaa looked at her. She seemed to have aged years since her visit the week before.

"How did she die?" she asked.

"In her sleep. It was . . . very peaceful."

He paused, thinking of the night when Sanna died, of the darkness and the overpowering thought that had weighed him down.

The thought of losing everything.

"It was very peaceful," he said again. "She was asleep." He looked at Merja. "To the very end she was in no pain."

He searched her eyes for consolation but found none.

He offered to make them some supper. They didn't want any, but he made some anyway, relieved to be able to retire to the kitchen.

He concocted some potato soup from leftovers, but they barely touched it. The three of them sat together for a long time, scarcely uttering a word. At some stage Merja said she was tired.

It took him quite a while to convince them that he intended to sleep on the sofa, and that they were welcome to the bedroom. He almost lost patience when Merja kept urging him not to go to any trouble.

He made up the bed afresh, trying not to notice how hard he found it to touch the sheets in which Sanna had slept, her blanket and pillow. He put the bedclothes in the top drawer of the wardrobe.

He waited for Merja and Jussi to go. It seemed an eternity before the bedroom door finally closed behind them.

He had meant to call Elisa, Sanna's best friend, but a glance at his watch told him that it was really too late, she might already be asleep. Although relieved to have an excuse not to call her, he forced himself to dial the number even so. He punched the keys quickly, avoiding all thought of how to dress up Sanna's death in words.

Elisa answered after the third ring. He guessed from her voice that she'd been asleep, but she sounded glad that he'd called and said she intended to visit Sanna now that she'd caught her breath at last.

She talked of pressure at the office.

"Sanna's dead," Joentaa said.

He waited for her to react. The silence persisted. He had visions of it never ending and thought how much he hated it, this wordless silence.

He wondered why no one ever laughed—why no one ever laughed him to scorn, shouted at him, exposed him as a liar.

He tried to describe Sanna's death in such a way that Elisa would find bearable. He told her that she'd been in no pain, that she'd been asleep, and wondered why he was doing so. Why should he, of all people, spare and console those who couldn't even guess at what was going on inside him?

Elisa eventually asked when Sanna was to be buried, and he promised to let her know as soon as the date was fixed. The flickering in front of his eyes began again when he hung up. He rose and fetched the blanket and pillow he'd removed from the sofa to make room for Sanna's parents to sit down on it.

Too tired to wash, he turned out the light and lay down. Stretched out on the sofa he could see the moonlit surface of the lake through the window.

Just before he fell asleep, he plunged into its dark waters.

17

The strident sound seemed to come from far away. Joentaa wanted to wake, but he couldn't. Sleep was pinning him down on the bottom of a dream he failed to understand.

A tormenting dream.

He could see the surface, but it was so far above him, he felt sure he would drown.

He heard a voice calling him.

He awoke filled with a panic fear of death.

"Telephone!" Jussi was bending over him in the gloom, shaking him to and fro.

"What . . ."

"The phone's ringing."

He jumped up, his knees buckling. Jussi handed him the receiver.

"Hello," he said. "Joentaa . . ."

It was Grönholm.

"Sorry, Kimmo, but you'll have to stir your stumps."

"What is it?" asked Joentaa.

"A young man has been murdered. At the youth hostel."

"What . . ."

"Ketola's completely lost it. All he does is yell."

"What happened exactly? How much do you know?"

"Not much. The guy was obviously knocked out first—there was a smell of chloroform. He was probably killed while unconscious, so Laukkanen thinks his death is reminiscent of the Naantali case. If he's right, the use of an anesthetic would indicate that the killer thought a man likely to offer more resistance than a woman."

Joentaa felt as if the ground was giving way beneath him.

He looked at Jussi, who was standing beside him with a worried, helpless expression.

"I'll come at once," he said into the phone. "The youth hostel? You mean the old one at Aurakatu?"

"That's right."

"See you soon." He hung up.

"Something wrong?" asked Jussi, trailing after him as he looked for his clothes in the dark.

"Please turn the light on," he said.

"What's happened?"

"A man has been murdered at the youth hostel. I'm sorry, I must leave at once." He gathered up his clothes and got dressed in seconds. Merja was standing in the bedroom doorway. "I'll explain everything later," he called, catching sight of her. "Please go back to sleep." He draped his overcoat over his arm. Merja and Jussi stared at him apprehensively.

"Go back to bed," he called, and left the house.

It was unexpectedly cold outside.

This is a false summer, he thought as he hurried to his car.

He drove along the narrow forest track to the main road.

He thought of the weekend he'd spent in Turku as a schoolboy. His first visit there had entailed a long journey for him and his class-mates from Kitee. He recalled their two nights at the youth hostel. One of his best friends had shared the bunk above him with a girl he himself had a crush on. He hadn't seen the friend for a long time, he reflected. He had no idea what he was doing or where he was living these days. Or even if he was alive.

He couldn't remember what the girl had looked like.

It seemed an eternity ago, he thought.

He thought of Sanna.

The youth hostel was situated right beside the Aurajoki, the river that divided the city in two. The grounds had been cordoned off by some uniformed policemen, who saluted him. He couldn't identify them in the darkness, but he returned their salutes.

He opened the big front door and felt he was entering a tunnel. He walked down a long passage toward a light and the sound of voices.

Niemi emerged from the gloom.

"Hello, Kimmo," he called, smiling as if everything was fine.

"Can someone turn a light on?" That was Ketola.

Just as Joentaa got to the room from which the strong yellow light was issuing, the passage, too, was suddenly bathed in the same yellow. He turned to see a familiar figure standing at the far end. It was the hostel supervisor, the same one, fifteen years older but still with the same gray hair and angular features.

"Sorry," he called. "Somebody switched it off by mistake."

Joentaa nodded. For a moment he felt sure the man must recognize him.

He turned and peered into the room from which the light had been coming. It was a big dormitory.

He saw Ketola, Grönholm, and Heinonen standing beside a bed with a man lying in it. Ketola, who was talking urgently to the other two, gave Joentaa a casual nod as he came closer.

Joentaa went over to the narrow bed and looked down at the lifeless body, which was that of a tall young man. He thought of the dead woman in the blue villa. This man was a victim of the same killer, he told himself.

He felt quite sure of it. He knew it.

On the bedside table were some playing cards and a cell phone. There was a dark-green, travel-worn carryall on the floor.

He heard scraps of conversation.

"I've had it up to here with this shit," Ketola was saying.

Joentaa saw Heinonen nod, looking thoroughly at a loss.

"You're going to interview the whole bunch and question them until you find out what happened here," Ketola bellowed.

Heinonen and Grönholm silently withdrew.

"Get a load of this," said Ketola, when Joentaa caught his eye. "It's beyond belief." He indicated the corpse and the other beds, shaking his head. "The guy was murdered with seven other people asleep all round him."

Joentaa nodded. He was going to say something, but he didn't because his muddled thoughts had been pierced by a sudden shaft of lightning.

For a moment he believed he'd fathomed the whole thing.

He had a vision of the person he sought walking along a tunnel.

"If Laukkanen is right and it's the same killer," Ketola said, "we must establish a connection between the woman in Naantali and this guy here."

"Who is he?"

"Johann Berg, Swedish, a twenty-nine-year-old student, allegedly a musician, resident in Stockholm. He had a little boy. The youngster's in the breakfast room, like the rest of the tour group. They're all in a daze."

Niemi came in with two of his assistants. Wide awake and

unflappable, he briskly issued some instructions. Joentaa thought Niemi was crazy. He had an urge to talk to him about Sanna.

"It seems the boy had a nightmare. He woke up and tried to rouse his father." Ketola was about to say something else, but he cleared his throat instead.

Joentaa knew what had been on the tip of his tongue.

That the boy's real nightmare had only just begun in earnest.

"He woke one of the women in the group because his father wouldn't stir, and she discovered he was dead. There was a strange smell, too. Chloroform, probably."

A police photographer came in and took some pictures without so much as an excuse-me. Looking at the man, Joentaa wondered if he ever really thought about what he was doing.

"The rest of them are completely distraught, of course," said Ketola. And, after a while: "What's the connection between this Swede and the Naantali woman?" His expression conveyed that Joentaa must know the answer.

"I've no idea," Joentaa said.

"Tomorrow, have another word with Ojaranta. If it really is the same killer, we must establish a link between them. Of course, it may be a coincidence . . ."

"I don't think so."

Ketola looked at him sharply. "Why not?"

"I don't know."

As if he considered it pointless to pursue their conversation, Ketola turned and went into the corridor without another word.

Joentaa remained standing beside the bed. He looked down at the young man who had still been alive a few hours ago—who had gone to sleep firmly convinced that he would wake up and go on living.

He looked at the man's motionless face. He looked at the closed eyelids and reflected that there was nothing left behind them, nothing at all.

He looked down at the man, who was exactly his own age.

He thought of his gun, which was at home.

He wondered if he would be capable of pulling the trigger.

He remembered thinking that Sanna was immortal.

"Where's the breakfast room?" he asked Niemi, who was carefully picking up the objects on the bedside table.

"Immediately on the left of the entrance," Niemi replied, giving him what looked like a smile of encouragement.

He walked back along the passage, which was now so brightly lit that the glare hurt his eyes. The light in the breakfast room, which was more subdued, came from some small white wall fixtures.

He scanned the tourists' petrified faces.

Grönholm, Heinonen, and around a dozen uniformed policemen were seated at the tables taking statements. They were having difficulty in making themselves understood in Swedish or English. Ketola, standing to one side, was talking angrily to the hostel supervisor, who kept shaking his head in a defensive way.

Joentaa surveyed the scene like a picture.

At one of the tables sat a trembling, weeping boy and a young woman, who had her arms round him. Joentaa went over and sat down facing them. He asked the boy his name.

"Sven," he said.

"My name's Kimmo," said Joentaa, extending his hand. "I'm a policeman."

The touch of the boy's fingers made him feel cold. He gave them a squeeze, wishing he could give Sven back his father. He let the hand slip from his own and decided not to say anything to him because there was nothing to be said.

Heinonen came and asked the young woman if she was ready to make a formal statement. She nodded and wearily got to her feet. "I'll be back in a moment," she whispered to Sven. She spoke fluent Finnish. Looking up, Joentaa caught a glance from her. He didn't know if he'd interpreted it correctly, but he rose, sat down beside the boy, and awkwardly put his arms round him. When Sven subsided feebly onto his lap, he started to stroke his head.

As he watched the woman go, he realized to his surprise that he found her attractive. He forced himself to look away and dismiss the thought.

It wasn't long before he felt infinitely remote from his surroundings. He saw Heinonen, who looked tired, and Grönholm, who was disguising his impatience with difficulty. He saw Ketola, who was barking at the bewildered hostel supervisor.

He tried to imagine how it would be if time stood still—now, this minute—and transformed the scene into a tableau: Ketola forever interrupted in mid-tirade, the hostel supervisor forever bewildered, Heinonen forever weary.

If time stood still, he himself would sit forever on the edge of the tableau stroking Sven's head.

He saw Ketola coming toward him. "The supervisor didn't notice anything suspicious, of course," he said. "No, no one was behaving oddly, no, everything was quite normal, no, he didn't see or hear a thing, no, everything was just the way it always is, in other words, fine." Ketola lit a cigarette with trembling fingers. "It's a regular hoot, this place, don't you think?"

"Could a stranger have got into the building unobserved?" asked Joentaa.

"Of course. The man didn't see or hear a thing, as I say. He claims to have locked the front door around one o'clock, but one of the visitors says he sometimes leaves it open all night." Ketola pulled at his cigarette. "There are roughly a hundred young people staying here at present, some of them for one night only. An unfamiliar face wouldn't attract attention."

"Is there a register?" Joentaa asked.

Ketola nodded. "Heinonen's checking it."

Grönholm came over and sat down in the chair beside Joentaa. Behind him came the young woman, who smiled faintly when she saw the boy's head on Joentaa's lap. He noticed only now that Sven had fallen asleep. He could feel his shallow, feverish breathing.

"Nothing at all so far," said Grönholm. "Nobody saw a thing. Anyone would think the man had simply gone to sleep and failed to wake up."

Joentaa saw Ketola greedily inhaling the smoke from his cigarette. His pale face looked tense and irate.

"The killer must have some nerve," Joentaa said after a moment. Grönholm nodded vaguely. Ketola didn't appear to be listening.

"It's as if he feels untouchable," said Joentaa.

"I don't care how he feels," Ketola snarled. "I want him, that's all."

Joentaa swallowed his irritation and looked away. He caught the eye of the young woman, who was standing alongside, looking down at him. "I tried to wake him," she said in a low voice. "But it was no use."

It occurred to Joentaa that she had a beautiful, open face.

The thought puzzled him, and he suppressed it.

He shifted his position a little—carefully, so as not to wake the boy—and motioned to her to sit down beside him.

"Were you traveling together?" he asked.

He immersed himself in her eyes and thought of Sanna.

She nodded. "There were eight of us, all students from Stockholm. We really intended to move on to Tallinn tomorrow."

"What time did you go to bed?"

"Around eleven, I think. My bed was right next to Sven and Johann." She drew a deep breath. "Johann laughed when I wished him sweet dreams because the bed was far too small for him. He was well over six feet."

"When did you arrive in Turku?" Joentaa asked.

"Two days ago. But I already told that to one of your colleagues."

"I'm sorry . . . Does the name Ojaranta mean anything to you? Laura Ojaranta?"

"No." She looked at him inquiringly. He returned her gaze, fighting off an absurd desire to touch her.

"What did you do yesterday? Did you spend the day with Johann Berg?"

"Yes, most of it. In the morning we visited the Handicrafts Museum on the Klosterberg. Johann really enjoyed it—he insisted on going into every one of the craftsmen's workshops. He was studying cultural history. Later he went off on his own with Sven for a while. I'm not sure, but I think they went down to the harbor for a boat ride."

Joentaa nodded.

"Do you have any . . . explanation for what has happened?" he asked. The woman shook her head. "There isn't one," she said.

No explanation . . . Ojaranta had said that too, and so had Jonna Koivuniemi, the painter of the missing picture.

Grönholm, looking thoroughly harassed, came over and asked if someone could find him an interpreter. "I'd no idea my Swedish was so appalling," he said. "There are also a couple of youngsters from France. I haven't been able to exchange a word with them so far."

"I speak French," said the young woman, getting to her feet. Grönholm's face brightened. He started dictating his questions to her as they went. Joentaa watched them go, then gave a jump: Sven had begun to mutter in his sleep. He couldn't understand what the boy was saying. He stroked his head, hoping he would sleep on, but Sven sat up abruptly and stared at him wide-eyed, as if he'd never seen him before.

I'm a stranger, thought Joentaa.

"What is it?" Sven asked. "What happened?"

"You've been asleep," Joentaa said. He tried to restrain the boy, but he broke away and burst out crying. Instantly, all eyes turned in his direction. Joentaa hurried after him. He saw Grönholm and the young woman turn to look in dismay. The woman caught Sven and held him tight until he gradually quieted. Grönholm, who was usually so imperturbable, equal to any situation and never at a loss for some flippant remark, stood beside them looking helpless and irresolute. Joentaa heard him ask one of the uniformed policemen where Laukkanen was, but the doctor had already left.

Joentaa shook off his inertia and asked the hostel supervisor if he had a single room somewhere. The man stared at him uncomprehendingly. "The boy needs rest," he said.

"Er, of course. This way." He showed Joentaa, the young woman, and Sven into a twin-bedded room on the top floor—the quietest room in the building, he explained.

Joentaa thanked him and went off to get Sven's bag from the dormitory in which his father had been murdered. The neon lights were still on. Niemi was examining the sheet on which the dead man had lain.

"They just took him away," he said when he caught Joentaa's look of inquiry. "We haven't found much to date, I'm afraid."

Joentaa located Sven's bag after a brief search. Sven was asleep when he returned to the little attic room. The young woman was seated beside the bed with the boy's hand in hers, looking down at him.

Joentaa paused in the doorway. It occurred to him that he had looked at Sanna the same way the night she died.

He tiptoed over to the bed.

"Sleep's the best thing for him," he said. The woman nodded without taking her eyes from the boy.

Joentaa pulled up a chair and sat down beside her. He studied the lines of her face, which was in shadow.

"What's your name?" he asked after a while.

"Annette Söderström."

He resisted an urge to tell her about Sanna.

"How long had you known Johann Berg?" he asked.

"A very long time. We were at school together." There was a brief silence. "I can't believe he's dead."

He looked up, sensing that her eyes were on his face. She's waiting for me to undo all that's happened, he thought.

He avoided her gaze.

He thought of Sanna and wondered why he wanted to tell this Annette Söderström about her. My wife is dead . . . The words were on the tip of his tongue, but he didn't utter them.

"Were you and Johann Berg . . . friends?" he asked instead.

She turned toward him again. To his surprise he saw that she was smiling, probably at his clumsy phraseology.

"We were very good friends," she said.

"Where is Sven's mother?"

"In Stockholm. Sven lives with her, actually, but Johann often used to visit him and take him away on holiday."

Joentaa felt vaguely relieved that the boy wouldn't be entirely cast adrift.

He took his leave without telling Annette Söderström about Sanna.

On the stairs he passed a gaggle of youngsters, some of whom were laughing uproariously. The only people left in the breakfast room were Ketola and the hostel supervisor. The latter, who sat slumped on a chair, was clearly hoping to be able to go back to bed at last.

Ketola was talking into his cell phone, his upright stance suggestive of a man taking orders. Joentaa surmised that he was speaking to Nurmela.

"That's it for tonight," he said when the call ended.

"Do we have anything yet?" asked Joentaa.

Ketola shook his head. He was evidently too tired to get irate about it. "Absolutely nothing," he replied. "Heinonen and Grönholm will carry on here tomorrow. First thing in the morning, look in on the Handicrafts Museum and have a word with the staff there. Maybe they'll have noticed something about the tour group." His tone conveyed that he doubted it. "Nurmela has scheduled a press conference for twelve noon. You can then submit a detailed report about the Naantali case."

Joentaa nodded.

"How's the boy?"

"He's asleep."

"Good. He'll be returning to Stockholm tomorrow. His mother has already been informed. The others must stay here, of course. See you tomorrow." He draped his coat over his shoulder and turned on his heel.

The hostel supervisor jumped up and escorted him out. "If I can help in any way . . ." he said halfheartedly.

"Just make sure all your guests remain available and nobody leaves," Ketola told him.

Joentaa followed them out. The place was now in darkness except for the dormitory at the far end of the long corridor. Niemi was still at work, it seemed.

Joentaa walked slowly to his car. He drew the cold air deep into his lungs and thought of winter, which was not far off.

He dreaded its approach, he realized.

The hostel supervisor came over to him.

"Remember me?" Joentaa asked him without thinking.

He looked puzzled. "I'm sorry?"

"I stayed here as a youngster, fourteen or fifteen years ago. I recognized you at once."

The supervisor nodded, but he still looked uncomprehending.

"It was my first long trip," Joentaa said. "I'm from eastern Finland originally."

The supervisor nodded again.

"See you tomorrow," said Joentaa.

"Oh, right. Till tomorrow."

He watched the man's receding figure until the door closed behind him.

Looking up in search of the window beneath the eaves, he tried to picture Annette Söderström sitting beside Sven's bed.

He hoped the boy was still asleep.

He drove home, sat down in the living room, and drafted the obituary notice. "I love you. Kimmo," he wrote at the end.

He dreamed of Sanna. He was lying with his head on her lap, telling her how he felt. She listened patiently and soothed him with words that undid all that had happened. He thought, when he awoke, that those words were on his lips.

He tried to utter them, but they were gone.

18

In the morning he drove to the Handicrafts Museum on the Klosterberg. The sunlight was even brighter than it had been for the last few days, but the air was growing colder.

It occurred to him, as he got out of the car and walked slowly toward the wooden buildings, that Johann Berg had seen all this only yesterday. He tried to imagine what the man had felt.

A young woman sitting in the little ticket office smiled at him as he approached. He showed her his warrant card and asked if she remembered the group of Swedish tourists. When she asked why he wanted to know, he told her that one of them had been murdered.

Her face conveyed suppressed curiosity and spurious horror.

"But that's terrible," she said.

"Did anything strike you about them?" he asked. "Anything in particular, I mean?"

She thought awhile, then shook her head. "They were just happy tourists."

Joentaa could tell that she was recalling their faces and wondering feverishly which of them was alive no longer. "I only sold them their tickets," she said. "Vesa showed them round the workshops."

"Vesa?"

"I think he's in the café," she said, pointing to the largest of the wooden buildings, which housed a postcard kiosk and a cafeteria. "Vesa is our jack of all trades," she went on with a smile. "The main thing is, he knows an incredible amount about handicrafts and the history of the buildings."

Joentaa thanked her and went over to the place where he and Sanna had once stopped off for tea and apple tart. It was in winter. Big fat snowflakes were falling, and Sanna remarked that they hadn't had to drive far to see something worthwhile.

He had to duck his head on entering, or he would have hit it on the lintel. He wondered why people had been so much shorter in centuries gone by, and recalled that the same thought had struck him when he visited the place with Sanna.

He could hear music—a tune that instantly appealed to him.

The interior was in shadow except where two thin strips of sunlight slanted down through the windows. A waitress in a white apron was just bringing an elderly man a coffee. He glanced up from his newspaper as Joentaa came in. The waitress said good morning and asked where he would like to sit.

"I'm looking for Vesa," Joentaa told her.

"That's him playing now." She smiled and pointed in the direction from which the music was coming. There was an upright piano at the far end of the room, Joentaa saw. A young man with shoulder-length hair was playing it with his head bowed and his eyes closed.

He was dressed entirely in black.

Joentaa went over to him. He could sense how soothing the pianist found the gentle melody.

"You play very well," he said.

The young man slowly raised his head. "Thanks."

"My name is Kimmo Joentaa. I'm a policeman." Joentaa showed his warrant card. The young man looked at him inquiringly. Joentaa got the impression that he was still in a dream, that he was very slowly returning from another world. He wished that he, too, could play an instrument. He wished he were capable of constructing an alternative world with music.

"What was that tune?" he asked. The young man stared at him. He didn't seem to understand. "The one you were playing, I mean . . ."

"Oh, nothing special. All my tunes tend to sound alike. That's because I can't read music." He smiled. "I simply play whatever I think will sound nice."

"You do it very well."

The young man looked down shyly and played on. Joentaa had the feeling that he was pleased with the compliment.

"Your name is Vesa?"

"That's right. Vesa Lehmus."

"You showed a group of tourists round the workshops yesterday."

"More than one, actually. Five in all."

"I'm talking about a group of Swedish tourists. Young people, students. Do you remember them?"

"Yes, they were the first batch, in the morning."

"Did you notice anything, well, unusual about them?"

"What do you mean?"

"One member of the group has been murdered." Joentaa paused, waiting for some reaction, but there wasn't any. The young man's eyes remained expressionless, as if he didn't understand.

"Murdered?" he said.

"I was hoping you might be able to help me . . . that you might have noticed something. It's a long shot, I know . . ."

"Which one was it?" he asked. "I remember them all quite well."

"But nothing struck you about them?"

He shook his head. "Which one was it?" he asked again.

"I'm afraid I'm not at liberty to disclose any details," said Joentaa.

The young man nodded slowly. "I'm very sad to hear that one of them is dead," he said at length. "They all seemed so nice."

Joentaa lingered for a while. The young man resumed playing, hesitantly at first, then with more assurance. Joentaa saw him close his eyes and lose himself in the melody once more.

He envied him.

Vesa Lehmus glanced up and smiled when he said goodbye.

19

While driving to police headquarters Joentaa thought of the press conference Nurmela had scheduled for midday and how unprepared for it he was.

On arrival he remained sitting in the car for a while, striving unsuccessfully to recall all he knew about the woman murdered at Naantali.

He tried to picture Laura Ojaranta and saw Sanna.

He got out of the car in order to banish the vision.

As he walked slowly toward the brown brick building, he contemplated letting out a yell and running away. He had an urge to run until he passed out from sheer exhaustion.

Two men were standing on the steps, talking excitedly into their cell phones. Joentaa recognized them when he drew nearer. Both were journalists with a fondness for embarrassing Ketola at press conferences with aggressive and unwelcome questions, particularly the younger of the two, Markus Helin, whose cocky manner Joentaa disliked as much as he disliked the *Illansanomat,* the rag for which Helin worked.

Helin smiled when he saw him coming. "Well, fancy that!" he exclaimed as Joentaa walked past.

Joentaa failed to grasp what he meant. For a moment he thought Helin was making a jocular allusion to Sanna's death, but he promptly dismissed the idea.

He took the elevator to the fifth floor, where he bumped into Grönholm, who was looking elated.

"We've got the would-be assassin," he said.

Joentaa recoiled.

"We've got the person who took a potshot at Sami Järvi," Grönholm amplified. "You should go and take a peek at the monster, it's worth a look." Joentaa noticed only now that Grönholm was grinning and in high spirits.

He merely nodded and walked on.

"In the interview room," Grönholm called after him.

He nodded again, absently this time.

His first thought had been that Grönholm was referring to the killer of Laura Ojaranta and Johann Berg. The idea that he'd been caught had filled him with dismay. The murderer's arrest would dispel the mystery that was preserving him from an emotional vacuum.

Tuomas Heinonen was standing outside the interview room's big window. Ketola's incisive voice could be heard through the glass.

"What were you thinking of?" he bellowed.

Joentaa went and stood beside Heinonen, who was quietly smiling to himself.

The would-be assassin who had been hunted by scores of detectives—who had dominated the airwaves and been the talk of all Finland—was a frail little woman with bobbed hair, spectacles, and a handbag. She clutched the latter tightly on her lap while Ketola harangued her.

Joentaa couldn't understand what Grönholm and Heinonen found so amusing. "Has she said anything?" he asked. Heinonen shrugged. "She has a screw loose," he said. "Says nothing most of the time, and when she does say something it's gibberish."

Ketola had got to his feet. He went round behind the woman and leaned over her shoulder. "If you don't say something sensible in the next ten seconds, I'll smash your face in," he said, and turned away. For a moment Joentaa thought he'd misheard. He looked at Heinonen, who raised his eyebrows.

Ketola leaned against the wall and started counting. "One, two, three, four . . ."

The woman sat hunched up on her chair, seemingly unaware of what was going on around her. She was wearing an old-fashioned regional costume familiar to Joentaa from the films of peasant life his mother used to weep at many years ago.

Ketola went on counting. He paused when he got to ten, then pounced on the back of the chair and proceeded to shake it until the woman fell to the floor. He kicked her in the back. "Start talking!" he yelled.

Joentaa froze. For several seconds he stared at the scene as if it were some weird, incomprehensible skit that had no connection with reality. Then he came to life and dashed into the interview room. Ketola was bending over the woman, who had shut her eyes and was muttering to herself. Joentaa seized him and tried to haul him to the door, but Ketola shook him off, grabbed him by the throat, and slammed him against the wall. "What are you doing here?" he shouted.

"Calm down," Joentaa stammered. He caught a glimpse of Heinonen staring through the window with his mouth open, utterly flabbergasted. "Calm down," he repeated. He strove to speak clearly and insistently, forcing himself to look Ketola straight in the eye. To his relief, he felt the hands around his throat relax their grip. Ketola avoided his gaze. He seemed to be slowly awakening from a dream. He grabbed Joentaa once more, then released him and stood with his shoulders drooping. Joentaa could tell that he was at a loss for words. Eventually Ketola said: "We'll speak later." He said it in his usual, peremptory tone, but with his head down.

He left the room without a backward glance.

Joentaa shut his eyes and wondered if this was the end—if he could work with Ketola again after this incident. He wondered what had happened, why it had happened, and whether he had done the right thing.

The woman was still lying on the floor, whimpering to herself. "He's a bad man," she mumbled. Joentaa went over and cautiously tried to help her up. "It's over," he whispered soothingly when she resisted. "Take it easy, everything's all right."

She let him lift her onto the chair. When their eyes met she looked at him inquiringly.

"Everything okay?" asked Heinonen, who had suddenly appeared behind him, flushed and breathless. Two uniformed policemen were standing irresolutely in the doorway.

Joentaa gave a hesitant nod. "I guess so," he said. He couldn't help laughing, he didn't know what at. Perhaps at Heinonen's expression or the stupid question he'd asked.

"Ketola seems to be cracking up," Heinonen said helplessly.

Joentaa drew a deep breath and suppressed his nonsensical laughter.

"Where's he gone?" Heinonen asked.

"No idea." Joentaa signaled to the uniformed cops to remain with the woman and shoved Heinonen out of the interview room.

"What's going on here?" he asked when they were outside in the corridor. Heinonen didn't understand. "I mean, where did this woman come from?"

"Grönholm arrested her this morning. He'd taken a bus from the marketplace to Paatinen. You remember, we had this tip that the perpetrator escaped on board a bus . . ."

Joentaa nodded.

"Well, the woman was sitting in the bus, and she kept smiling at him. He asked if she often used that route because he thought she might have seen something. She said she used it every day and invited him to have coffee at her apartment. Grönholm spotted the pistol on the table in her living room. It was just lying there."

Heinonen fell silent, as if that said it all.

"I see," Joentaa said.

"Grönholm pulled her in at once, of course."

"I see," Joentaa said again, although he didn't see at all. "And there's really no doubt that she's the . . ."

"Kari Niemi is working on the assumption that her gun is the one we're looking for. And when Grönholm raised the subject of Sami Järvi with her, she said something about him being a bad man, and that something had to be done about him."

Joentaa nodded.

"That's all we know at present," said Heinonen. "The whole thing's only an hour old at most. Grönholm is busy trying to get hold of the woman's friends and relations."

Nurmela strode briskly up to them. "Where's Ketola?" he demanded. "The press are waiting. The show starts in five minutes, and I don't want to hog all the kudos." He gave a hearty laugh, thoroughly satisfied with himself and with life in general.

Heinonen started to say something, but limited himself to a shrug.

"I'll go and look for him," Joentaa said.

"Please do. Tell him to get a move on, they're already getting itchy. I must go. If Ketola isn't there in five minutes I'll open the proceedings myself. By the way, give Grönholm a big pat on the back." He underlined his words with a thumbs-up, nodded to them, and hurried off to enjoy his triumph.

He was quite as impatient as the representatives of the press, Joentaa reflected.

He told Heinonen to go on questioning the woman and went off to look for Ketola. He found him in their office, sitting bolt upright at his desk and staring vacantly at the wall.

"Nurmela wants you with him at the press conference. He says to hurry."

Ketola didn't react.

Looking down at him, Joentaa felt himself break out in a sweat. It occurred to him that he would never again feel comfortable in Ketola's presence.

"Time to go," Joentaa said.

Ketola shook his head. "I'm staying put." He looked up, and Joentaa was surprised to see that he was smiling at him, sadly and wearily. His eyes were bloodshot. Joentaa wondered if he'd been weeping.

"Sit down, Kimmo," Ketola said. Joentaa hesitated, then sat down at his desk.

He waited for Ketola to say something, but he didn't.

The silence persisted. For an eternity, or so it seemed to Joentaa. His head was in a whirl, but he relaxed by degrees, and at some stage he began to enjoy the silence. He wondered what story Ketola was hiding. Who exactly was this man he worked with every day? He thought of the young man who had been playing the piano in the Handicraft Museum's cafeteria, and who had seemed genuinely saddened by the death of a Swedish student he'd seen on only one occasion. The young man had been quite unaware how deeply affected he, Joentaa, had been by his piano playing. Joentaa wondered what went on in the young man's head when he played the piano. There were so many stories he didn't know and would never know.

He thought of Sanna.

He looked at Ketola staring motionless into space.

His muddled thoughts were scattered to the winds when Nurmela came in with two bottles of champagne and good-humoredly suggested drinking to the successful outcome of their investigation.

He saw Ketola smile and get to his feet with an effort. Although he couldn't interpret the look he gave him, he felt he'd been closer to the man during those minutes of silence than in all their conversations to date.

20

At lunchtime a congratulatory fax arrived from the wounded politician's party headquarters. Nurmela was jubilant. The murders at Naantali and the youth hostel might never have occurred, they counted for so little now. Infected by the general euphoria, the police commissioner seemed to assume that those cases, too, would solve themselves. In the end, having initially been deferred in favor of some television interviews, the meeting scheduled to discuss them lapsed into oblivion.

Grönholm, in his gruff, unemotional way, was pleased with the praise Nurmela had heaped on him.

Ketola went home early. "Sure, take the rest of the day off, you deserve it," Nurmela told him, clearly unconcerned that the would-be assassin's motives were obscure.

Joentaa and Heinonen spent the whole afternoon trying to get through to the woman, but without success. She simply repeated that Sami Järvi was a bad man, and that she had needed to do something about him.

Grönholm's preliminary interviews with the woman's neighbors yielded little. Her name was Mari Räsanen, and she and her mother led a very secluded life. No one seemed to be particularly interested in the pair. The mother had yet to show up.

Grönholm reported that their three-room apartment was filled with flowers and house plants. The woman had "simply flipped," he said, tapping his forehead.

Joentaa wondered why Grönholm was taking the whole thing so lightly—why everyone seemed to find it unexceptional that this woman had shot a politician. Everyone except Ketola, who had lost his nerve and gone home long before the end of office hours for the first time since Joentaa had been working with him.

Heinonen sat facing Mari Räsanen and patiently asked her questions. Joentaa stood to one side and watched her as she gave her answers in a faint, tremulous voice. Occasionally she smiled a remote smile, as if she were in another world. He was fleetingly reminded of the young pianist in the museum café.

Mari Räsanen told Heinonen that she was forty-two, that her mother worked at a laundry, although she was nearly seventy, and that Sami Järvi wanted to take their money away. "I had to do something about him," she said.

Early that evening Heinonen lost patience.

"I've had it," he told Joentaa when they withdrew to the corridor.

Joentaa said he would carry on by himself for a while. When Heinonen had gone he stood watching the woman through the window. She was sitting quietly on her chair, muttering to herself. From time to time she firmly shook her head.

Joentaa went back inside and sat down facing her. He turned on the tape recorder again and tried to make eye contact, but she stared past him.

"What was going through your mind as you walked toward Mr. Järvi in the marketplace?" he asked. She didn't answer, but her eyes swiveled in his direction.

"Can you remember the moment when you pulled the trigger?" She merely stared at him.

"Did you see him fall to the ground?"

She went on staring.

Joentaa was finding his own questions meaningless.

In a low voice, the woman asked why her mother hadn't come yet.

Joentaa drove home. In the city center he was brought to a standstill by the rush-hour traffic. He had read recently that Aninkaistenkatu, the wide boulevard that traversed Turku, was more heavily polluted with exhaust fumes than any other place in Finland. On the other hand, he doubted if any other country had so few big cities and so many lakes and trees.

He felt relieved when he left the city behind him. He turned on the radio and listened to some vapid music. It didn't appeal to him, but he left it on.

He parked in the shade of the apple tree and looked over at the house, which was bathed in evening sunlight. The house that had ceased to be his home.

Now that Sanna was gone, he thought, he would have no home.

He remembered the smile of the estate agent who had plied Sanna with compliments.

He remembered Sanna's smile.

He got out of the car. A renewed urge to flee assailed him as he walked toward the house. He felt the urge and yet, at the same time, dreaded it.

He pictured himself running away and plunging into nothingness.

Reluctantly, he opened the front door and entered the hallway.

He hoped Jussi and Merja weren't there. He hoped they'd simply gone home, never to return.

He had no desire to see their grief-stricken faces, which only reminded him that Sanna was alive no longer.

She could still be alive, he thought, as long as he denied her death and no one reminded him of it.

His mother was making coffee in the kitchen.

For one unreal moment he thought she was an illusion, and that she too was dead.

"Kimmo," she said, "I didn't hear you come in." She came over and gave him a hug. He shrank away.

"What are you doing here?" he demanded. "I said I'd call you."

Anita gently patted his hand and smiled. "Well, I'm here now," she said.

It had always been that simple.

She had aged, he thought, and felt he ought to be annoyed. It occurred to him, as she deftly arranged some cups on a tray, that she would die before long.

She turned to leave the kitchen. Joentaa wondered why he found it hard to look at her.

He wondered what she was thinking and whether she had shed many tears since his phone call. He felt sure she had, but she would do her utmost to conceal it from him. She would talk nicely to everyone, dispense words of consolation and listen patiently and attentively without changing the subject to herself. She asked him where the sugar was and carried the tray into the living room.

When she smilingly slid a cup toward Jussi and rested her hand on Merja's arm, he felt glad of her presence after all.

He sat down in an armchair and waited for her to say something, but she didn't. As the silence continued, he felt his thoughts grow steadily lighter until they became airborne.

At some stage he heard his mother talking quietly to Merja. Merja replied. He didn't catch what she said, but it relieved him to hear her speaking.

He tried to imagine the day of Merja's death, wondering where he would be and how he would feel when he heard the news.

He thought of the woman in the blue villa and the young man at the youth hostel, who had been his own age.

He thought of Sven and of his inability to help the little boy.

He heard the subdued murmur of his mother's voice.

He heard the rattle of cups on saucers.

He tried to imagine the last moment of his life and the first moment thereafter, which wouldn't happen.

He tried to imagine that nonexistent moment.

His head was filled with an ever-recurring melody whose provenance escaped him.

21

He wound down the window and stuck his head out into the airstream.

He looked up at the dark, cloudless sky and imagined it slowly descending on him.

It was a pleasant notion, a euphoric notion.

He wasn't afraid. He would never be afraid again.

He reached for the little silver stars and crushed them in his hands.

He was zigzagging. A car overtook him, horn blaring.

He thought of the policeman who had spoken to him that afternoon. He had played his role quite effortlessly. He was relieved it had all been so easy.

No one would ever guess who he really was.

He laughed and flattened the accelerator, recalling how he had walked along the passage in the youth hostel.

It was dark.

He was floating.

He had spent a long time waiting in the parking lot beside the river.

Waiting until he knew he was invisible and invulnerable.

He had suppressed his fear and changed worlds. The chloroform-soaked cloth he had inserted in a plastic bag to hide the smell.

In the passage he had smiled at the faces that brushed past him without a second glance. He opened several doors. In some of the rooms, which were wrapped in silence, he tiptoed over and studied the faces of the sleeping occupants.

He was infinitely powerful.

In one room some youngsters were playing cards. He laughed when they demanded to know what he wanted. "Sorry, it won't happen again," he called to convey that it was just a silly joke on his part.

Rock music had been coming from somewhere.

No one paid him any attention.

At last he had found him. It was only a matter of time.

He sighted the crescent moon through a narrow crack between the curtains.

He stood beside the bed for a long time, inhaling the man's regular breathing.

He was so silent. So omnipotent.

He had waited patiently until he sensed that he would do it without thinking.

He anesthetized the sleeping man, then slid the pillow from beneath his head and pressed it down on his face.

He shut his eyes.

When he was sure it was over, he released the pressure.

He took the dice cup from the bedside table.

He turned away and walked back along the dark passage toward no-man's-land.

He vented his elation in a cry.

He was immortal.

He was death itself.

22

Summer ended on the day of the funeral.

Joentaa shook hands and thanked people for their condolences. His mother tried to shelter him under her umbrella, but he pulled away and stood in the downpour on his own.

He thought of Sanna and how fond she had been of rain.

He saw her dancing in the rain.

He was cold.

He stood beside the pastor of Lenganiemi, who was talking about Sanna, but he didn't hear what he said.

Everyone assured him later that the pastor had said the nicest things.

His thoughts went back to the day he'd spent at Lenganiemi with Sanna. Years ago, an eternity ago. He couldn't understand why he hadn't been able to remember it properly when he'd visited the place to consult the pastor after her death.

It had been a fine day. Sanna had talked a lot, and he'd nodded without listening. He had nodded and failed to listen far too often when she was talking. He had never dreamed how precious her every word would become.

He yearned to hear her voice again.

And her laugh.

Many of her friends and colleagues had turned up, as well as many of his own friends.

They looked like strangers to him.

Pasi and Liisa Laaksonen were there. So was Niemi and—to his surprise—Ketola.

He hadn't seen many of those present for a long time. What surprised him most was that Markku Vatanen had turned up, a schoolfriend from Kitee whom he hadn't spoken to since their graduation party.

The sight of him reminded Joentaa that he'd sometimes thought of Markku, just before going to sleep, and wondered how he was getting on. He had often toyed with the idea of calling him sometime soon, but it had always evaporated by the morning.

He reflected that Markku could have died without his ever learning of it.

Although glad that he had come, he couldn't bring himself to say so. He couldn't speak to anyone. His one thought was that this was the worst day of his life.

He heard earth falling onto Sanna's coffin and resolved to take his life that night. He saw himself on the dock beside the lake. It was cold and windy. He was holding the gun to his temple, no longer afraid of pulling the trigger.

He pictured what would happen after that. He had a vision of himself reunited with Sanna, embracing her, holding her tight for evermore. But he didn't believe in it.

He envied the pastor his incomprehensible faith.

He told himself that the notion of eternal life was even more terrifying than death.

His mother had wanted to arrange a meal at a small inn near the parish hall, but he'd quashed the idea. When she started to argue he shouted at her. Shut up, he told her. That's the last I want to hear of it.

He would sooner have buried Sanna by himself.

As he shook people's hands and gazed into their sad, sympathetic faces, he regretted not having done so.

And then it was over. Most of the mourners had left without his noticing. He realized it only when they'd gone. He stood beside the grave in the pouring rain and felt that it was all unreal—that everything should be different.

His mother came over and gingerly asked if he was coming.

He shook his head.

Merja and Jussi Sihvonen were already waiting beside the car, he saw. Merja was weeping, Jussi standing frozen-faced behind her. He was talking vehemently in a desperate attempt to calm her.

"I'm going to stay a little longer," Joentaa told his mother. He handed her the keys to the car and to the front door. On the ring was a lucky charm Sanna had given him, a polar bear in white wood. "Jussi can drive," said Joentaa. Anita nodded and took the keys.

He watched her go, saw her get into the car. She settled herself on the rear seat, beside Merja, and put an arm round her shoulders. He saw Jussi drive off down the narrow track through the trees with feverish, jerky movements. He waited for the hum of the engine to fade and die away altogether.

The sexton was at work in the rain outside the red church—the one who had looked up at the sun, only a few hours after Sanna's death, and called out what a glorious day it was. Joentaa tried to catch his eye, but the man didn't recognize him. Ill-humoredly, he pulled the hood of his waterproof cape over his head and drove his spade into the soil.

Joentaa wondered when the man would die and whether he often thought of death.

Looking down at Sanna's grave, he found it impossible to grasp that she was lying in the coffin. He couldn't conceive of the fact, and never would, that she no longer existed. He thought of his mother, of Merja and Jussi. And of Markku Vatanen, who had probably spent hours in a train or his car in order to attend the funeral of someone he'd never met. He hadn't said goodbye to Markku—hadn't even noticed that he'd left. He thought of Kari Niemi, whom he liked, and of Ketola, who was an enigma to him, and of the fact that none of these people meant anything to him.

No one meant anything now that Sanna was dead.

He stared at her grave and felt nothing.

He turned away and walked down to the ferry.

He crossed the cold, windswept stretch of water and walked home.

At times, when Sanna was still in good health and all was well, he'd felt that he would be unable to live without her—that he belonged to her, body and soul. The idea had vaguely perturbed him, but it was always quick to subside.

Especially when Sanna looked at him and asked what he was thinking.

He had smiled and left the question in the air.

He set off along the road through the forest. Every step was taking him a little further away from Sanna, he thought. By the time he reached home it would be as if she'd never existed.

He wondered if that was what he wanted—if he wished he'd never met her.

He tried to banish the thought. When this didn't work he resorted to violence: he eradicated it by talking loudly to himself so as not to have to think anymore.

He shouted her name.

He shouted until he wept.

When he got home his mother was standing in the doorway as if she'd been waiting there the whole time.

He was cold. His sodden clothes were clinging to his body.

Anita took his coat and peeled off his sweater. She told him to take a shower at once and change.

She disappeared into the kitchen to heat up some soup.

Merja and Jussi were in the living room, she lying on the sofa with her head on her husband's lap. Jussi looked blankly at Joentaa when he came in.

Merja was breathing evenly. Joentaa hoped she was asleep.

He sat down in the armchair and looked out of the window at the lake, on which thin strands of rain were falling.

He saw Sanna sitting on the dock wrapped up in blankets. Standing behind her, he described how he'd watched the dawn breaking. He told her exactly what he'd seen.

He waited for her to react, but she didn't.

He closed his eyes. When he opened them a gray sun was breaking through the clouds.

Sanna turned and smiled at him.

He knew she was smiling but couldn't see it.

Sanna had no face.

She stood up and jumped into the gray water.

The pale-blue sky was gray too.

She called: Come on, you coward!

He waded toward her, cried out when he felt the chill of the lake, looked down at his gray legs in the gray water.

He tried to catch her eye as he waded nearer. Another five or ten yards and he reached for her, stumbled and pulled her under.

They embraced under water.

She regained the surface, coughing and spluttering.

I love you, he cried.

He kissed her, but he couldn't feel a thing.

Her lips were gray.

Still seeking her eyes, he plunged into a bottomless pit.

PART TWO

I

Jaana had been looking at the boy for a long time.

Behind her, Kati called to her to hurry up and come in.

"It isn't cold," she called. "What's the matter with you?"

Jaana didn't answer. She dropped the towel she was holding and walked over to the boy, who was sitting on a bench, watching the surface of the water.

He was dressed entirely in red.

He didn't stir as she drew nearer. It was this stillness of his that attracted her, she thought.

She sat down beside him and asked if he'd care to join them.

She pointed to Kati, who was waving at them.

He slowly turned his head in her direction.

The sun was behind him. She had to screw up her eyes to see his face.

"No, I wouldn't," he said.

His voice was low.

Jaana said nothing for a while. "Are you from around here?" she asked eventually.

The boy nodded.

"From Naantali, or Turku?"

"From Maaria," he said. "It's on the outskirts of Turku."

She was debating what to ask next when he went on, "I work at the Turku Handicrafts Museum. I know all about the old buildings. Ever been there?"

Jaana shook her head. She looked over at Kati, who was gliding slowly through the water and deliberately paying no more attention to her.

"I could tell you all about the buildings," the boy said.

He looked into her eyes.

He had lovely deep eyes.

When she returned his gaze he looked away.

"I'd like to see the museum sometime," she said.

The boy stared at the water and said nothing. She wasn't sure if he'd been listening.

"Do you work there every day?" she asked.

No response. She was about to repeat the question when he nodded slowly. "I'm always there. From ten till five, then we close."

"I could come in the next day or two. I'll be in Turku anyway on Wednesday."

He looked at her as if he hadn't understood.

After a while he got up and walked off.

Jaana watched him go. She waited for him to turn and look back at her, but he didn't.

Kati called to her to hurry up and come in.

Today was definitely the last day for swimming this year, she'd said that morning as they walked along the dock toward the glittering water. Kati's forecasts tended to be accurate.

She got up and walked down to the shore.

"Who was that guy?" Kati asked.

Jaana shrugged.

"You mean you didn't know him?"

"No."

"So what did you want with him?"

"He was . . . all by himself."

Kati laughed, "I think you're crazy sometimes." She reached Jaana in two strokes and pulled her under.

Jaana screamed.

Kati grinned at her when she surfaced again. "And sometimes one has to use force to get anywhere with you."

2

J oentaa looked at Liisa Laaksonen's expectant face. She placed the basket of fish on the dock and patted her husband's shoulder.

Pasi cast his line with panache. He'd always been fond of fishing, he said, even as a boy. He told how his four older brothers had snapped his rods, they were so resentful of his catches.

Pasi laughed. Liisa laughed too.

Joentaa nodded and smiled, not listening.

He knew why the couple had invited him and was grateful to them. They were merely casual acquaintances of a couple of years' standing, so it wasn't axiomatic that they should be taking all this trouble to summon him back to life.

He ate Pasi's fish and Liisa's apple tart.

He took another slice when Liisa proved implacable.

He looked at his mother, who was covertly watching him and trying to swallow some of her maternal solicitude with every morsel.

He thought what a lovely day it would have been if Sanna were sitting beside him, joining in their laughter at Pasi's eventful past.

That night he told his mother to leave.

She stared at him.

"I need to be alone," he said. "I need some peace and quiet."

Anita gave him a hug and promised to take the morning train back to Kitee. She made to release herself from his embrace, but he held her tight. He closed his eyes and rested his head on her shoulder.

After a minute or two he released her.

While Anita was packing her bag he sat in the living room and gazed through the window at the dark green lake. Jussi and Merja Sihvonen had returned home two weeks ago, shortly after the funeral. He wondered how they were.

Jussi hadn't stirred from Merja's side, doing his best to interpret her every wish and fulfill it. For all that, Joentaa got the impression that he was powerless because there was no way of breaching the wall his wife had erected around herself.

The last time he'd spoken to Jussi on the phone, he'd assured him that Merja was bearing up. He hoped it was true.

Anita made some supper and they ate in silence.

He was relieved when she went to bed not long afterward.

Sitting up straight on the sofa bed in the living room, he tried to relax his tense muscles. After a while the silence became unbearable. He got up, turned on the light, and skimmed through the newspaper without absorbing its contents.

He wondered if he'd been right to ask Anita to go. He didn't know. He didn't know whether he wanted solitude or company, because neither seemed to achieve anything. When alone he was at least spared the sensation that other people were staring at his back with sympathy or concern, or sometimes only with curiosity.

The feeling that his life was at a standstill had grown even stronger than it had been in the week after Sanna's death.

He was alive, but nothing moved.

The pain had simultaneously receded and become more immediate. It didn't strike as deep—its sudden onset had ceased to take his breath away—but it was ever-present. It numbed him.

He strove to conceal it from others so as not to have to answer any questions. As long as he remained equable they regarded him as normal. As long as he remained equable no one felt duty-bound to worry about him.

As long as he didn't draw attention to himself their sympathy would remain within bounds.

He performed his work conscientiously, sometimes staying at the office until late at night. By now, although he had never exchanged a word with her, he felt he had known the dead woman at Naantali for a long time. Whenever he thought of her, he thought first of the blue villa and then of the corpse in the bedroom.

He now knew that Laura Ojaranta had been a first-class orienteer.

This had surprised him, he couldn't have explained why. As a girl she had even competed in the Finnish national championships.

He pictured her as an almost invariably amiable, contented woman who had done a lot of gardening, and whose husband had often been away on business.

Several of her neighbors had told him that she often used to sing while gardening.

There was no trace of her murderer. There didn't even seem to be a motive.

Nurmela had dismissed the possibility of a connection between the murders at Naantali and the youth hostel as quickly as Laukkanen had mooted it. The pathologist had established during the autopsy that, unlike Laura Ojaranta, the victim at the youth hostel had indeed been drugged with chloroform. Nurmela pronounced this a definite discrepancy and saw no reason to suppose that a serial murderer had been at work. It was now regarded as certain that Laura Ojaranta and Johann Berg had never crossed each other's paths.

The cases had been divided up. Ketola and Heinonen were investigating the murder of Johann Berg, Joentaa and Grönholm that of Laura Ojaranta. It did Joentaa good to work with Grönholm. Grönholm laughed a lot. He was always cracking jokes and seemed to have forgotten that Joentaa had ever had a wife. Joentaa sometimes wondered whether he'd really forgotten, or if he realized that the best way of helping him was to exclude Sanna from their conversations.

The press was devoting surprisingly little attention to the two murders. Joentaa surmised that they had been too close in time to the attack on Järvi and the arrest of his mysterious assailant to be of any great editorial interest. Even the local paper had printed only brief reports on the subject.

Joentaa further surmised that Nurmela's main reason for splitting up the investigations had been to keep media interest to a minimum.

Interest in the attempt on Järvi's life had also waned in the interim. His would-be assassin, Mari Räsanen, was clearly incapable of accounting for her actions, although there were times when she suddenly emerged from her torpor. Joentaa found this perplexing.

It transpired from the long interviews he conducted with her that she had really been acting on an idea of her mother's.

He was surprised when Ketola asked him to conduct these interviews. Ketola himself usually stood in the background, saying nothing. He had said very little since losing his self-control on the day of Mari Räsanen's arrest.

He had merely nodded when Joentaa thanked him for coming to the funeral.

Under interrogation, Mari Räsanen stated at some point that Sami Järvi had spoken out in favor of the death penalty, and that this was wrong. Taken aback, Joentaa had checked her statement and found it to be true. During a television interview three weeks before the attempt on his life, Sami Järvi had parenthetically described the enforcement of the death penalty in America as "essential."

When informed of this by Joentaa, Ketola had laughed grimly at the thought that Mari Räsanen had tried to kill a politician because he considered killing justified.

At some stage Joentaa fell asleep. He awoke feeling chilled and looked out at the lake, which was suffused with dim blue light. It was a quarter to six on a gloomy morning. He didn't know how long he'd been asleep because he didn't know when he'd dozed off.

He washed and dressed. After breakfasting on a slice of bread and a glass of milk, he drove to the office. By now, Ketola was probably used to the fact that he often got there before him.

He had written a note to Anita, but it gave him a pang to think she wouldn't be there that evening. I shouldn't have left like that, he thought as he came to a standstill in the rush-hour traffic.

He couldn't think why he hadn't woken her.

He resolved to call her as soon as he got to the office.

The big parking lot in front of the brown brick building was almost empty. He remained sitting in the car for a while.

This would be the coldest winter of his life, he thought.

The porter at the reception desk nodded listlessly as he walked past. The corridors were deserted. He felt he was going to find it hard to work—to concentrate on dead people and the question of who had killed them.

For an instant life seemed pointless. That thought occurred to him more and more often. It went as quickly as it came, but it kept returning. The thought that life held no meaning when a much-loved person died. A person who had done nothing that would invest her death with meaning.

If death was meaningless, so was life.

He recalled a conversation he'd had with Markku Vatanen just after they graduated from high school. They were sitting in a smoky disco, drinking beer and shouting at each other in the hope of making them-selves heard above the diabolical din. At some point Markku had leaned across the table and shouted that life was tragic because it always entailed the approach of death.

He saw Markku sitting there, saw him downing beer after beer, talking ever faster and louder, and suddenly coming out with that remark.

Once more he heard the blaring music and saw his schoolfriend's sparkling eyes.

He saw himself laugh.

He had laughed to disguise the fact that those words, shouted in his ear by a tipsy friend, had impressed him as an incomprehensibly simple and terrible truth.

He'd never told Markku how deeply they had affected him.

It would be nice, he thought, to be once more sitting in that disco with Markku.

How strange it was, he thought, that he still hadn't met Sanna that night—that he had never even dreamed of meeting her.

He resolved to call Markku and thank him for having come to the funeral.

3

J ust before eight Arto Ojaranta called and said something that astonished Joentaa.

He'd been holding a photograph of Laura Ojaranta in his hand
when the phone rang. He continued to stare at the dead woman's
expressionless face while her husband announced that a key to his
front door had disappeared.

"It's been hanging on the board for years as a spare, in case the
other one got mislaid," he said. "And now it's gone."

"Are you sure?" Joentaa asked.

"Of course I'm sure."

"How often did your wife use the key?"

"She never used it, in fact, because she never mislaid anything. It
was me that used it, if anyone."

"Did she ever lend it to anyone—a neighbor, perhaps, or a friend?"

"Why should she?"

Joentaa didn't reply. He wondered what Ojaranta's information
signified. If the murderer had a key, Laura Ojaranta wouldn't have
had to open the door to him. On the other hand, he could only have
got the key from her. This supported rather than cast doubt on the
assumption that the murderer was someone known to her.

Joentaa nonetheless sensed—or thought he sensed—that this was
a turning point.

Then again, he was probably imagining the whole thing.

"What exactly are you getting at?" Ojaranta demanded.

It took him a moment to grasp that Ojaranta was alluding to
his supposition that Laura had given the key to some neighbor or
friend.

"I'm simply trying to account for the key's disappearance," he said.

"Really? I get the impression you're trying to conjure up some lover
who borrowed the key from my wife while I was away."

That's precisely what I'm *not* trying to do, thought Joentaa. Although it was the logical explanation.

Or *because* it was the logical explanation?

"I don't think that's so," Joentaa said.

Ojaranta was obviously taken aback. "Why not?" he asked after a brief pause.

"I don't know." Joentaa thought for a moment. "I don't think your wife had a lover."

"I see."

"Do you think it's conceivable?"

"I . . . no. You're right, of course. But where's that key?"

"How much longer are you going to be there?"

"Why?"

"I'm coming over. I'll leave right away."

"I've got an appointment at—"

"I'll leave at once—be with you in half an hour. Please wait for me," Joentaa said, and hung up.

4

To Joentaa, as he drove toward it, the blue villa looked untouched. It was as if nothing had changed since he first set eyes on the house.

He had the feeling that, if he went into the bedroom, he would see the dead woman once more: Laura Ojaranta, lying motionless in bed like Sanna.

He heard the gravel crunch beneath his feet as he walked up to the front door. Some inexpert piano-playing—isolated, disjointed notes—was faintly audible through the windows.

Arto Ojaranta opened the door moments after Joentaa rang the bell. He invited him in, promptly adding that he was pressed for time. He was already wearing his overcoat and holding a black briefcase in his hand.

In vain Joentaa searched his face for the desperate, bewildered giant he had interviewed on the first day of the investigation.

"This may take some time," he said.

Ojaranta nodded as if his worst fears had been confirmed and ushered Joentaa into the living room.

"Coffee?" he asked. Joentaa shook his head.

Seated at the piano was a little girl who smiled at him when he looked over at her.

"This is Anna, my sister's daughter," Ojaranta said. "Anna, this is Mr. Joentaa, a policeman."

Joentaa nodded to the girl, who turned away and clumsily proceeded to play a well-known folk song he'd liked as a child. He tried to remember the title, but it escaped him.

Ojaranta invited Joentaa to sit down and lit a cigarette. He really hadn't anything more to tell him, he said. "The key's gone, that's all I know."

"The reason for its disappearance could be most important," said Joentaa.

"I'm sorry, I can't suggest one."

Joentaa was finding it hard to concentrate. Ojaranta's lack of emotion intrigued him, and he secretly condemned the man for seeming so self-possessed, as if his wife's death was over and done with. That was unfair, of course. Ojaranta probably lived behind a façade just as he himself did.

The little girl's rendering of the tune he'd liked as a child was so slow and maladroit it infuriated him. He was tempted to tell her to give it a rest.

He looked in her direction and saw that she was smiling at him again in an inquisitive, expectant way, as if hoping for a word of praise.

"You play very nicely," he said, returning her smile.

She grinned and reapplied herself to the piano.

"My sister's away," Ojaranta said. "Anna always stays with me when she's away."

Joentaa wondered why he'd thought it necessary to explain the girl's presence.

"You could always ask your neighbors whether your wife left the key with one of them," said Joentaa.

Ojaranta frowned impatiently.

"It would be a great help to us," Joentaa went on.

"I can try, but I'm sure we won't find the key that way."

"You puzzle me," Joentaa said.

Ojaranta stared at him in surprise.

"Surely you want to know who killed your wife?"

It was a moment or two before Ojaranta answered. "Of course I do," he said.

"Then why are you so reluctant to help us?"

Ojaranta looked Joentaa in the eye. He seemed to be working out his answer before putting it into words. "Because I don't think there's any point. Because I don't believe you'll get anywhere, and because I don't think I'll ever fathom why my wife was killed."

Joentaa avoided his searching gaze. He had no idea how to respond, and the longer the silence lasted the more annoyed he felt.

The girl had stopped playing and was covertly watching them.

"We're doing our best," he said at length, sensing how hollow that sounded.

He got up. At the front door he shook hands with Ojaranta and forced himself to look the man in the eye. "I shall do my utmost to get to the bottom of your wife's murder," he said. "It's very important to me personally."

Ojaranta stared at him. Not for the first time, Joentaa felt an urge to tell him about Sanna. He knew he would do so if Ojaranta prompted him by asking what he meant.

But Ojaranta said nothing, just released his hand.

By the time Joentaa turned onto the main road to Turku he had forgotten about the blue villa. All his thoughts were of Sanna.

5

Vesa Lehmus stood at the open window, breathing the chilly air. The playground was steeped in the golden glow of the setting sun.

A little boy was busy building a castle out of moist sand. Vesa had been watching him for quite some time. The boy didn't see him. He seemed oblivious to his surroundings.

His mother was sitting opposite on a bench, leafing through a magazine. When her son tried to draw attention to himself and his castle she glanced up and pretended to be impressed.

Vesa Lehmus knew them. They lived on the third floor of the neighboring block. He sometimes saw the boy standing at the window. The youngster always waved and he waved back.

Vesa couldn't understand why the boy's mother was showing no interest in his sandcastle. He felt like shouting at her. Instead he nodded to her when her weary eyes caught sight of him.

He thought of the girl who had spoken to him on the beach at Naantali.

Jaana.

He wondered why she had accosted him. He pondered the question for a while but came to no conclusion.

He winced: the boy had swiped at his sandcastle and destroyed it. He yelled and laughed and hammered the turrets flat with his little green plastic spade.

His mother, still sitting on the bench, told him not to shout like that. She didn't even look up to see what he was doing.

The boy shouted louder still and battered away at the shapeless mound of sand that had once been his castle. His mother rose, went over, and snatched him up in her arms. He started crying.

Vesa watched them until they disappeared into the building. He stared down at the sandpit in the deserted playground, trying to discern traces of the castle on which the boy had worked so long and patiently, only to subject it to wanton destruction. Why had he done that? His red plastic bucket and little green spade were still lying on the sand.

Vesa waited for the mother to come and retrieve them, but she didn't reappear.

The playground was already swathed in blue shadow when his door-bell rang. He ran to answer it. He knew it was Tommy. It had to be.

It was.

"How goes it?" Tommy asked. "Everything okay?"

Vesa flung his arms round his neck. Tommy laughed and said, "Take it easy."

They sat down on Vesa's bed. Tommy did most of the talking; he always had plenty to say. Listening to him, Vesa thought what he thought whenever he saw Tommy: that Tommy was different. Tommy was tall and tanned. Tommy had a loud, infectious laugh.

And masses of friends.

Although there were times when Vesa didn't like Tommy, he loved him. Tommy was the most important person in his life.

He stayed a long time this evening. Longer than usual.

In the end he got up and left as nonchalantly as he had arrived. Tommy came and went at will.

They were already at the door when Vesa heard his own voice speaking. "What would you say," he asked, "if I told you I had a powerful friend?"

Tommy, who had just draped his jacket round his shoulders, paused. "Say what?" he said with a faintly puzzled grin.

"What would you say if I told you I had a friend who was stronger than anyone else in the world?"

"I'd say congratulations, because he'd be bound to protect you from all the minor dangers of everyday life." Tommy's grin had changed to one of genuine amusement. "Are you talking about anyone in particular?"

Vesa hastily shook his head and clamped his lips together. Tommy nodded and turned to go.

"What would you say if I was completely different from the way you think I am?" Vesa called when Tommy was already at the head of the stairs.

Tommy swung round and stared at him keenly. "What's eating you?" he said.

"Nothing."

Tommy's face relaxed. He retraced his steps and laid a hand on Vesa's shoulder. "If you were different I'd be very sad—I like you the way you are," he said with a smile.

Vesa savored his smile.

"See you," said Tommy, and continued on his way.

6

When Joentaa got home that night he found a note from his mother on the hall table. Needless to say, he'd forgotten to call her from the office that morning.

He tried to persuade himself that Ojaranta's surprising news had prevented him from doing so. The truth was, it had simply slipped his mind.

Not that it mattered.

Thinking it over, he realized that he'd welcomed an excuse to forget about it.

Anita had written that she would always be there for him, and that he must call whenever he wanted, any time of the day or night.

He made no attempt to fight off his sense of guilt.

He called her at once, but she didn't answer.

He let the phone ring for a long time. After only a few minutes he tried again. He wondered if she'd had an accident. It was an absurd idea, he knew, but he couldn't shake it off.

He had visions of her lying in a hospital bed. He pictured a train crash. He called her again, imagining that she was dead and that he would never speak to her again.

He kneaded the idea into shape until he believed it was true.

He got through at the eighth attempt. His mental images exploded at the sound of her voice. He felt relieved and vaguely annoyed with himself for having devised such a horrific scenario.

Of course all was well.

Listening to himself and his mother talking, he wondered why Sanna was dead when Anita was alive.

Why was Sanna dead when he was alive? When everyone was alive?

He promised to call again.

He promised to take care of himself.

He was about to hang up when Anita stopped him.

"Sooner or later," she said, "you'll be able to make a fresh start."

He heard the desperation in her voice.

He fell asleep in front of the television.

He dreamed of Sanna.

He dreamed of her continually. It no longer relieved him that she was alive in his dreams because he knew, even in his dreams, that he was dreaming.

He dreamed that he was touching her and knew she didn't exist.

He wept.

He was awakened by his own sobs.

7

It was something different, something new and unfamiliar. A feeling he couldn't define.

She was laughing so loudly, Mara couldn't fail to hear. Mara was reading a book in the ticket office, but he sensed that she was stealing occasional glances at them.

Mara must surely be wondering what this girl was after.

He'd been sitting on the steps outside the old bakery, listening to the rain, when she suddenly loomed up in front of him and touched him on the shoulder. He opened his eyes, not knowing what to say.

"Forgotten our date?" she asked with a smile.

He jumped to his feet and brushed the hair out of his eyes.

"We didn't have a date," he said.

"You weren't exaggerating, it's really nice here," she said as if she hadn't heard his denial. "Not many visitors, though."

"There never are when it's raining," he said.

He dived into her eyes, trying to fathom what he was feeling.

"I'll show you round the workshops if you like," he said.

"Great."

She hung on his every word.

She laughed when he told her the story of Oscari, the master baker who got into financial straits because of a predilection for his own pastries.

He inhaled her laughter.

She thanked him for the leather dice cup.

He dived into her eyes and realized that he'd killed two people.

In his imagination, she was able to undo what he'd done.

In his imagination, he took her in his arms.

When she'd gone, Mara asked who she was. "Jaana," he said.

He imagined never letting her go.

He imagined that all was well.

Nothing had happened.

He was Vesa, and he was alive.

8

"So we've got a missing key and some unidentifiable fingerprints," said Ketola. "Anything else?" He looked round the room. Heinonen was nervously toying with a pen, Grönholm grinning wryly. Niemi, ever cheerful and straightforward, was looking Ketola in the eye as if he hadn't noticed the irritable note in his voice.

"I think we should reexamine the possibility that the two murders are connected," said Joentaa.

"Why?"

He sensed that Ketola was controlling himself with an effort and wished he hadn't spoken.

"I don't know," he said.

"Exactly. You don't know, which means you know as much as the rest of us, in other words, zilch. We've had two stiffs on our hands for nearly a month and we don't know a thing. That not only worries me, it bugs me."

Ketola got up and walked to the window. Joentaa saw that he was trembling. He remembered the bottle and glass in his boss's desk and wondered if he was still capable of heading the investigations. He wondered what ailed the man he'd known for years as a self-controlled and almost obsessively self-disciplined person, although he'd always sensed that this might be a façade concealing a violent temper.

"What about these prints?" Ketola demanded.

"As I said, we still haven't managed to identify them," said Niemi. "I don't know if it's important, mind you. The killer was obviously wearing gloves."

"All the same," Grönholm put in, "if Laura Ojaranta knew him— if he was a friend or lover—he might not have worn them on some previous occasion." He looked over at Ketola, but there was no reaction. Ketola didn't seem to have heard.

"It's a crock of shit," was all he said, staring out of the window.

Joentaa resolved to speak to him, to ask him what was wrong and whether he could help. Even as he made this resolution, he feared he wouldn't have the courage to approach him.

He tried to guess the reason for Ketola's increasing irritability but failed. He didn't even know if Ketola was married, if he had children or people who mattered to him.

He knew nothing about the man. He knew only what he could see, which was that Ketola was losing his grip.

Grönholm's gruff but amiable voice broke the silence. "It's not as if we're completely clueless," he said. "We know pretty well all there is to know about the Ojaranta woman, and we also know a certain amount about Johann Berg. The problem is, neither of them provided anyone with a motive for killing them."

"The fact remains that they're dead," Ketola said without looking round. "Where Johann Berg is concerned, we know little more than that he studied cultural history, worked in a factory, and fathered a son by mistake."

"Our colleagues in Stockholm have discovered that he did drugs and sold them on a small scale," Heinonen said. "Soft drugs, admittedly, but there might be a motive there."

Ketola snorted impatiently. "Ridiculous, even my son smokes dope. They say the stuff's quite harmless."

He continued to gaze out of the window, apparently unaware that the others were staring at him with their mouths open.

So Ketola has a son, Joentaa thought, and he wondered why this surprised him. What had he thought Ketola was? Probably single and unattached. After all, how many women could sustain a long-term relationship with a perpetually moody man?

Ketola himself broke the silence. He turned away from the window and resumed his seat at the table. He spoke of the missing key and the pathologist's findings, which were of little help to them, but Joentaa had stopped listening. He wondered if this son was the cause of Ketola's outbursts. Why had he suddenly broadcast the fact that his son smoked dope when he'd never once so much as mentioned his existence all these years, at least not in Joentaa's presence?

Eventually they all got up and left. Joentaa had absorbed almost nothing of what Ketola had said. He waited—he forced himself to wait—until the two of them were alone in the room.

"What's holding you?" Ketola asked.

"I never knew you had a son," Joentaa said.

Ketola raised his head and looked him in the eye.

"I could say the same," he said, turning to go. "Got any kids?" he asked when he was already at the door.

Joentaa shook his head.

"Consider yourself lucky," Ketola said, and walked out.

9

That night Vesa took a blank sheet of paper and wrote down all he knew about Jaana. The first thing he wrote was her name.

Jaana.

Jaana lived in Naantali. Her flat was over the beach café where she worked.

In the summer she sold ice cream.

She'd told him he'd better hurry if he wanted one of her ice creams because the café stopped selling them at the end of October.

If he didn't hurry, she said, he would have to wait till next summer.

He painted the building in which she lived. People were sitting in the sun outside the café. Jaana was looking out of an upstairs window, smiling at him.

He painted the building green.

Jaana had told him it was a green clapboard building.

He painted the sun yellow.

She'd laughed when he asked what her flat looked like. "You can be really nosy," she said, and added that the place was always in a mess. "There's never anything in the fridge I feel like eating."

Jaana had fair hair and lots of freckles.

Jaana was twenty-five years old. She worked as a waitress, but she had also studied acting. She acted in children's plays at a small theater in Turku. At the moment, because no male actor had volunteered for the part, she was playing Peter Pan.

He must definitely come and see her, she'd said.

Jaana's parents lived far away in the north, and she'd lost touch with them. Why? The question had been on the tip of his tongue.

But he hadn't asked it.

He'd felt the thin ice beneath his feet, the dread of her own questions.

But she hadn't asked a single one.

He tried to draw her face in his imagination and reflected that it would be nice to have a photo of her.

To be able to look at her whenever he wanted.

Before he went to sleep he took down the picture, the one of the hazy landscape, and put it under his bed.

He never wanted to see it again.

He would ask Jaana for a photo when he paid her a visit at the café. Soon, maybe even tomorrow.

10

Joentaa spent most of the day on the phone in his office.

He was working his way through a list of people who had been in contact with Laura Ojaranta. Friends, relations, acquaintances, neighbors.

He elicited nothing new. None of them could tell him anything about the missing key. They all tried to shake him off as quickly as possible, their prosaic, purposeful, businesslike tone conveying that the death of the woman they had known well was only one of many facts that had to be accepted.

The one person who did not conceal her grief was Kerttu Toivonen, the dead woman's sister. She had no idea where the key could be, but she felt sure her sister wouldn't have given it to a neighbor.

"It wasn't that Laura was mistrustful—far from it, she was very open with people—but she liked to have everything under control. It would have worried her, a key to her home in someone else's possession."

Those words echoed in Joentaa's head as the conversation gradually petered out.

Laura always liked to have everything under control . . .

He'd had several telephone conversations with Kerttu Toivonen in the past few weeks. Whenever he called her he felt vaguely uneasy because he sensed that he looked forward to hearing her voice.

Joentaa had paid two visits to her flat on the university campus. He had attended some lectures at the university as a police probationer, and had always found the campus depressingly ugly, but Kerttu had furnished her little flat in such bright, vivid colors that one forgot about the gray façade outside.

He had felt at home with her.

He looked into her eyes while she was talking about her sister, and his own grief had briefly found solace in them.

Afterward he had reproached himself and failed to understand his own feelings. Why was he seeking the company of a woman he didn't know at all? Why, on the night of Johann Berg's murder, had he sought the proximity of Annette Söderström—another female stranger?

A woman who was also grieving for someone. Like himself, like Kerttu Toivonen.

Why did his thoughts keep turning to Annette Söderström and Kerttu Toivonen when Sanna was dead and her death was what governed his life?

"How are you?" Joentaa asked just as Kerttu was about to hang up.

She hesitated for a moment. "Not too good . . . I keep remembering Laura isn't there anymore, and I can't understand why it happened. That's the worst thing: the fact that there's absolutely no explanation."

"We're doing our utmost to get to the bottom of your sister's death," he told her.

He waited for a response, but none came.

"We'll find the murderer," he went on, for something else to say.

"You won't bring her back to life."

He fell silent.

He thought of Sanna and saw himself lying in the arms of Kerttu Toivonen, who was caressing him.

He bade her a hasty goodbye and hung up.

He sat there unmoving for a while and waited for the vision to dissolve into other images.

He tried to concentrate on Laura Ojaranta.

He shut his eyes and saw the blue villa in the darkness behind his eyelids. He wanted to open his eyes but kept them closed because he noticed he was drawing nearer.

He was already at the front door. He went inside.

He had a key.

He made his way into the bedroom. Slowly. He looked down at the sleeping woman. He bent over her and felt her breath on his cheek.

He took a pillow and pressed it down on her face.

He waited until she was dead.

In the passage he took a worthless picture from the wall.

In the living room he drank some wine. Then he left.

It was a quiet scene.

A quiet death.

Circumspect, Laukkanen had said.

No altercation, no raised voices, no secret lover.

No secret lover took a worthless picture home with him.

A moonlit landscape. Pale colors, the painter had said.

The picture she showed him had been beautiful.

A quiet picture. A quiet person.

So quiet that no one in a crowded youth hostel had noticed him.

He had been invisible, and he had felt so while walking along the dark passage to the room in which a Swedish student was lying asleep. Asleep like Laura Ojaranta.

"Zero results, but I see you're taking it easy."

Joentaa opened his eyes and saw Grönholm's grinning face.

"Any more luck than I've had with that missing key?"

Joentaa shook his head.

"I'm quite sure now that there was only one killer," he said.

Grönholm raised his eyebrows.

"One killer for both murders," Joentaa amplified.

"So you keep saying, but why?"

"I think the killer is a quiet sort of person."

"I'm afraid I don't follow you," said Grönholm.

"There are times when I feel I'm close to him in some way."

"Who?"

"The murderer."

"Huh?" Joentaa saw that Grönholm was staring at him with his mouth open. He couldn't help laughing. "Don't take me seriously," he said, hoping that Grönholm would drop the subject, but he didn't.

"Of course I take you seriously. I don't see what you're getting at, though."

"It's probably something to do with Sanna, but I can't explain exactly."

"Please try, because I just don't get it."

"Laura Ojaranta died the day after Sanna, also in her sleep. That's all."

"I see," said Grönholm, but Joentaa could tell from his voice that he didn't.

Of course not. He didn't understand it himself.

"The killer saw Laura Ojaranta. He saw her asleep and he saw her dead."

Grönholm stared at him expectantly.

"Somehow, I feel . . ."

"Well?"

". . . that the killer may have been as desperate as I was."

Joentaa was surprised by his own words. He looked at Grönholm, who still hadn't shut his mouth.

"What are you talking about, Kimmo?"

Joentaa got up and strode to the door.

"Let's forget it. I'll explain when I've worked it out myself."

I I

I n the morning he saw the moon.

He was glad.

It was good to know that he would never escape, however much he wanted to.

He hung the picture of the hazy landscape in its old place.

Soon he would be strong.

Soon the world would be upside down and turn and make him laugh.

He shut his eyes and softly started to sing.

The gentle strains bore him off into the no-man's-land that struck fear into him, but his fear was only there to be mastered.

He opened his eyes.

Vesa was standing beside him.

Vesa was sad. He was weeping and frightened, but there was no need for him to be frightened as long as he protected him.

He shouted at Vesa for being so stupid.

He got up and showered.

The cold water froze all that had happened in the last few days.

When he turned off the shower he heard the doorbell. He pulled on his bathrobe and answered it. He was unsurprised by the sound of the bell and uninterested in knowing who was at the door.

It was Jaana.

She transfixed him with a high-pitched laugh.

"You're looking pretty frazzled," she said.

He asked how she'd found him.

"Even *you* are in the phone book, sweetheart," she said.

He saw out of the corner of his eye that Vesa was glad, that he stepped forward to invite her in, but he thrust him back.

"I'm not feeling well. Let's postpone it."

"What . . ."

"Please."

"But . . ."

He shut the door.

He saw Jaana's confused face.

He stood quite still for a moment, breathing deeply.

Looking through the peephole, he saw Jaana going down the stairs with her head down.

You've ruined everything, Vesa shouted.

He merely laughed and slammed him against the wall.

He would show Vesa what was what.

He went out onto the balcony and, with a smile, leaped into the abyss.

He was lying on the ground.

He got up.

He strode into no-man's-land, erect and self-assured.

He waved to Vesa, who was staring after him.

Vesa was safe because he was Vesa's best friend, and he was immortal.

12

He caressed the keys with his eyes closed.

He inhaled the fresh, bracing air of the house he'd taken possession of.

It had worked.

Of course. Everything was working. Everything he wanted.

The girl he didn't know came and asked if he'd care for some coffee. Like Laura Ojaranta.

Everything was repeating itself because he wanted it to.

If he wanted it to, the cycle he'd initiated would continue ad infinitum.

He hadn't known Laura Ojaranta either.

If he wanted it so, Laura Ojaranta had never existed.

If he wanted it so, the youth hostel beside the lake didn't exist.

He thanked the girl and took the cup from her. He patiently answered all her questions. Her piano lessons were a drag, she told him. But perhaps it would be better when the piano wasn't so out of tune.

He nodded. Perhaps, he said.

She was very pretty, he thought. Vesa wouldn't have got a word out in her presence.

He caught sight of the man who had suddenly appeared in the doorway. "Hello, Daddy, this man wants to tune our piano," the girl said, half mischievous, half shy. She hugged her father, who was staring at him suspiciously.

He felt sure the man was going to seize him and push him down into hell.

He saw himself falling.

When the moment passed the man was smiling. Tuning the piano was a good idea, he said. "Perhaps your lessons will bear fruit at last. What's it going to cost?"

He named a price the man liked.

He explained to the girl how to tune a piano. She hung on his every word.

He pictured himself kissing her.

After a while he said he had to fetch something from his car.

While going through the keys hanging on the board in the passage he stared fixedly at the man, who was reading a newspaper in the kitchen only a few feet away.

He knew he wouldn't turn round. The man wouldn't move for as long as he didn't want him to.

He found the right key. It was attached to a ring, so he had to remove it first. But that wasn't hard. He sensed how deft his movements were. He didn't have to do a thing.

He slipped the key into his trouser pocket.

He went back into the living room and sat down at the piano. He played.

The girl said he played very well.

He asked her name. Margit, she said.

Her father called that it was nearly time for volleyball practice, but she didn't want to go. She stayed till he'd finished. It didn't bother him. He knew his job and enjoyed her approbation. When they were outside in the passage the man proffered some notes. He thanked him and said he would come again to carry out the finishing touches. The piano hadn't been tuned for ages, he pointed out.

"You can say that again," the man said. "Would the end of the week suit you?"

He nodded and asked for his phone number.

Margit had run over to the piano and was timidly trying the keys. He called goodbye.

He shook hands with the man and left.

For a moment he thought of Jaana, but that was unimportant. It wasn't real.

If he wanted it so, Jaana had never existed.

13

That night Joentaa called Markku Vatanen.

He found the number in his address book. It had been there for several years, but he'd never dialed it. Markku had sent it to him when he moved to Helsinki to read for a degree.

He sat on the sofa for a long time, phone in hand, and tried to map out the conversation in advance. For each of his remarks he devised a potential reply on Markku's part.

What if they had nothing to say to each other?

He dialed the number. While waiting he hoped Markku would be out. When Markku answered he noticed at once that his schoolfriend announced himself the way he'd always done, first name only.

"Markku here."

He couldn't help laughing.

"Same old Markku," he said.

"Kimmo?"

Joentaa went on laughing. He didn't know why, but he felt relieved. It was as if the years that lay between their friendship and estrangement were already over.

"Kimmo, is that you?"

"You still refuse to say your surname," said Joentaa. "Why is that?"

"Old habits die hard. Good of you to call."

"I wanted to thank you."

How simple it was, suddenly.

"I was so glad you came . . . to the funeral."

"It was a pleasure. I mean . . ."

"I know what you mean," said Joentaa. "And I want to apologize for taking so long to call."

"Nonsense, I didn't call either."

"All the same . . . How's your degree going?"

"Don't ask." Markku forced a laugh. "I'm thinking of packing it in. I'm really only carrying on because I don't know what else to do."

It occurred to Joentaa that he had no idea what Markku was studying. He strove to remember.

He'd known it at one stage. Markku helped him out. "I've been working on my thesis for the past two years. Two stupid plays by Shakespeare."

Of course, English language and literature. Markku had been in England, even in America, at a time when Joentaa still hadn't known there were bigger towns than Kitee, with its few thousand inhabitants.

"I'd still like to become an interpreter, maybe translate books or work as a foreign correspondent, but I won't get anywhere without a degree. I've already used up my government grant."

"You'll make it," Joentaa said without really listening. He felt his thoughts veering away from Markku's life and concerns.

What do Markku's problems amount to? he thought involuntarily as his friend fell silent. He sensed that Markku wanted to bring up the subject of Sanna's death but couldn't find the right words.

"I'm sorry I never met your wife," he said eventually.

"It would have been nice. Sanna was . . . special."

He couldn't think of a better word.

"Tell me about her," Markku said.

Joentaa was taken by surprise. "She was an architect," he said at length. I couldn't have said anything more absurd, he instantly thought.

Markku seemed to be waiting for him to go on, but he couldn't.

"How are you feeling?" he asked.

"I still haven't grasped that she's gone, I guess. I don't know if I'll ever really take it in."

Markku said nothing.

"The night she died I thought my life would come to a standstill, and that's just what happened. No matter what I'm doing, I'm never really alive." Joentaa wanted to go on, but he couldn't find anything to say that would make his meaning clearer.

"If you like," said Markku, "I could pay you a visit soon. This weekend, maybe."

Joentaa welcomed the offer but was simultaneously unsure whether he wanted to see Markku—or anyone at all.

"May I call you nearer the time?" he asked.

"Of course. I'll quite understand if you want some peace and quiet at the moment."

"You once told me that life is tragic because it entails the approach of death, do you remember?"

Markku was taken aback. He didn't speak for a moment.

"Vaguely," he said. "The disco at Kitee?"

"Right first time," said Joentaa. It relieved him that Markku could remember.

"I've been thinking of that remark these past few weeks. At the time I laughed, but it really scared me. I only laughed to cover my embarrassment."

"I don't see things so black and white these days," Markku said. "You shouldn't either. I'd read it somewhere and wanted to impress you, that was all."

"You succeeded," said Joentaa.

He liked Markku, he told himself. He couldn't understand why they'd lost touch.

He promised to call him again.

Sitting there in the silence that followed, he resolved to call Markku tomorrow and invite him for the weekend.

He turned on the television and promptly turned it off again.

He looked out at the lake glittering in the darkness.

Snow would fall before long, and the children would soon be playing ice hockey on the lake. Sanna was always laughing, but his attempts to skate had tickled her more than most things.

It was Wednesday, he remembered. He had occasionally played volleyball on Wednesday nights. Competitively. So competitively that the others sometimes laughed at him. A colleague of Sanna's had introduced him to the group. Once or twice he'd accompanied the others for a beer and listened to them holding forth. Their own lives were a mess, they told him. He was the luckiest of the lot.

He wondered why he'd ever been interested in winning a game of volleyball.

There was no one in Turku he really cared about, he reflected. He thought of Kerttu Toivonen. He had a hazy recollection of her face and eyes, saw her sitting alone in her flat.

He contemplated calling her and asking how she was.

Involuntarily, he saw himself lying with his head on her lap. She was caressing him. He lay there quietly and listened to her talking about her sister.

Her soft voice lulled him to sleep. At some stage she told him who had killed her sister. She told him this in one short sentence, the meaning of which escaped him at first. It wasn't until she stopped speaking that he realized she'd said something important.

He wanted to ask Kerttu Toivonen to repeat herself, but she bent down and licked his face. He tried to fend her off and ask what she'd just said, but before he could speak another woman came and fondled his neck. Although he couldn't see her, he knew it was Annette Söderström. He smelled the sweet scent she'd worn at the youth hostel. He tried to turn around but failed, sensing that he had to ask her an important question.

Before he could do so he awoke.

He got up at once and groped for the light switch in the dark. When the room was brightly lit he calmed down by degrees.

He went into the bathroom and sluiced his hands and face. As he looked at himself in the mirror, he had a feeling that Sanna was lying in bed, waiting for him. He pictured her reading the book she'd been unable to finish.

He heard her laughing, opened the door to the passage and heard her laughter more distinctly. Against his will, he walked along the passage to the bedroom. The door was closed.

He could still hear her laughing.

He quickened his steps and flung open the door. He thought he could sense that Sanna was there, and that everything else was collapsing like the most terrible dream he'd ever dreamed, but the room was cold and deserted. He'd forgotten to shut the window.

He turned away and shut the door.

He wouldn't call Markku tomorrow after all.

14

Tommy turned up just as he was leaving.

He was very chipper and in no hurry. He told Vesa about an old man who'd learned to walk again after spending years in a wheelchair. Tommy worked as an orderly at an old people's home. He always laughed when he talked about it, although most of his anecdotes were sad.

Vesa sensed that the story of the old man who could walk again was interesting.

He wanted to ask questions and elicit more details, but he didn't speak.

He sat facing Tommy and didn't welcome his presence. It had never been like that before. He heard him talking and hoped he would leave as abruptly as he always did, but today, of all days, Tommy had all the time in the world.

Tommy had brought a bottle of red wine.

Tommy fetched some glasses and filled them.

Tommy asked where the painting above his bed had come from but didn't seem to notice when he got no answer.

Tommy talked and talked.

Vesa saw his words trickling to the ground.

It was getting dark outside.

At some point Tommy asked how he was doing and whether the old museum buildings were still standing.

He nodded.

Tommy gave a wry grin and asked again if everything was really okay.

He nodded.

He would have liked to tell Tommy who he really was, but he would never do that. He couldn't.

He knew Tommy so well.

He admired him. He loved him. Tommy was all he had.

He despised him.

He said nothing. He waited until Tommy had run out of anecdotes and waved to him as he went down the stairs. When Tommy had gone he felt a sharp pain and ran to the window.

He saw Tommy disappearing into the darkness.

He imagined that Tommy was now in no-man's-land, and that they would meet there.

He wept.

He wished Tommy would come back.

He washed up the wineglasses and put the half-empty bottle in the fridge.

He shut his eyes and pictured Tommy coming back—pictured him climbing the stairs and standing outside the door.

But Tommy didn't come back, and it was all his fault.

He put on his jacket and went out. When the cold engulfed him he felt infinitely free. Infinitely strong and invincible.

He said hello to Seppo, his fat neighbor, who was walking his dog.

While driving he felt his face break into a smile, and the void containing all that had once existed burst like a bubble.

His world was simple.

His world was a road and a destination.

He parked the car in a side street and made his way slowly toward the house. A light was on, he could see that from a long way off. He would have to wait, but that was no problem. His patience was boundless.

It was cold, but he didn't feel it.

He walked toward the light and saw the girl Margit through the kitchen window. She was sitting at the table where her father had sat reading the newspaper that afternoon, while he was looking for the key. Gripping the key in his jacket pocket, he remembered with a pleasurable thrill how sure he had been that the man wouldn't turn round and see him.

He went up to the window and watched Margit.

She was drinking a glass of milk and looking unhappy.

A woman came in, and he flinched because she promptly started shouting. He could hear her shrill voice through the windowpane. The woman had to be Margit's mother. She slammed a book down on the table in front of the girl, shouted that things couldn't go on this way and that the days when Margit had done as she pleased were over.

Margit burst into tears.

Her father came in. He didn't say anything, just went over to Margit and slapped her face. She let out a yell, and the mug that had been on the table in front of her fell to the floor.

Vesa shrank back into the darkness, staring at the man's infuriated face through the glass. He looked quite unlike the affable person he'd been that afternoon.

Margit's mother was leaning tensely against the wall. The girl sat rooted to the spot for several seconds. Then she jumped up and ran from the room.

He inhaled the fear in her eyes.

Her mother was weeping too. She shouted at her husband. "What do you imagine Margit thinks of you after that affair of yours?" she demanded.

Vesa went up to the window again. He heard the man trying to justify himself, heard his anger subside and peter out into some half-hearted remarks. "Things don't always go the way Margit expects, it's time she learned that."

Vesa laughed.

He thrust out his arms, seized the father, and yanked him over to

the mother, who was still leaning against the wall. The man gesticu-
lated helplessly, absurdly, as he towed him over to her, and he got
the mother to tell him to go find Margit and apologize.

These people were his puppets.

He made the man go up to the woman and forced the couple to
embrace, but only briefly. Then he wrenched them apart. He made
the mother weep. The father he sent upstairs to Margit, whom he
knew to be sobbing on her bed. She had locked her bedroom door
and was weeping with her head buried in the pillow. He could read
her thoughts. He knew she was thinking of the nice young man who
had tuned the piano and listened to her that afternoon.

If he wanted, he could have all she had to offer.

He shut his eyes and saw the moon.

Leaving the window, he crossed the small front garden in a few
long strides and reached the front door. He turned the key in the lock
and found himself standing in the dark, the epicenter.

He held his breath. The kitchen light was on, the door ajar. He
could hear Margit's mother stifling her sobs.

He slowly climbed the narrow staircase and made his way along
the passage to Margit's door, which was shut. He put his ear to it and
heard the muffled voice of Margit's father.

"I'm sorry it happened," he was saying, "but what's done is done."

"Go away," said Margit.

"I love your mother as much as ever," her father said.

Margit didn't speak.

Vesa shut his eyes and saw her lying in bed. She was staring at the
wall and waiting for her father to leave the room.

"We'll have to talk about it sometime," her father said.

Margit still didn't speak.

Vesa retreated into the gloom. He shrank back into the cramped
niche between two cupboards and waited. He heard the door open
and saw a shadow as Margit's father walked past him and went
downstairs.

He heard his breathing.

Margit's mother was standing at the foot of the stairs.

"Well?" she asked coldly.

Her husband didn't reply. He went into the living room, where he flopped down in an armchair and turned on the television.

Vesa heard the voice of a game-show host whose program he watched occasionally. A quiz show for couples. He withdrew into the niche again and leaned against the wall.

The clear, resonant voice of the man on television made him drowsy. He felt quite weightless.

After a while Margit's mother started laying into her husband. He made no response until she said she wanted a divorce.

Vesa heard him laugh.

"You don't believe that yourself," he said, and turned up the volume.

The quizmaster asked a candidate which his fiancée liked better, the cinema or the theater.

"I told you I was sorry," Margit's father said.

The television audience laughed because the candidate had got his fiancée's preferences wrong.

"I'm going to bed," said Margit's mother.

She went to the bathroom and cleaned her teeth. A few minutes later all was quiet. The game show came to an end. The audience clapped, the music over the final credits began.

Then came a break for commercials. Vesa didn't like commercials. After the break came an old Finnish film. Vesa had seen it. He sometimes watched those films. He knew it was silly of him—Tommy had told him so more than once—but it was nice that all ended well in those old Finnish films.

Margit's father eventually turned off the television.

Vesa could hear him sobbing in the silence.

He closed his eyes and savored his sense of power.

He emerged from the darkness and went over to the banister. A few minutes later the man got to his feet with an effort and disappeared into the bedroom without washing.

Vesa lingered at the top of the stairs for a few moments.

Then he went down to the kitchen.

The kitchen light was on. The mug Margit had drunk from was still lying on the floor. He picked it up and put it on the table.

He poured some milk into the mug.

Looking through the window, he saw his reflection in the glass and the vague outlines of the street and the house next door.

He trembled as he raised the mug to his lips and drank.

He closed his eyes again and waited for his thoughts to revolve, to dissolve into the fast-flowing stream and make him dizzy.

He rose and went upstairs.

He climbed slowly, but without pausing.

He opened the door and entered the room, which was very warm and in darkness.

She was asleep.

He pulled up a chair and sat down beside the bed.

He watched her breathing.

He took the drug from his jacket pocket and anesthetized her. He had trickled only a few drops of it onto the cloth. That would be enough, and it was better that way. He didn't want her to know a thing.

He was trembling.

He sat down again and waited for his agitation to subside.

He waited for the flickering yellow-and-red moon to fill the entire picture.

He stood up, slid the pillow from under her head, and pressed it down on her face.

He closed his eyes and saw Jaana.

Jaana was standing there in the dark.

Jaana was screaming.

Screaming at him to stop.

Jaana screamed until he laughed and the moon in his head exploded.

He let go of the pillow.

He looked down at the girl, took the pillow from her face, and saw her closed eyelids.

He took hold of her limp body and pulled it to the floor. He kicked her in the back, kicked her legs. He kneeled down and kissed her on the lips.

Then he ran.

On the stairs he slipped. He felt a dull pain in his legs and heard voices behind him.

He didn't look round until he was sitting in his car.

He drove toward the cry, which grew steadily louder.

He didn't know how long he drove for, he simply drove until he got there.

Even in the dark, the building looked as she had described it and as he had painted it.

He hammered on the door until lights came on and windows opened. He heard several voices, one of which he knew.

"Come in," said Jaana, drawing him into the warmth.

She made some tea and put her arms round him.

She didn't ask why he'd come.

She didn't ask anything at all.

He told her about an old man who could walk after spending years in a wheelchair.

15

Of course it wasn't normal, thought Jaana Ilander.

Of course it wasn't normal for a distraught young man to be sitting at her kitchen table at four in the morning, staring at the floor and telling her about his life.

Of course Kati was right, these things only happened to *her*, and of course she herself was to blame. If Kati had gone over to the boy on the beach that morning, he would now be sitting with Kati, not with her.

She poured some tea into a mug and, out of the corner of her eye, watched him slowly look up as she put the mug on the table in front of him.

He smiled and thanked her, and she smiled back.

She was glad of his presence. She liked him. She liked it that he was different and mysterious. It was this element of mystery that had attracted her to him.

Having preserved a stubborn silence for some minutes, he started to talk—feverishly, restlessly. He told her about a man who could walk after spending years in a wheelchair. He told her about Tommy, his brother. He told her about his parents, who had died in an accident when he was little. He told her about being brought up in an orphanage with Tommy.

Jaana sat across the table, facing him, and listened intently. She didn't interrupt—she never interrupted when people were telling her things. You didn't get to know things unless you were capable of listening, and Jaana always wanted to know everything, especially about people she didn't understand.

All that Vesa told her brought her closer to the person she'd sensed when she went over to him on the beach. She hadn't been able to put her finger on it—she still couldn't—but there was something underlying the look in his deep-set eyes.

Eventually he broke off and apologized for not inviting her into his apartment yesterday morning. "I wasn't feeling well," he told her.

"No problem. I like springing surprises on people," she said with a laugh. "Besides, you're here now."

"You must be angry with me, though."

"Just forget it."

He nodded and fell silent. When she was sure he wouldn't go on talking of his own accord she asked why he always dressed in one color.

Vesa stared at her in surprise.

"Sometimes you wear red, sometimes blue, and now you're all in black. Yesterday, when I paid you that unwelcome visit, you were all in white. What is it, a fad or a fashion statement?" She grinned.

"I like it, that's all."

"I see." She shook her head and asked if he wanted something to eat.

"I expect you have to get up early," he said.

"No earlier than you do. You start work at the museum at ten, don't you?"

Vesa nodded. "Nothing to eat, thanks. Who's the guy in the photos?"

Jaana followed the direction of his gaze.

"Daniel," she said.

"A boyfriend?"

"No."

"There's a photo of him in the living room as well."

"We were together at one time, but it's over. He lives in Germany."

"But you must be fond of him if you have his photos everywhere."

"I wouldn't have let you in if I'd known you were *this* nosy."

"I'm sorry."

"What would you say to grabbing at least a couple of hours' sleep?" she asked.

He stood up hurriedly. "Of course. I'll go."

"You can sleep here," she said. "I've got a sofa and a bed. You take the bed."

She had expected him to play coy, but he merely nodded and said, "Thanks."

She went to the bathroom and washed her face. He was already stretched out on the bed when she returned. Before she turned out the light she asked why he'd come to see her in the middle of the night.

He didn't reply at first.

She heard his voice as she lay on the sofa in the dark.

"What did you say?"

"Because I'm scared."

"Scared of what?"

"Everything."

She got up and went over to the bed. He turned away from her, but she could tell he was trembling.

She stroked his back.

"Sleep well," she said after a while, and he fell asleep with her voice reverberating in his head.

16

Her vision was blurred and her head was spinning.

Her father asked what had happened, her mother looked tearful.

"I don't feel well," she said.

"Did you fall off the bed?" her father asked.

"I don't know."

"You must have," he said. "We heard a bump, and when we came in you were lying on the floor."

"I feel sick," Margit said.

"I'll call Järvenpää right away and get him to examine you before you go to school," said her father. "You may be suffering from concussion—" He broke off. "There's a funny smell in here."

"Can you remember falling?" her mother asked.

Margit shook her head.

"Can you remember last night?" asked her father.

Margit nodded.

"We had a fight," said her mother.

Margit tried to laugh. "I remember that all right. It's a pity I *didn't* fall on my head. Then I'd have forgotten all about it."

Her father awkwardly took her hand, her mother hugged her tight.

"We won't quarrel anymore," she said. "Never again."

17

He spoke slowly, pausing now and then as if he had to concentrate on finding the right words, but in his eyes she saw a fire that hadn't been there before.

In his eyes she saw the conflagrations he was describing as vividly as if he had witnessed them in person.

The castle of Turku had gone up in flames on three occasions, in 1365, 1614, and 1941, and each time it had been rebuilt, bigger and better than before.

Vesa turned on the spot with his arms outstretched. He had a story to tell about every painting, every old chest, even about the wallpaper on the walls.

He stared at her in disbelief when she said she'd never been inside the castle.

When they were sitting on the edge of the rocky island, dangling their legs in the cold seawater, she put her arm round him and kissed him on the cheek. He shrank away, got to his feet, and stared at her as if she'd assaulted him.

Jaana laughed.

"Take it easy," she said, and pulled him down beside her. She kissed him on the lips. He didn't respond, but he didn't shrink away either.

They went into the cathedral, and Vesa was relieved when she claimed to have visited it quite often. He told her about the fires again. The big cathedral tower had burned down six times, and it had been rebuilt each time, bigger and better than before.

Vesa told her about the fire that had almost destroyed the city in 1827. "Everything except the buildings on the Klosterberg," he said, and told her about a farmer who had lived quite close to them but on the wrong side. "He lost everything, his farm and his family. His neighbor, whose farm was situated in the lee of the Vardberg, survived together with all his possessions. Do you know what the first farmer did a few months after the fire?"

Jaana shook her head.

"He murdered his neighbor and hanged himself in the ruins of his farm."

She stared at him.

If Vesa had started to laugh she would have joined in, but he didn't.

"Did you make that up, or did it really happen?"

"It really happened. I read it in an old chronicle. The farmer's name was Arho and his neighbor's was Kustavi. They'd been friends before the fire broke out."

"You seem to have a weakness for horrible stories," she said.

Vesa didn't seem to grasp that she was trying to put a humorous gloss on the whole thing.

"I've always wondered what went on in Arho's mind when he saw his farm on fire and knew that his wife and children were in the midst of the flames," he said. "Know what I mean?"

"No," she said, "and I'm not sure I want to."

When they were sitting over an ice cream at the Fontana Café in the city center, she asked what he was scared of.

"Scared?" he said.

"Yes. Yesterday you said you were scared. What exactly did you mean?"

He seemed to be deliberating.

"I don't think I said that."

"Of course you did, I was right beside you."

He shook his head.

"What was the matter? Why did you turn up at my place in the middle of the night?"

He didn't reply.

"You rang the bell like a madman and kicked the door. You were in tears when I opened it."

He looked at her for a moment.

"I wanted to be with you," he said. Just that.

18

S o she, too, had started to ask questions now, but he didn't mind. She didn't question him like other people. She really wanted to know something about him, and she refrained from pressing him when he didn't answer.

If he didn't answer she smiled at him as if she'd understood all the same.

Perhaps she really had.

He'd gone all hot when she kissed him, and he'd felt a stabbing, lingering pain in the gut.

That evening she played Peter Pan.

She was wonderful. She was quite different from him—his diametrical opposite, in fact.

She was life.

Although he was sitting in the front row, she was far away. He closed his eyes, hearing nothing but her clear voice, which bore him away to a land he didn't know. A land where he wanted to live.

Later that evening he asked her if she could imagine living with him in that land.

Jaana didn't reply. She was annoyed because she'd had to go looking for him. He'd been waiting for her outside the theater.

"I was beginning to think you'd simply run off," she said.

He apologized and asked her again if she could imagine living with him in that far-off land.

Her face relaxed. She laughed.

"It's a fairy tale," she said.

"But you must be able to see the place when you're acting," he said.

"I imagine it, certainly."

"What does it look like?"

"If my acting's good enough, you should be able to imagine it yourself."

He said nothing.

"We'll go looking for it if you like," she said, slipping her arm through his.

He drew back and looked at her inquiringly.

"How would you like a swim?" she asked.

19

The sky was dark and the moon veiled in cloud.

Jaana laughed and called to him that the water was cold. He was sitting on the sand beside the clothes she'd removed before going in.

"Come on," she called.

He got undressed and walked down to the water's edge. He recalled having gone swimming one night not long ago.

He'd been burned and frozen.

He'd been far bigger than he was now.

He'd been immortal.

He hadn't felt the water then, but now it was cold. So cold it frightened him.

"You're looking doubtful," Jaana said, tugging at his arm.

"Don't!" he shouted.

She let go. "All right," she said, "take it easy."

She eyed him mistrustfully for a moment or two, then smiled again. "Scared of a little cold water?" she asked. He shook his head.

Two strokes brought her to his side. He felt her smooth, cold skin as she embraced him.

"We're making progress. You've told me what *doesn't* scare you, so now you can tell me what *does*."

He sought her eyes in the gloom.

"What did you mean last night when you said you were scared of everything?"

He released himself from her embrace and duck-dived.

He let himself sink until he felt his head would burst.

"What are you playing at?" Jaana cried when he surfaced after an eternity. "Does that give you a buzz, or something?"

It pleased him that Jaana had been worried. He wondered what she would have done if he'd never surfaced again.

"Who is Daniel?" he asked.

"What are you scared of?"

"No, you first."

She made a face and swam away from him on her back. She didn't speak again until there were a few yards of water between them. "If Daniel is still alive, he'll now be twenty-nine years seventy-two days old. He's German. He was studying philosophy when I met him, but that was nine years ago. I've no idea what he's doing today."

"And?"

"And what?"

"Go on."

"It's your turn."

She swam up and made a grab for him, but he evaded her and dived until the distance between them was as great as before.

"Why is Daniel important to you?" he called.

"He isn't important to me."

"So why do you keep photos of him in your living room?"

"Let's say they're there to remind me that even an idiot can look really nice."

"Why is Daniel an idiot?"

Jaana laughed. "You're incredible," she called, and struck out for the shore. Vesa dived and quickly overtook her. He grabbed her and pulled her under, sought her lips with his, and held her tight.

She didn't release herself until they reached the shore. She ran her fingers through his hair, then turned away and got dressed.

He watched her.

He glimpsed the outline of her body in the darkness.

He felt cold.

He enjoyed feeling cold.

"Would you say I'm an idiot too?" he asked.

"You're certainly idiotic enough to go swimming in this temperature. Why do you ask?"

"If I'm an idiot, you can hang a photo of me on your wall."

She laughed.

"But first I'd have to get one made," he said. "Tommy's in most of the ones I've got."

"Come on," she said, and walked off.

He followed her.

She hadn't taken his arm. For a moment he thought she would press him, force him to talk and spoil everything, but she didn't.

20

She took a Polaroid of him when they got to her apartment. She caught him unawares. He was just coming out of the bathroom, drying his hair on a towel, when she snapped him.

"Got you!" she said. "Without Tommy." She looked at the photo, which developed within seconds, and said: "I like it."

She showed it to him.

He looked different, he felt sure he'd never looked like that before. He'd laughed just as he saw the flash.

"Pretty silly," he said, and asked if he could have a photo of her. "A real one."

"A real one?"

"A nice one, not one like this." He pointed to the Polaroid print.

"Sure." Jaana rummaged in a drawer and tossed him some envelopes. "Pick one, but take care. On most of them I look just the way you do on this one." She flapped the photo at him.

Vesa looked through the snaps. Jaana looked good in them. She was grinning at the camera and doing unusual things: Jaana halfway up a rock face, Jaana on a surfboard, Jaana moments after landing by parachute.

"You're athletic," Vesa said. "Parachuting?" He showed her the photo. Jaana nodded. "Possibly the finest sensation imaginable," she said. "However, I broke my arm a few years ago, and I haven't jumped since. Maybe I will again. Maybe the two of us will."

"Maybe," said Vesa.

One of the photos showed Jaana with Daniel. They were standing in the sun outside a small, seedy-looking hotel, smiling at each other.

"Daniel," Vesa said.

Jaana groaned. "Looking at these photos was probably just an excuse to start on about him again."

"Where were you?" he asked.

"In Italy."

"Is that where you met?"

"Listen, I've no desire to talk about him anymore. I don't like him because he promised to come to Finland and he never has. If it'll set your mind at rest, he probably will come to Finland sometime. For my sake."

"What do you mean?"

"What I said. I always get what I want," she said, kneeling on the floor beside him. She drew him down to her and kissed him on the lips. He felt her hair in his face and her tongue against his teeth. The pain in his gut intensified. Just when he felt he could stand it no longer she jumped up and asked if he'd like a drink.

He hurriedly sat up and shook his head.

She laughed and lit some candles, poured two glasses of red wine. "You're funny," she said when they were sitting on the floor side by side, drinking.

He didn't speak.

"I'd like to know a lot more about you," she said. "Everything, preferably."

He closed his eyes.

"Can you remember the day your parents died?"

No answer.

"What happened, exactly? What sort of accident was it?"

He kept his eyes shut, but he could sense that she was looking at him, staring at him fixedly, trying to divine his thoughts, coming closer.

She took the glass from his hand and licked his cheek. She ran her fingers over his neck and along his arms, then carefully slipped off his trousers. He felt nothing for a while after that. When he opened his eyes she was standing naked before him. She took him by the hand and led him into the bedroom.

She stretched out and pulled him down on top of her.

He felt the pain slowly permeate his body.

He heard her voice. She moaned and cried out, but her words were unintelligible to him.

Just before the pain dissolved he saw the end.

He heard himself cry out.

She laughed full in his eyes.

He turned on his side.

She fondled his back and bent over him.

"Everything all right?" she asked.

He nodded.

After a few minutes the hand on his back relaxed. Turning toward her, he saw that she had fallen asleep.

He felt his fear subside. His thoughts were safe.

As long as she was asleep all was well.

As long as she was asleep she would ask no questions.

He lay there for a long time without moving.

Then he realized that it had been good, his best experience ever. He realized that, in the end, everything had dissolved into nothing.

Slowly, he got up. Her arm, which had been lying limp on his back, slid off onto the bedclothes. He got dressed without looking at her.

He sensed the void in which nothing remained but the truth.

He turned out the light.

He stood over her and watched her breathing.

He withdrew the pillow from beneath her head and pressed it down on her face until it was over.

He heard her cry out, but he knew that the cry was coming from a world that wasn't his.

He blew out the candles, picked up the two photos and the camera, took a key from her jacket pocket, and ran out into the void.

He sensed that this time he would remain there—that he had to do so. This time it was different.

He let himself fall.

While falling he gave an exultant cry. He had accomplished a difficult task, and it had been so easy, he hardly knew why he'd ever been afraid of failing.

He hadn't failed.

Jaana's laughter had been extinguished.

Jaana's laughter, in which he had discerned his death.

21

When Joentaa heard what Heinonen was saying, he sensed at once that something was wrong, that his reaction wasn't what it should have been.

He had no chance to think this over because Ketola distracted him. Ketola had initially stared open-mouthed at Heinonen, who had stood in the doorway and conveyed the news in a few brief, hurried sentences. To Joentaa the silence that followed seemed endless. Then Ketola laughed. He got up and strode toward Heinonen, who drew back, but halted halfway there and started yelling. He stood in the middle of the office and yelled so loudly he must have been audible throughout the building.

"I don't believe it!" he yelled. "This is such a load of shit! Just what I needed! Fuck you! Yes sir, no sir, whatever you say, sir, always at your service!" Looking at Ketola's contorted face, Joentaa resolved to have a word with him when this was over, when his shouting fit had run its course. He would ask him what was the matter.

He would tell him about Sanna.

Nurmela suddenly appeared in the doorway. He pushed past the dumbfounded Heinonen and went over to Ketola.

"What's going on here?" he demanded when he was face-to-face with him.

Ketola made no response.

Nurmela seized him by the collar and thrust him toward the desk. "You're starting to get on my nerves," he said. "I suggest you go home at once and come back tomorrow in a normal frame of mind. What do you say?"

"That won't be possible." Ketola wrenched himself free and sat down at his desk. He straightened his jacket, squared his shoulders, and gave Nurmela a businesslike look as if nothing had happened.

"What do you mean?" Nurmela demanded.

"I mean we've got a problem," said Ketola. "Just a minor problem, scarcely worth mentioning."

Nurmela said nothing. He waited.

"A woman's been murdered," Heinonen said from the doorway. "In Naantali. She was suffocated with a pillow."

Nurmela didn't bat an eyelid. Joentaa waited for him to say something, but he didn't. He merely nodded and left the room without looking at any of them.

"Asshole," said Ketola.

On the drive to Naantali he preserved a steadfast silence until Joentaa turned on the radio. "I don't feel like that tango shit," he growled, and turned it off. Joentaa said nothing. He thought about various things. About Ketola, who wasn't himself anymore, about the blue villa in which Laura Ojaranta's body had lain, and about the dead woman they would soon be looking at. He tried to picture her, but all he saw was Laura Ojaranta lying in bed, seemingly asleep.

The house was a clapboard building painted green, and it stood on the slope that led down to the beach.

The beach Sanna had liked so much.

He saw himself lying on the sand.

He had been watching her swimming, convinced that things would go on like this forever.

The ground floor of the building was a café. *Kahvila Rheno*, it said in yellow on the wall, and some fat white lettering on the windows announced that fresh apple tart was on the menu. A stout woman came out to meet them.

"Are you from the police?" she called before they reached her.

Ketola nodded.

"Thank God."

"Where's the apartment?" Ketola asked.

"Up there." She pointed to a window under the eaves.

"Was it you who discovered the body?"

The woman nodded. "Jaana hadn't come downstairs although we were open already. She worked in the café. After a while I went upstairs to look . . . The door was open . . ."

"Thanks," said Ketola, striding past her.

They had to go through the café to get to the first floor. An elderly man was sitting at a table by the window, drinking coffee and reading a newspaper. He seemed quite indifferent to what was going on. Evidently he hadn't gathered that a woman had been murdered on the floor above.

They climbed a narrow staircase. Two uniformed policemen were standing outside the door of the apartment.

"Anything important?" asked Ketola.

They looked puzzled.

"Anything to report?" he demanded irritably.

The older of the two shook his head. "Nothing, sir. The forensics boys are still in there. The woman's in the bedroom. Jaana Ilander, twenty-five. We waited till you came."

Ketola nodded and walked in. Joentaa followed him.

The apartment was light, that was the first thing that struck him.

Light, although it was misty outside and had been raining for hours. The living room was surprisingly spacious and dominated by a wide window. The balcony faced the sea.

Lying on the floor were some photographs. They all showed a young woman, usually smiling with her lips slightly parted. Beside the photographs stood two wineglasses, a pair of tall candlesticks containing the stub ends of two candles, and a half-empty bottle.

"Hello, Kimmo."

Joentaa turned to see the ever-smiling face of Kari Niemi.

"Hello, Kari," he said.

"Seems you were right," said Niemi.

Joentaa looked at him questioningly.

"You suspected there was only one killer from the outset."

Joentaa nodded.

"I'm starting with the bedroom," said Niemi, and went out into the passage.

Joentaa pictured him entering the bedroom, patiently examining everything in sight and building up an overall picture of the smallest objects in which the dead woman was only one of numerous details. He liked Niemi, but his unfailingly cheerful mood was a mystery to him. Perhaps that was a false impression—perhaps he was far more thoughtful than he seemed at first sight.

Joentaa recalled the hug Niemi had given him after Sanna's death. Niemi had come to the funeral although they scarcely knew each other. He had met Sanna on only one occasion, at the headquarters Christmas party a year ago. Sanna was seriously ill already, but she'd pretended all was well—very convincingly, too.

So convincingly that Grönholm had later asked him if she was completely cured.

"Enjoying the view?" said Ketola, "or would you care to take a look at the victim?"

Joentaa followed him to the bedroom. On the way he felt a recurrence of the tension, the strange nervousness he'd experienced when Heinonen informed them of the murder.

He couldn't account for this tension, but he sensed that he would have to give it some thought before long.

The bedroom was so small that the bed, a flat sofa bed, took up most of the available space. Lying on the bed was a young woman. She was naked, and her eyes were still open.

There was nothing left behind those eyes, Joentaa reflected.

Turning away, he saw a photograph of a young man on the bedside table, presumably her boyfriend. A framed photo of the same young man had been hanging in the living room.

Niemi was kneeling on the floor, examining the carpet.

"Seems you were right all along, Kimmo," said Ketola, calm and businesslike all of a sudden. "A serial killer."

Joentaa looked at him.

"Why were you so sure from the first?"

He didn't know how to respond. His answer would certainly sound odd. "Laura Ojaranta was murdered the day after my wife died," he said after a pause.

Ketola stared at him intently.

"I think that had something to do with it," Joentaa went on. "Perhaps . . . perhaps I adopted a different approach to the scenario we found at the time."

"I don't see the connection," said Ketola.

Joentaa shrugged. "I don't know. I discussed it with Grönholm recently. He didn't understand what I meant either. I think the murderer's MO is important . . . He kills in silence while his victims are asleep. I picture him as a quiet, self-effacing person . . ."

He broke off, scanning Ketola's face for signs of derision and waiting for some flippant remark, but Ketola merely nodded. He looked unconvinced, but made no sarcastic comment.

"That sounds interesting," Niemi said without looking up from the carpet.

Ketola nodded absently, then bent over the dead woman. His gaze lingered on her face as if in search of something specific. Joentaa couldn't understand why he had calmed down so suddenly—there was no hint of his former, furious self—but Ketola was a mystery to him at the best of times.

He turned away and went downstairs to speak to the woman who had found the body. She was sitting at a table beside the window, staring out at the rain. The man who was quietly reading the paper when they arrived had already left.

"My name is Joentaa," he said. "I'd like to ask you a few questions."

"By all means," she said.

He sat facing her.

"You're the owner of this establishment?"

She nodded. "Krista Somervuori. The place belongs to me and my husband."

"Where is your husband?"

"In Turku. He left early, before I . . . before I started to wonder why Jaana hadn't come downstairs."

"Jaana Ilander worked for you?"

"Yes, she was an actress as well. She worked here during the day and at the theater at night. She was very good. We saw several of the plays she appeared in."

"How long had she lived here?"

The woman thought for a moment. "Six years. She moved here from the north to take drama lessons. She wasn't just a tenant. She bought the apartment with her parents' help. It's near the beach, that's mainly why she liked it. She intended to live here permanently, so she said at the time."

"Do you know anything about her parents? Are there any other next of kin we should inform?"

She shook her head. "Jaana didn't talk much about her parents. I seem to recall her saying that they lived in Rovaniemi. They're pretty well off, I think, but she had very little contact with them after moving south."

Joentaa paused briefly. He could guess what the woman's answer to his next question would be.

"Have you any idea who could have killed her?"

The woman stared at him as if she hadn't understood a word he'd said. Kerttu Toivonen and Arto Ojaranta had looked at him the same way, and so had Annette Söderström in the dim light of the youth hostel.

"No one could have had anything against Jaana," she said. "Jaana was . . . a very nice person."

Joentaa stared past her at the rain outside the misted window panes. For one brief moment he had the crazy notion that he'd found the key to the mystery: that the killer deliberately murdered nice people.

He dismissed the idea.

The woman began to weep. She apologized and went behind the counter to get a tissue. "I just can't understand it," she said when she was seated facing him again.

"Did you see or hear anything unusual last night?"

She shook her head, then stiffened. "There was one odd thing," she said.

"Yes?"

"Two days ago."

"What was it?"

"Someone rang the doorbell in the middle of the night. Like a madman!"

Joentaa felt his stomach muscles tighten.

"Who was it?"

The woman subsided again. "I don't know. Jaana ran downstairs and let someone in. We were standing in the passage, me and my husband, when she came down to answer the door. We didn't know what to do. It was the middle of the night, after all, but Jaana called to us not to worry, it was a friend of hers."

"A friend? The young man whose photo she kept on her bedside table?"

"Oh, him. No, no, he's an old flame. A German. She told me about him once. It was over long ago, I think."

"But his photo is on her bedside table, and there's another on the wall in the living room."

The woman shrugged. "I don't know why. I think she . . . well, still had a thing for him. She told me once he'd promised to visit her, but he never came."

"I see," he said. "This man who rang the bell in the early hours, did she tell you anything about him? Did she mention his name or describe him in any way?"

She shook her head.

"And you didn't see him?"

"No."

It was him, Joentaa thought. He came here in the night. He rang the doorbell violently, he was agitated but careful not to be seen.

Or was he simply lucky?

Above all, he was acquainted with Jaana Ilander. Had he also known Laura Ojaranta and Johann Berg?

"How long did he stay? Was he still here in the morning?"

The woman nodded deliberately. "He was here all right. Jaana smiled when I asked about him. I did ask her who he was, naturally. After all, he'd startled us to death . . ."

"What did she say?"

"She simply said he was a friend, and quite harmless."

Joentaa felt his stomach muscles tighten again.

Harmless.

Harmless and quiet.

Self-effacing, unobtrusive.

He seemed to see the man in front of him. At the same time, he felt he was mistaken.

"What else did she say?" he asked. "Every little detail matters."

She shrugged. "Nothing else. That's all I can remember. Late that morning Jaana came and asked me for time off. She did that some-times—she knew I wouldn't be annoyed, especially now that busi-ness is so slow. I didn't see the man when he left. They were gone before I knew it."

Joentaa nodded. That wasn't fortuitous, he told himself. The man had been careful not to attract attention. He'd known he was going to kill the girl, he must have done.

But why hadn't he done so right away, that first night? Why had he hesitated? And why had his victim regarded the person who killed her as a friend?

"Did Jaana Ilander say anything else at all? Whether he was young or old, at least?"

She deliberated briefly, then shook her head. "I didn't raise the subject again. I didn't like to pry."

Very laudable of you, thought Joentaa. And very regrettable.

He got up. "I'll come back to you in due course," he said. He had already turned away when another thought struck him. "Was the bedroom light on when you found her?"

She shut her eyes and thought for a moment.

"No," she said.

Joentaa went back upstairs. Nothing had changed there except for the forensics team. Two men in white overalls were examining the wine bottle, glasses, and photographs in the living room.

Ketola was leaning against the bedroom wall, watching Niemi at work. Seemingly engrossed in his thoughts, he gave a start when Joentaa spoke to him.

"I think we're on to something," he said.

"Like what?" Ketola looked uninterested.

"I've been interviewing the lady who owns the café. She says a man rang the doorbell like mad in the small hours two days ago. He spent the night here."

Ketola pricked up his ears. "What man?"

"She doesn't know. Evidently a friend of the girl's, that's all. She never saw him."

"She didn't see a man who woke her up in the middle of the night?"

"The girl answered the door, and he didn't show his face the next morning. Either he was very lucky or he deliberately kept out of sight, maybe both. In the night he was out of control and lucky. The next day he was back in control and careful not to be seen."

For several seconds Ketola fixed his subordinate with the alert, piercing gaze Joentaa had avoided ever since his first day at work. "This man may have absolutely no connection with the murder," he said at length.

"I'm sure he's the killer," Joentaa replied.

Ketola stared at him in a way he found hard to interpret. "And that's all the woman knows?" he said eventually.

Joentaa nodded.

"I'm sick of this!" Ketola detached himself from the wall and went out, presumably to interview the owner himself.

Joentaa stood there irresolutely, conscious that he was avoiding the sight of the dead woman on the bed.

"Ketola thinks a lot of you," Niemi said. "Did you know that?"

"Huh?" Disconcerted, Joentaa was about to make some rejoinder when one of the forensics team came in from the living room. "There's a photograph missing," he announced.

"What?" said Joentaa, still perplexed by Niemi's remark.

"The envelopes contained the negatives of the photos that were lying on the floor, and one of the corresponding prints isn't there."

"Which one? What's it of?"

"A woman. The one who's in all the others. Jaana Ilander, I guess."

Joentaa nodded. "I'd like to see the negative," he said, setting off for the living room with Niemi at his heels. One of the forensics team handed him the negative. He held it up against the window and saw, in brown and black, the figure of a woman with a grounded parachute. She was laughing at the camera.

Jaana Ilander.

Joentaa couldn't be sure, not having looked closely at the dead woman in the bedroom, but it had to be her.

A nice picture, and the murderer had taken it away with him.

There were other possibilities, of course. It was conceivable that the photo had gone missing earlier, or that the Ilander girl had given it away at some stage, but Joentaa felt sure it was in the murderer's possession. He had taken it away, just as he had taken the painting, the landscape that had been hanging in an inconspicuous niche in the Ojarantas' home.

What had prompted the man to do such a thing?

Could he also have pocketed photographs of Laura Ojaranta and Johann Berg?

"May I see?" asked Niemi.

Joentaa handed him the negative. Niemi held it up against the light and scrutinized it for some time. Then he turned his attention to the photos that were now lying in their plastic sleeves on a circular glass table. "To my mind," he said after a moment, "she was a very beautiful young woman. Genuinely beautiful, I mean, not just pretty." He continued to examine the photos, apparently searching for some phrase that would make his meaning plainer. "Special, somehow," he said eventually.

Joentaa nodded, but he'd been listening with only half an ear.

He was wondering why he'd avoided looking at the corpse. Why had he found it so hard to remain in the bedroom—why had he promptly gone downstairs on the pretext of having to interview the owner?

For that was all it had been: a pretext, an excuse to turn his back on the sight of the dead woman before he'd actually seen her.

Why had he been afraid of looking at her? What was the nature of the tension he'd felt when Heinonen informed them of the murder?

He turned and went back to the bedroom. Niemi said something else, but he didn't catch it.

He forced himself to go inside.

He approached the bed and bent over the dead woman.

As he absorbed the lines of her lifeless face, he realized what he had felt.

His prevailing emotion when Heinonen informed them of the murder had been relief. Relief at being distracted once more. Relief at having to examine another crime scene and solve another mystery. Relief at his ability to go on living for as long as the murders overlaid his awareness that Sanna was dead.

He was secretly glad that the murderer still hadn't been caught. A corner of his mind wanted the man to go on killing, and he had offset the disequilibrium of his world of ideas by simply not looking at the dead woman.

When he looked into Jaana Ilander's face—when he looked down at her as he had looked down at Sanna, who had stopped breathing from one moment to the next—it dawned on him that her murder, the death of another human being, had breathed life into himself.

22

Joentaa set off for Stockholm the same night.

He gave the matter no thought until he looked over the rail at the glittering water and felt the ship getting under way.

He had acted on impulse after standing in his living room and staring out at the lake as he had done for weeks now, night after night.

Haunted yet again by the past, by images of Sanna, he had got into his car and driven off into the darkness, accelerating until he was going fast enough to lose control and shatter the images into a thousand fragments.

He parked the car down at the docks and bought a ticket for the ferry. The young woman in the ticket office looked puzzled and queried his lack of baggage.

Once he was sitting on the bunk in his cabin, the images returned. He left the cabin and drifted up on deck, borne along by a tide of fellow passengers and trying to redirect his thoughts by concentrating on other people's conversations.

When they got under way he realized that his attempt to escape was doomed to fail because the ship harbored memories, just like the house beside the lake, the beach at Naantali, and every corner of the city.

Memories he would never escape.

As he watched the lights of Turku steadily dwindling he recalled a brief sea voyage he'd made with Sanna one weekend in summer, when she was still immortal.

He was a trainee at the time, and Sanna had just started work with her firm of architects. That had been the occasion of their weekend cruise, a cause for celebration. Sanna got smashed and he lost a mint playing blackjack and the slot machines. They'd had a whale of a time, and Sanna—who usually liked to think in terms of the geometrical figures that underpinned her world of ideas as firmly as the buildings she designed—had told ludicrous, tipsy anecdotes, laughed herself silly, and hugged him to the point of asphyxia.

Sanna had had many faces.

Sanna, who always knew exactly how life should be lived.

After a while it became freezing on deck. A steward appeared and called to him to come inside. It was madness to stay out there, he said.

Joentaa made his way downstairs to the big red saloon where he'd sat with Sanna—yes, it was the same ship, he was sure of that now. The same hubbub, the same weird little tunes from the one-armed bandits as they swallowed your coins, the same laughter, shouts, and beaming faces everywhere. It had been like that before. Only the band was different. The singer had been a dark-skinned chanteuse whose voice appealed to him. This time it was a blond giant, but the music was the same, an unpleasant mixture of tango and disco that never seemed to vary.

He sat down on a red sofa and ordered some mineral water. As he watched the couples on the dance floor, he felt the one-dimensional melody and the singer's monotonous voice lulling him gradually to sleep.

He awoke to find a glass of mineral water on the table in front of him. On the dance floor several closely entwined couples were swaying to a protracted guitar solo. The blond giant was smiling at the guitarist and mimicking his movements.

Joentaa sat up straight and drank some water.

He wondered what he was doing aboard this ship—what he proposed to do in Stockholm.

He shut his eyes and thought of the dead woman in the light, airy apartment above the beach café.

Jaana Ilander.

A beautiful woman, Niemi had said. Special, somehow.

What was special about her was that she had known her murderer. Jaana Ilander had regarded him as a friend, and the man who killed her had sought her company.

Why?

He had rung her bell in the middle of the night, panic-stricken, and found peace with her.

What had he previously done to make him so agitated?

Jaana Ilander had thought him harmless, and the owner of the café hadn't seen his face.

He was careful not to attract attention.

He enjoyed being inconspicuous.

He had killed a man in a crowded youth hostel—committed the murder in a room in which seven people were asleep.

He had felt immensely powerful. More than that, he had felt invisible. He had deliberately sought a hazardous situation so as to prove to himself and everyone else that nothing could happen to him.

He had felt invulnerable.

He had felt strong, invisible, and invulnerable.

Joentaa asked the waiter for a pencil and jotted the three words down on a coaster: *Strong, invisible, invulnerable.*

He put the coaster in his wallet.

Then his thoughts blurred.

When they took shape again he saw himself. He saw the dead woman, Jaana Ilander, lying on the bed. He saw himself bending over her.

The killer had bent over her like that before pressing the pillow down on her face.

Why had he done it? Why had he killed a woman who had helped him when he was in despair?

The bedroom light had been off when the body was discovered in the morning. Had the man turned it out during the night, before he took the pillow and smothered his victim?

It must surely have been dark in the youth hostel as well.

The man felt at ease in the dark.

Yes, he'd turned out the light. He'd always killed in the dark. He created darkness so as not to have to see his handiwork.

Joentaa shut his eyes, clamped his eyelids tightly together, and was back in Jaana Ilander's apartment. He looked through the big window at the beach, which was in darkness.

He moved swiftly along the passage and into the bedroom.

He saw the man's shadowy figure standing beside the bed.

He saw that he was trembling—that he didn't want to do what he was about to do.

Abruptly, the man bent down and clamped the pillow to Jaana Ilander's face, exerting all his strength. He was very determined.

The man was relieved she was asleep. Why? Because he didn't want her to suffer.

So why had he killed her?

Joentaa followed the man into the living room and tried in vain to discern what he was feeling.

All he saw was that he took a photograph from the floor, one of Jaana Ilander moments after landing by parachute.

Did it embody some reference to himself?

Or did he want to keep the woman he'd killed alive with the aid of a photograph?

Then the image broke up. Joentaa didn't see the man leave the apartment. He didn't see whether he was calm or on edge, whether he walked or ran.

He opened his eyes.

The blond giant was crooning a well-known tune. He saw couples on the dance floor bathed in the unnatural red glow from the spotlights focused on the stage.

He paid for the mineral water and went to his cabin. Two of the four bunks were already occupied by sleeping men.

He didn't wash for fear of waking them. He lay down fully dressed on his bunk, relieved to feel that he wouldn't find it hard to sleep. As he listened to the two men's breathing, it occurred to him that no one could feel safe if a murderer who killed sleeping people was on the loose.

At first he dismissed the idea as banal, exaggerated, and nonsensical, but shortly before he fell asleep he wondered if that was the killer's intention.

Perhaps he killed so that no one could feel safe anymore.

No one but himself.

23

"Hey, wake up, we're there!"

Joentaa opened his eyes and found himself looking into the face of a man he didn't know.

"We've reached Stockholm. You'd better hurry if you're going ashore, this ferry'll be going straight back to Turku."

Joentaa sat up. "Thanks."

The man nodded, picked up his bag, and went out into the passageway. Joentaa continued to sit there for a moment, striving to wake up. Then he rose and tottered into the bathroom. While washing and shaving he seriously considered returning to Turku.

He thought it over, knowing at the same time that he wouldn't do so.

Upstairs he bumped into the man who had woken him. His benefactor was wearing a well-pressed beige suit. He himself must have presented a rather peculiar sight in his crumpled, slept-in clothes.

"You slept like the dead," the man said. "Had a heavy night, eh?"

"I didn't, actually," Joentaa replied when they were standing side by side. "Thanks again, though. I'm afraid I'd have been halfway back to Turku by the time I woke up."

"Don't mention it," said the man.

They parted on the cold, windswept quayside. The man purposefully hailed a cab and called another "Goodbye" as he got in.

Joentaa didn't move for a while, wondering how long he would have to stand there before he froze to death.

He went over to a phone booth and leafed through a torn, dog-eared directory on which several cigarettes had been stubbed out. The name Söderström took up almost half a page. There were three Annettes and seven A. Söderströms. He recalled the entries in the Turku directory.

Ojaranta, Arto and Laura.

Joentaa, Kimmo and Sanna.

He tore out the page, then hailed a taxi.

While the cab was gliding slowly through the snowy streets he wondered what Annette Söderström would say when she found him outside her door. If she was at home, of course. He couldn't think what to say to justify his visit. There was no good reason for it. He himself had no idea of its true purpose.

All he'd known when leaving Turku was that he had to get out of the city and wanted to see Annette Söderström without delay. He'd ignored the question of why. It delighted him not to have to think, to be on the move at last, preferably forever.

When they reached the first address he got out and told the driver to wait.

The name Annette Söderström appeared on a card beside a whole row of bell buttons, handwritten in clumsy capitals. Annette Söderström lived on the ninth of fourteen floors in a high-rise block of apartments. Joentaa was sure he'd come to the wrong address, but he rang all the same. The voice that answered belonged to an old woman who was clearly uninterested in receiving visitors.

"Annette Söderström?" said Joentaa.

"Yes. What is it?"

He hesitated for a moment. "I'm sorry," he said, "I've made a mistake. I'm obviously looking for another Annette Söderström, a young woman. Do you by any chance have a young relation of the same name?" Even as he spoke, he wondered if he'd offended the woman by guessing her age on the strength of her voice.

"What exactly do you want?" she asked irritably.

"I'm sorry," he said. "Goodbye." He went back to the waiting taxi. The driver was lounging behind the wheel and had turned up the music on the radio. Joentaa got in and read out the second address in the phone book.

They drove for quite a while. Some children at a bus stop bombarded the cab with snowballs. The driver didn't take offense at this, in fact he seemed unaware of it.

The second address, too, was a washout. It was a big private house, and none of its occupants knew the Annette Söderström he was looking for.

While the driver was threading his way back into the heavy traffic, Joentaa reflected that it would, of course, have been wiser to call the various Söderströms first. The Annette Söderström he was looking for might be unlisted.

Her address and phone number were in his notebook at the office, he remembered. A little forethought would have spared him this wild-goose chase. He could have gone to get the notebook last night, before driving to the harbor.

He glanced at his watch. Ketola would be fuming because he hadn't turned up for work. He was probably taking it out on ever-amiable Heinonen while Grönholm stood there nonchalantly, waiting with a faint grin for his boss's outburst to subside.

At some stage he would have to call the office and let them know where he was, but not now.

The third address was the right one. He found himself face-to-face with Annette Söderström before he'd worked out what to say. She flung the door open as if expecting someone, certainly not him.

"Good morning," Joentaa said. "You've probably forgotten who I am. I'm one of the police officers from Turku who were called to the youth hostel when—"

"Of course I remember. You helped take care of Sven . . ."

"That's right."

"I had no idea you were coming. One of your colleagues was here a few weeks ago. I think I told him all I had to say . . ."

"I know . . . I've been in Stockholm for a couple of days, so I thought I'd pass by and ask if anything else has occurred to you." Joentaa felt himself break out in a sweat. He couldn't understand why he was talking such nonsense.

"Yes, well . . . I have to go to a lecture in a minute. Actually, I was expecting a girlfriend of mine—she's giving me a lift. My car gave up the ghost yesterday." She laughed. "This time for good, I fear." She pointed to an insignificant little runabout parked on the verge, its white bodywork almost indistinguishable from the snowy background.

Joentaa's taxi was waiting beside it with the meter running. The driver was engrossed in a newspaper, he saw.

"Look, I hope you won't think I'm crazy . . ." he began.

She looked puzzled.

". . . but could you possibly skip this lecture of yours?"

She didn't understand. "I could, but I'm afraid I wouldn't be of any further help to you. I wish I could—"

"It's not about that," Joentaa broke in. "Everything I told you just now was nonsense. I've only just got to Stockholm, and my sole reason for coming was to see you. Not about Johann Berg, not professionally . . . I simply wanted to see you . . . I thought of you when I couldn't stand my own company any longer."

"Oh . . ."

"This is unusual, I know . . . The thing is, my wife died a few weeks ago, and whenever I think of it and wonder who could help me, you come to mind. Don't ask me why I think of you rather than people I know well. They're the last ones I want to see. Mostly I think of you . . ."

She simply stood there for a while.

"You'd better come in," she said.

"One moment," he said, and ran to pay the cabby. Annette Söderström's apartment consisted of a big living room with a little alcove of a bedroom on a mezzanine reached by way of a spiral staircase. The décor was as white as the snow outside.

She brought some coffee and biscuits.

"I suppose you think this is all rather . . . peculiar," Joentaa said when they were sitting facing one another.

She gave him a long look before she replied. "No. I'm surprised, that's all."

"Do you often think of Johann Berg?"

"I try to switch off."

"That's just what I can't do," he said. "The thought of my wife never leaves me, no matter what I do. I never have a moment's peace. I can't listen to music anymore because every tune reminds me of Sanna. I can't watch films because I saw them all with her and still remember what she said and when."

"What did your wife die of?" she asked.

He was about to answer when the doorbell rang. She removed her gaze from his face and went to answer the door. He heard her talking to the friend who had come to pick her up for the lecture. She told her she had an unexpected visitor. The friend tried to pump her and asked what all the mystery was, but she said no more.

"Sanna had cancer," Joentaa said when she returned. "Lymph glands. A kind of cancer that attacks men in eighty percent of cases."

"I'm . . . very sorry," she said. She was disconcerted, he could tell.

"She was never ill. I'd never have thought it possible that such a thing could happen. Even now that it's over I sometimes get the feeling that it's a mistake, that it hasn't really happened . . ."

She nodded and put the cup to her lips. Her hand was trembling, he saw. "Sometimes, when I think of Johann and that night at the youth hostel, I get the same feeling—that it can't really have happened . . ."

"How is Sven?" he asked.

She drew a deep breath. "I don't really know. He has his mother, which is a very good thing, and when I visit him he always seems . . . well, his old self. But I'm not sure. It can't have simply passed him by. I doubt if he's really grasped the truth yet either."

Joentaa had a vision of the boy and recalled how he had stroked his head. He remembered Sven's uncomprehending gaze and the way he'd burst out crying. He would have liked to pay him a visit, but what would the sight of him be, other than a reminder of a night that was best forgotten forever?

He looked at Annette Söderström. Their eyes met. She asked if he would like to stay for lunch, and he said yes.

He'd been right, he thought. He'd been right to come to Stockholm. "I'm glad I came," he said. "I'm not sure why, exactly, but it's true."

She smiled. "I don't know if I can really be of help to you."

"You're helping me simply by sitting there. Simply by being there."

24

That evening, when Joentaa was standing on the quayside with the sleet coming down, he gave her a farewell hug. She waved to him as she boarded a bus for the city center. Turning, he joined the passengers streaming up the gangway and went straight to his cabin.

He stretched out on his bunk and reflected that it had been a good day. It had been a good day because Annette Söderström had listened to him talking about Sanna for the first time since her death.

He had told her a great deal. He had painted a picture filled with Sanna, and he had believed, while speaking, that she was still alive.

Sanna, puce in the face, had beaten him at arm-wrestling. Sanna had sat in their living room and, wielding her pencil with a light touch, designed fanciful buildings—surrealistic, crazily cambered houses that would never be built and were occupied by cheerful-looking match-stick people. Sanna had got terribly annoyed when she lost at party games.

To the very last, Sanna had behaved as if she wasn't afraid.

He wondered what she would have said if she could have seen him. Whether she would have understood why he was telling all these things to a woman he didn't know at all. He wondered what her reply would be if he could ask her what to do next. He wondered why Annette Söderström, of all people, had been able to help him, and why he had found the peace with her that neither friends nor relations had been able to give him.

He sat up abruptly to break this train of thought. Taking the cell phone from his jacket pocket, he called the office. He closed his eyes and braced himself in readiness for a tirade from Ketola. To his surprise and relief, it was Heinonen who answered.

"Kimmo, where are you?" he asked. To Joentaa's ears, his tone conveyed more concern than annoyance.

"I'm . . . on my way back to Turku. I've been in Stockholm."

"In Stockholm? About Johann Berg?"

"Er, yes. I went to see Annette Söderström."

"But we had no idea. It wasn't on the schedule."

"Yes, I'm aware of that. I'm sorry, I simply had to get away. I'm in rather a muddle at the moment . . ."

"I understand," Heinonen said. Joentaa thought how wonderfully sympathetic he was being. He must have borne the brunt of Ketola's anger, which had really been directed at himself.

"The boss will be pretty sore tomorrow morning, naturally, so you'd better be prepared. He was furious when you didn't turn up and couldn't be reached anywhere."

"I'm sorry. I hope he didn't take it out on you too much." Joentaa looked at his watch and pictured Heinonen sitting at his desk just after nine, the last to leave the office.

"It wasn't too bad," said Heinonen.

"Any news?"

"Not really. That's to say . . ."

"Yes?"

"We've now identified the German whose photo Jaana Ilander kept on her bedside table. His name is . . . just a minute . . . Daniel Krohn, and he probably lives in . . . Wiesbaden. As things stand, he's now the proud owner of a two-room apartment overlooking the beach at Naantali."

"What?"

"We've found a will in which the Ilander girl left it to him."

"Jaana Ilander made a will?"

"Yes. We don't yet know if it's legally valid, but it looks that way."

"Why would she have made a will? She was in her mid-twenties at most, surely?"

"Twenty-five," Heinonen said. Joentaa caught his breath when he grasped the absurdity of what he'd just said.

Sanna had also been twenty-five.

"She made the will six years ago, just after she bought the apartment."

"That's surprising," said Joentaa.

"Ketola thought so too. He reckons we should try to get in touch with the man."

"I'll handle it," Joentaa said. "Do you have a phone number for him?"

"No, and the address is probably out of date."

"Say the name again."

"Daniel Krohn. He was living in Wiesbaden six years ago, according to the will. Are you going to try calling him now?"

"Possibly."

Joentaa said a monosyllabic goodbye. He didn't know why, but he really did want to call the man right away. Why had Jaana Ilander left him her apartment, and why had she kept his photo on her bedside table when they hadn't seen each other for years? The owner of the café had said that much, at least, and she should know.

It took him about ten minutes to discover the number. There were several Krohns resident in Wiesbaden, but only one of them was a Daniel.

Joentaa stared at the slip of paper on which he'd noted down the name and number. He wondered what he expected of this man and why he was so set on informing him that Jaana Ilander was dead—that she had died before he'd come to Finland to see her again.

25

Vesa groped his way along the ice.

The water was so cold, he'd ceased to feel it.

He couldn't breathe.

He wanted to—he knew that he could and must—but it was no use.

Starved of air, he sensed that fear was overlaying his mental processes and paralyzing him.

He felt his way along the ice, seeking the surface where his life would begin anew.

He remembered lying on the bottom.

He'd been asleep. It wasn't until he awoke that he realized he couldn't breathe.

He groped his way along the ice but sensed that he was searching in vain. To survive he would have to go to sleep again, but how was he to sleep if he couldn't breathe?

Through the ice he glimpsed the sky and the white trees surrounding the lake.

He saw the pallid moon, which held no significance.

It dawned on him, as he groped his way along the ice, that everything was quite unlike his expectations.

How could he have been so mistaken?

When fear had permeated him completely, he allowed himself to sink.

That was better.

The deeper he sank the warmer it became and the more the burning sensation in his throat abated.

He was breathing.

He was lying on the bottom.

He felt very warm.

He was released, this time forever.

He saw the color he didn't know.

Just before he went to sleep, he awoke.

PART THREE

I

Daniel Krohn had known she meant trouble.

That was his first thought on shaking off his inertia after the surreal seconds in which his sole emotion had been amazement.

He was standing in the hallway, still holding the receiver although the caller had hung up long ago, and Marion was shouting at him.

Why was she shouting?

The caller had spoken with a curious accent he'd heard before. He couldn't place it or remember where he'd heard it until the voice at the other end of the line informed him, after a brief preamble, that Jaana Ilander had been murdered, and that she had left him, Daniel Krohn, a two-room apartment in her will.

The man had spoken quietly and deliberately. His German was strongly accented but grammatically correct. And crystal clear. Harsh.

Jaana Ilander.

Of course!

He'd known she meant trouble.

That had been his first thought.

The thought had been there even when he first kissed her on the lips all those years ago, in an entirely different life.

The man at the other end of the line had given his name and phone number and waited patiently for him to note down the particulars on a slip of paper. He could fly from Frankfurt to Helsinki and travel on to Turku by long-distance coach. If Daniel informed him in good time he would pick him up at the coach station.

The man had seemed in no doubt that he would catch the next plane. Daniel glanced at the slip of white paper while he was still speaking. The name meant nothing to him, but it imprinted itself on his mind nonetheless.

Kimmo Joentaa, Finnish CID.

Jaana Ilander had told him about Finland while they were lying on a white beach in Italy. He nibbled her lips, reflecting that Finland lay at the other end of the world, inaccessible but very near. He unbuttoned her blouse and closed her eyelids with his tongue, and Jaana Ilander laughed.

He'd never forgotten Jaana's laughter. It was the only thing he could really remember about her.

Marion was shouting at him.

"That was her, I suppose!" she snapped. "Do you think I'm blind? Do you think you can do as you damn well please?"

"It was a policeman," he said. "A Finn."

She'd been about to renew the attack, but she stopped short.

"Years ago I had an affair with a Finnish girl—no need to raise the roof, it was long before we met, ages ago . . . Her name was Jaana. She's dead."

"So what?"

"She's been murdered, the policeman said, and I've inherited her apartment."

Marion stared at him, and he himself felt just as bewildered by what he was saying.

"One second," he said, and strode off to the bedroom. Opening the door of the wardrobe, he kneeled down and rummaged in the bottom drawer, looking for the shoebox.

He sensed that Marion was standing behind him.

He'd suddenly remembered that the shoebox was there. He knew exactly what it looked like, white with green stripes. It had contained some tennis shoes, he now had a vivid recollection of the day he'd bought them.

He continued to rummage in the bottom drawer of the wardrobe. He brought to light a white paper bag of old clothes, two broken tennis rackets, and a Walkman whose defunct batteries had leaked.

He heard Marion say "Ugh!" as he deposited it on the floor beside him.

He hadn't looked in this drawer for ages, it occurred to him.

The shoebox was right at the back.

White with green stripes.

He took it out and placed it on the floor in front of him.

"What's that?" Marion asked.

"Letters."

"Letters? From her, from that . . ."

"Jaana."

"You never told me."

"I didn't answer a single one," he said, opening the box to reveal a stack of torn-open envelopes and letters written in blue ink.

"There must be scores of them," Marion said.

Shutting his eyes, he seemed to hear the Finnish policeman's voice, distinct but very quiet.

"I've no idea how many there are," he said. "I got one nearly every day for the first few months. They dried up completely in the end."

"And you never answered them?"

He raised his head and looked at her. Seeing her bewildered, reproachful expression, he felt the whole scene was a bad joke. He laughed.

"What's so funny?" Marion shouted. "Why did you never tell me about this woman?"

He went on laughing till it hurt, then abruptly got to his feet. Planting himself in front of Marion, he drew a deep breath and shouted back at her. "I haven't had a thing to do with her! I haven't even thought of her for years. I'd forgotten all about the shoebox until five minutes ago, and I've no need to justify myself!"

He saw her recoil.

He stared at the blue handwriting and the envelopes he'd torn open in a hurry, eager to get his hands on the letters inside. Yes, he remembered now: he had enjoyed reading them, been pleased to get them at first. He hadn't shown them to anyone, just read them and tossed them into the shoebox. Jaana Ilander was slightly cracked, he'd told himself, but he would visit her someday, give her a surprise when the time was right.

He recalled that the letters had begun to irritate him after a few weeks, then make him feel a trifle uneasy. After some months he'd started to detest the sight of them. But he'd kept every last one.

He'd occasionally toyed with the idea of replying, he remembered, and once he'd even sat down in front of a blank sheet of paper and tried to find the words.

He recalled how relieved he'd been when the letters finally stopped coming. He couldn't remember exactly when he'd forgotten about Jaana Ilander and the shoebox, but it had to be quite a while ago.

"Well, what happens now?" asked Marion. She had backed off and was standing in the doorway.

She was looking him hard in the eye. He looked back at her, forcing himself to hold the gaze of the wife with whom he'd been arguing only a few minutes before—the wife who had claimed he was cheating on her. He had denied it although it was true, but that was wholly beside the point now.

He looked at her and spoke without hearing what he was saying.

"I'm going to fly to Finland. Tomorrow."

2

D aniel Krohn took roughly two hours to reach the country he'd thought of as being at the other end of the world.

The flight attendant never stopped smiling at him—at least, he got that impression—and the gray-haired man beside him, a Finn, never stopped talking and drinking beer. The man winked at him benevolently when he spilled his Diet Coke. The flight attendant smiled and mopped it up with a cloth.

The man told Daniel about himself in halting but surprisingly proficient English; about his life in Finland, about the friends he'd just been visiting in Germany, about the compensations of retirement, about the leisure time he now had at his disposal, about his grandchildren. He showed Daniel a snapshot of them: two little girls posed against an expanse of snow in thick, bright red overcoats. The photographer, presumably the man himself, had persuaded them to laugh.

He looked at Daniel, expecting some reaction. Daniel went on nodding in silence until the Finn produced a newspaper from his briefcase and started reading it.

Daniel turned away and looked out of the window.

Grayness.

He imagined kissing the flight attendant.

Marion had waved when he looked back at her through the window of the cab. The driver had been humming to himself. Marion meant a lot to him, Daniel reflected.

From the airport he had called Tina and told her he had to go away for a while. When she asked why, he surprised himself by telling her the truth. Tina, who was surprised in her turn, hadn't immediately grasped what he was talking about, but she asked no questions. Tina, the theology student who had absolutely no qualms about carrying on with a married man, just as long as the situation was clear-cut.

Tina was extraordinarily attractive, no doubt about it.

Tina and Marion had both asked him to call when he got to Helsinki.

Marion meant a great deal to him, he reflected, even though he'd been unfaithful to her with numerous women over the years and they'd long spent most of their time together bickering.

He wondered why Marion meant so much to him.

He wondered what had been going on in Jaana Ilander's head when she picked up her pen and proceeded to write, day after day: *Dear Daniel, I hope you are fine . . .*

Letters that had never been answered.

Invariably friendly, affectionate letters.

Intriguing, perturbing letters.

He'd read every last one.

He thought of the photograph the elderly man beside him had taken from his wallet, the one of the two little girls in red overcoats. Jaana had also shown him a photo that time in Italy, a photo of her nephew, who had just been born. He suddenly had a precise recollection of the occasion. They were lunching on spaghetti Bolognese at a restaurant on the beach. Jaana told him he simply must see little Teemu—that was the nephew's name—and that he must definitely come to Finland. He would do so without fail, he promised.

Jaana had called him once, some weeks after they met in Italy. He immediately sensed that she'd been worried about him. She sounded relieved to hear his voice and said she would enjoy getting a letter from him sometime. Her tone wasn't petulant, just insufferably affectionate. When she suggested coming to see him on her next holiday, he'd said he would bear it in mind.

He could now recall their conversation in every detail.

He'd waited until she ran out of things to say.

Then he'd said goodbye and hung up.

Jaana's letters hadn't changed in the least after that. Long, affectionate letters in a legible, unaffected hand, well written and interesting, but she never referred to her proposal to visit him, nor had she asked any questions about his future plans and present circumstances.

Dear Daniel, I hope you are fine . . .

After her phone call, that had to suffice.

He wondered what had inhibited him from telling her he hadn't taken their affair as seriously as she had. He wondered what had prompted him to joke to his friends about this holiday romance and, at the same time, to keep all Jaana Ilander's letters.

When the pilot announced that they would be landing shortly, the man beside him started talking again—feverishly this time. He asked

Daniel what he planned to do during his visit, what his profession was, what he liked best about Finland. He stumbled over the English words and his hands shook. Scared of flying, Daniel realized. The man had seemed thoroughly relaxed throughout the flight, but now, during the approach, he'd gone completely haywire.

He was afraid he would never again set eyes on the little girls he'd persuaded to laugh, Daniel surmised.

He told the man he worked as a copywriter in an advertising agency and was visiting Finland for the first time. Why? For a holiday. On his own? Yes, on his own. The man nodded. Daniel got the impression that he wasn't listening at all and merely wanted some distraction from his fear.

He himself was seldom afraid, he reflected. He had never been afraid of not seeing Jaana Ilander again.

The old man smiled at him when the plane taxied to a stop. He reverted to the subject of his grandchildren while they were making their way along the tunnel and into the airport terminal, quite at ease once more. It was a shame, he said, that his wife hadn't lived to see them.

Daniel nodded. All at once he pictured a completely different scenario. Jaana Ilander hadn't been murdered at all. Jaana, who had persisted in sending him affectionate letters for years on end, had devised a means of seeing him again. The man who had called him, the Finnish policeman, was no policeman but a friend of Jaana's who had lured him to Finland with a cock-and-bull story.

Jaana wasn't dead at all. She would be waiting for him at the exit. She would be lying in wait somewhere, behind a column or a newspaper, and would put her hands over his eyes. He would turn round and see her face.

She would laugh at him and kiss him hard on the mouth.

"What are you laughing at?" the old man asked.

"Nothing special," he said.

Jaana wasn't waiting for him.

He followed the instructions given him by Joentaa, the Finnish policeman. Joentaa had been wide awake when he'd called early that morning. He had given him precise details, and they all proved correct: the coach for Turku departed from stop number 11, right outside the international terminal. There was one at 13:30 and another at 14:01. As the Finnish policeman had predicted, Daniel landed just in time to catch the 13:30.

While the coach was gliding slowly along the snowy roads, his thoughts turned to this policeman who had radiated a strange calm. Daniel had seemed to detect a note of reproach in his voice. He must have been mistaken, of course.

Why had he been contacted by a policeman and not a solicitor or someone who dealt with testamentary matters? And why should Jaana Ilander, who was several years younger than himself, have made a will? He had never for a moment considered doing so.

The longer he thought about it, the more he suspected that the whole thing was a bad joke.

Jaana would probably be waiting for him at the coach station in Turku.

He shut his eyes and tried to recall her face, but without success. Jaana had sent him some photos enclosed in one of her earliest letters. He remembered that perfectly, and he also remembered being annoyed. He'd put the letter in the shoebox and the photos in the dustbin in case they fell into the hands of his current girlfriend.

He tried to remember the girlfriend in question. Her name was Cornelia, and he hadn't seen her for years.

After half an hour he had to change, as the Finnish policeman had told him. The second coach was bigger, more comfortable and nearly full. He sat down beside a young woman. She was reading a book with an unintelligible Finnish title. He'd laughed when Jaana Ilander had given him some samples of her mother tongue. He'd laughed and said he was sure he would never understand a word of it. Jaana looked disappointed at this, he noticed, but it hadn't worried him.

He found the young woman at his side attractive. She was a blonde like Jaana.

Jaana Ilander had been an exceptionally attractive girl, that was undeniable.

He settled himself more comfortably in his seat and wondered what he was doing on board this coach. He'd decided to fly to Finland without a second thought, and he was beginning to regret it.

What on earth was he doing here?

A woman in uniform addressed him in her strange and unintelligible tongue.

"Sorry," he said irritably, "I don't speak Finnish."

"Your ticket, please," she said, in English this time.

The woman in uniform remained steadfastly polite, which irritated him all the more. He handed her his ticket. The young woman beside him asked where he came from.

"Germany."

She nodded, smiled, and—to his surprise—left it at that. She re-immersed herself in her book. He eyed her with deliberate ostentation—he liked doing that when he was irritated, it soothed him. Fair hair and big blue eyes. If he remembered rightly, Jaana had looked much the same.

He turned away and stared out of the window. Snow-laden trees slid past for minutes on end, punctuated now and then by frozen lakes.

Silver. Gray. White.

"I like your country," he said to the young woman. "It's really beautiful." He didn't know why he'd said it, whether he really meant it or was only being provocative.

The young woman looked up from her book and smiled at him.

Jaana Ilander must have smiled like that.

She wasn't waiting at the coach station.

It was snowing heavily. A young man came toward him. It was the Finn he'd spoken to on the phone, Daniel grasped that at once and sensed that he wasn't a victim of some joke in poor taste. This man made a thoroughly bona fide impression.

Jaana Ilander was dead.

"Herr Krohn?" said the man.

"That's right. You must be . . ."

"Kimmo Joentaa. We spoke on the phone." Again the deliberate, precise German.

"Many thanks for coming to meet me."

"Not at all. May I?" He took Daniel's bag and walked over to a small, dark blue car. Before they drove off he seemed to deliberate briefly. "I was going to invite you to stay at my place," he blurted out.

Daniel was too surprised to reply at first.

"I can always take you to a hotel, of course . . ."

"No, no, only too glad to accept your offer . . . It took me by surprise, that's all."

The man nodded and drove off.

"I'm glad you came," he said after a while.

Daniel looked at the young man he didn't know. He found him likable somehow, but also rather weird, and it struck him that Jaana Ilander had succeeded after all: she had actually managed to throw him off his stride—with a vengeance, what was more.

He had even forgotten to call Marion on arrival. And Tina.

"Why?" he asked.

The policeman glanced at Daniel and raised his eyebrows.

"Why are you glad I came? I'm a total stranger."

The policeman pondered this for an exasperating length of time.

"I'm glad you came because there were other courses of action open to you. For instance, you could have said you were uninterested in Jaana Ilander and her will. I'm glad you didn't."

"But why are you glad? And why have you invited me to stay with you?"

The man relapsed into silence.

"Are you really a policeman?" Daniel asked at length.

The man looked surprised. "Yes, of course."

"During the flight I thought this whole thing might be a practical joke on Jaana's part. I wouldn't have put it past her."

The policeman gave him a long look. "I'm sorry to hear you thought that," he said.

They drove on in silence for a while.

"She was . . . murdered?" Daniel said eventually. The policeman nodded. The car had headed out of the city and into a snowy landscape. Daniel knew he had many more questions to ask, but none of them occurred to him. They turned off onto a forest track, snow crunching beneath the wheels and adhering to the tires. This is the strangest day of my life, Daniel told himself.

He would call Marion and Tina and Oliver, who was bound to be waiting for him at the agency. Where's Daniel?—Oliver would be asking impatiently—has he got writer's block again? He had taken the copy on Glanz, the politician, home with him to work on. He knew exactly what to do, he even had a slogan in his head, but the wording still wasn't snappy enough.

He had the situation under control, though.

The man beside him drove ever further into the snow-white forest. Timber-built houses loomed up to left and right of them, and from time to time Daniel glimpsed the icy sheen of a frozen lake between the trees. Finland is a beautiful country, he thought, and recalled that Jaana Ilander had said precisely that. Finland is a beautiful country, she'd told him, and he simply must see it sometime.

He banished the memory by asking if they had far to go.

"Not far," the policeman replied.

A few minutes later he pulled up beneath a tree in the drive of a wooden bungalow. It was a handsome building, but Daniel's first impression—he didn't know why—was that the house was empty and dead.

The policeman took his suitcase and went on ahead. For a fleeting moment Daniel expected Jaana Ilander to be waiting behind the door when he unlocked it.

There was no one waiting inside.

The policeman deposited Daniel's suitcase in the hallway and took his coat. "I have to go back to the office," he said as he was hanging up the coat. "There's some beef casserole if you're hungry . . . it's in the oven."

"Many thanks," said Daniel, instinctively reaching for his cell phone. He must call Marion. Tina too. And Oliver. He must return to reality.

"I must call home," he said. "My wife . . ."

"You're married?"

Daniel nodded. "And my boss is waiting for some copy I was supposed to deliver today, at least a draft. I caught the plane this morning without notifying him."

The policeman smiled.

"Why are you smiling?"

"That makes two of us."

"How so?"

"I went to Stockholm without informing my chief."

Daniel didn't understand. What was he getting at?

"Why did you go to Stockholm?"

"Why did you fly to Finland this morning?"

The policeman was still smiling. Amiably. Sadly.

Daniel couldn't think of a suitable reply.

"I must go," the policeman said. "I'll try to get away early. The sofa bed in the living room is for me, by the way. You'll be sleeping in the bedroom."

Daniel nodded. He was feeling bemused.

"See you later," said the policeman, and went out.

Daniel stood there irresolutely for a moment or two. Then he turned on the cell phone and started to key in his home number, Marion's number.

The policeman suddenly reappeared in the doorway. "You can always use my phone, it'll be cheaper," he said.

"Thanks," said Daniel.

The policeman nodded and then left. Daniel stopped dialing and waited until the hum of the car's engine lost itself in the forest.

He stood there for a while, trying to collect his thoughts.

He didn't know what this policeman expected of him, nor could he understand why he had come to Finland in the first place.

He put off calling Marion.

He toyed with the thought of not calling Tina at all.

He went into the kitchen and removed the casserole from the oven. He really was hungry, very hungry. He felt he hadn't eaten for ages. He filled a plate, sat down at the kitchen table, and stared through the window at the snowscape outside.

He thought of the publicity material for colorless Herr Glanz's election campaign and of the slogan he was meant to supply for it. He thought of Oliver, who would be waiting impatiently, but the thought soon passed.

He thought of Jaana Ilander and recalled the enthusiastic way she'd talked about Finland. He thought of the unknown policeman who was putting him up in his home.

Later he would ask the man a lot of questions and insist on getting some answers.

3

Joentaa paused outside the office door and drew a deep breath.

He'd been lucky enough not to run into Ketola that morning, but Grönholm had come up to him in the lobby and told him that the boss had arrived. "I'm afraid he's hopping mad this time," he said with a laugh, as if this was the greatest news ever.

Joentaa spent several seconds trying to work out some acceptable excuses. Then he abandoned the attempt and jerked the door open.

"Hello, Kimmo," said Ketola, who was bent over a file lying on his desk. He merely glanced up for a moment. "I have to face the press with Nurmela in a few minutes. The jerks are in full cry, needless to say . . . Heinonen said you'd gone to pick up that German. Is he here already?"

"Yes. I called him last night and—"

"Why?" Ketola demanded.

"Why what?"

"Why did you call him? The man isn't that important, not if he was at home in Germany at the time of the murder. Besides, you took yesterday off as well. A little joyride to Sweden . . ."

"Yes, I was going to have a word with you about that."

"Know what? Forget it."

"I'm sorry?"

"Forget it. Yes, sure, you could have informed us. Your cell phone was turned off, and I sent a squad car to your home because I was afraid something might have happened to you, but never mind."

Ketola didn't look at him. He was leafing through the file and seemed wholly engrossed.

"I . . . You sent a squad car to my home?"

"Heinonen says you had a word with Annette Söderström," Ketola muttered as if unaware of what Joentaa had said. "Did she have anything new to tell you?"

"No . . . No, I . . ."

"Yes?"

"I'm sorry I didn't phone in yesterday. I simply had to get away. It's hard to explain, but—"

"I drove my son to the hospital yesterday morning," Ketola broke in. "He's . . . in a pretty bad way." He began to laugh, loudly and hysterically, then choked and subsided after a protracted fit of coughing. "That, Kimmo, is equally hard to explain, but the absurd thing is, I'm quite sure you know how I feel. And because you know how I feel, I know how you feel, and that's why I said to forget it, follow me?"

Joentaa nodded slowly.

"This business with your son . . . I hope . . . What's the matter with him?"

"Nothing, nothing at all," said Ketola. "One of those little human failings that are always cropping up in life."

And he reapplied himself to the file.

4

Nurmela was adept at saying very little at very great length, but this time his listeners weren't having any of it.

Joentaa, standing at the back of the room, listened to the verbal hostilities with mounting suspense. The journalists' questions became more and more waspish and impatient, until Nurmela, usually so eloquent, began to hem and haw. "No, but we're well on the way to . . . Yes, of course, we're following up certain leads . . . No, we're not at liberty to . . . You'll understand, I'm sure, that I can't . . . The whole thing will resolve itself very quickly provided one or more of our leads . . . You must surely realize that we're still at an early stage in our . . ." Nurmela mopped his brow with a handkerchief. Ketola was sitting motionless beside him, fixing the representatives of the press with the piercing gaze that Joentaa had never managed to withstand.

It didn't seem to bother the journalists.

Nurmela was endeavoring to bring the press conference to a close with a few soothing, platitudinous phrases when Ketola suddenly exploded. Nurmela gave a start, and the reporter who had just asked a question stopped short with his mouth open.

"Who the hell do you think you are?" Ketola bellowed. "Do you think we get a kick out of people dying? Do you think we sit around all day, laughing at the shit that happens? Do you think you know all the answers, just because some rag prints the garbage you write?" He had risen to his feet and was bending over the table like an orator at a lectern.

Nurmela sat frozen to the spot, and even the journalists were speechless, at least for a moment or two. Before they had a chance to recover their wits, Ketola strode toward the exit. Joentaa prepared to follow, but Ketola didn't seem to notice him. "Scumbags!" he muttered to himself, and slammed the door behind him.

Nurmela hurriedly took the floor again and tried to play the incident down. They must surely realize that all his colleagues' nerves were a little . . . well, on edge at present. One or two of the reporters laughed, others were already streaming out, presumably to inform their editors of this latest sensation.

Joentaa went upstairs to the office. Ketola wasn't there. He briefly considered going to look for him but thought better of it. He was relieved not to find Ketola there.

He pulled the phone toward him and dialed the first number on a list Ketola had given him before the press conference. Friends, acquaintances, and relations of Jaana Ilander. Right at the top of the list was the name Kati Itkonen. Beside it, in brackets, Ketola had added something in his spidery handwriting. Joentaa deciphered it with difficulty: *Best friend of the deceased.*

It occurred to him while he was waiting to get through that Kati Itkonen mightn't have heard what had happened. This idea was instantly dispelled when he heard the tearful voice at the other end of the line.

He introduced himself. "Kimmo Joentaa, CID. Is that Kati Itkonen?"

"Yes."

"I'm with the team that's investigating Jaana Ilander's murder. I'd like to ask you a few questions, if I may."

"Of course. Just a moment."

He heard her blowing her nose. When she picked up the receiver again her voice was loud and clear, studiously normal.

"What do you want to know?" she asked.

"We have a lead. It concerns a young man, a boyfriend of Jaana Ilander's, someone she probably hadn't known for long."

"I find that hard to believe. Although . . ."

"Yes?"

"I know nothing about any boyfriend, Jaana never said much. She was . . . a very good listener. She could coax you into confiding your innermost secrets, but she never talked about her own problems. Perhaps she simply didn't have any."

He heard her draw a deep breath.

"So you don't know anything about a man she may have met quite recently?"

"No, absolutely not. Unless . . . You surely don't mean . . ."

"Yes, go on."

"It was a few weeks ago. We'd gone swimming. She spoke to a young guy who seemed rather . . . well, odd. He'd been sitting on a bench, staring at the water for minutes on end. His clothes were odd too—he was all in red."

"So she spoke to this man although she had no idea who he was?"

"Yes, but that wasn't so unusual if you knew her. Jaana was . . . very impulsive. She tended to do the first thing that came into her head. And she always took a special interest in oddballs like that guy."

"Did she mention him subsequently?"

"No, but we didn't see a lot of each other after that. We spoke on the phone a few times. As I told you, she never said much about herself."

"But you saw this man . . ."

"Not properly."

"You were there when she spoke to him."

"Yes, but he was sitting on a bench at least a hundred yards away, and I was in the water."

He cultivates invisibility, Joentaa thought.

"All the same, what do you remember about him? What did he look like?"

"I told you. All in red, longish hair. Slimmish too, neither tall nor short. Inconspicuous, if he hadn't been wearing that funny get-up."

"Do you think you'd recognize him again?"

She thought for a moment. "I'm afraid not. I don't have a definite picture of him in my mind. Besides, I don't think Jaana had anything more to do with him."

Joentaa nodded to himself, convinced that she was right.

He asked some more questions and received answers that got him no further. Answers reminiscent of the responses he'd elicited from Arto Ojaranta, Kerttu Toivonen, and Annette Söderström: utter incomprehension in the face of an occurrence they would never have believed possible.

He made some more phone calls without learning anything definite about the young man who had shared a bottle of wine with Jaana Ilander and was probably her killer. Two actresses from the theater where she'd worked did say something of interest, but it got him no further, nor did it surprise him particularly. Yes, they recalled that Jaana had met a young man, and that he'd attended a performance.

No, they hadn't actually seen him.

No, Jaana had merely mentioned in passing that he was a bit unusual, a bit of an oddball. She sounded rather amused, they said.

"She was annoyed after the performance," one of the actresses said, "because she had to go looking for him."

"Why did she have to go looking for him?" Joentaa asked.

"He'd left. She wanted to introduce him, but he'd disappeared."

"Did she find him?"

"I'm not sure . . . Yes, I think so . . . He was waiting for her outside, and they went off together."

"And you really didn't see him?" Joentaa asked. "Not even for a moment, not even in the distance?" He already knew the answer.

"No. I'm sorry."

Invisible . . .

The word haunted him as he drove home that evening. When he tried to escape from this train of thought, it occurred to him that Ketola hadn't reappeared.

As he labored through the evening rush-hour traffic in a light dusting of snow, it suddenly dawned on him where Ketola must be. He had told Nurmela, truthfully, that he was afraid he had no idea where Ketola was—Nurmela, who had stormed into the office, red in the face with rage, while he was working his way through the names and phone numbers on his list. He genuinely hadn't known where Ketola had gone, but he knew now. To the hospital, of course, to see the son he'd mentioned just before the press conference.

Even though Ketola had talked in riddles, Joentaa now felt sure that his son had a drug problem. Ketola had disclosed this in his strangely detached way, but it was uncharacteristic of him, most uncharacteristic, to have mentioned it at all.

Joentaa turned off the main road and onto the forest track. It was snowing more heavily now. He sighted the house, Sanna's house, through the trees and the whirling snowflakes. There was a light on.

He parked beneath the snow-laden apple tree. Of course there was a light on, he had a visitor.

He welcomed the fact. It was a comforting thought, not being on his own tonight.

5

Daniel Krohn hadn't called anyone.

Not Marion. Not Tina. Not Oliver.

He'd spent the afternoon on the sofa in the living room, gradually lulled to sleep by the snow-white landscape outside the window. He found the view extraordinarily soothing—indeed, he felt his annoyance with Jaana Ilander and the policeman, but above all with himself, slowly subside and ebb away to nothing.

He lost his sense of time and felt free in a strangely disagreeable way: weightless, insignificant, lethargic. He amused himself by checking his voice mail every now and then.

The messages were piling up, he noted with satisfaction. Four from Marion, sounding irate but worried. Three from Oliver, merely irate. Tina evidently had better things to do than phone around after him.

He sat on the sofa, looking out at the frozen lake and white trees, listening to his cell phone occasionally, and chuckling at the thought of Marion and Oliver.

He absorbed the whiteness outside the window until it stung his eyes so much he had to close them.

He was awakened by the little rattletrap's engine. He sat up, trying to shake off his drowsiness. When he felt he wasn't succeeding fast enough he jumped to his feet, he didn't know why. For some reason, he didn't want the policeman to find him half asleep. He went over to the television, picked up the remote control, and turned it on.

He heard the key in the lock and wondered why he was feeling so apprehensive. Why should he be nervous about a man who had given him such a cordial reception?

"Hello?" Joentaa called.

Daniel turned in his direction. "Hello."

His fear had already evaporated—in fact he couldn't understand where it had come from. The TV screen was showing some ice hockey. Highlights of goals being scored in quick succession. He changed channels. A cartoon, a black-and-white film, the weather forecast, ice hockey again.

"Have I pressed the wrong buttons, or are there really only four channels?"

Joentaa nodded. "Just four."

"I like that," said Daniel, "even though I don't understand a word. Back home we can get around forty channels. I like this, though. You don't feel so inundated."

"Inundated?" Joentaa looked puzzled.

"With garbage. I'm sure they don't show as much tripe here as they do on German TV. I shouldn't be saying that, of course. Television is one of my agency's principal sources of income."

"One can get plenty more channels in Finland too, with a satellite dish, but I don't watch much television . . ."

Daniel looked round because the policeman had broken off. He was gazing at the screen, apparently immersed in some private reverie.

On the screen an elderly man was presenting the weather forecast.

"What is it?" Daniel asked.

"Nothing . . . That's our best-known weather forecaster. There was a long article about him in the paper recently. It was his thirtieth anniversary in the job."

"Really."

"He says we're in for a lot of snow in the next few days."

"I see."

"Do you think he's . . . funny?" Joentaa asked.

"Who?"

"The weather forecaster."

Daniel looked back at the screen. "Funny? No. Why?"

Joentaa didn't answer. He seemed to be lost in thought again. "Would you like something to eat?" he asked after a long pause.

"Yes, please. The casserole was excellent, by the way."

Joentaa nodded and set off for the kitchen. Daniel followed him. As he did so, he felt a resurgence of anger. Why did the man keep speaking in riddles? What was all that about the weather forecaster? What was he withholding? Daniel felt sure he was concealing something important.

"I think you owe me a few explanations," he said when he was standing beside Joentaa in the kitchen, watching him lay the table.

Joentaa looked at him inquiringly.

"Why have you put me up in your home? Why did you call me rather than a lawyer or an executor? You seem to have a special interest in me, and I simply can't think why."

Joentaa had continued to lay the table while he was speaking. "Do sit down," he said. "Which would you prefer, milk or water?"

"Milk," said Daniel.

He normally drank wine with his evening meal, but why not milk for once? He couldn't help chuckling when the policeman poured him a glass of milk. If Oliver could see him now . . . Besides, for some reason he had always assumed that the Finns were permanently drunk. On milk?

"What's so funny?"

"Nothing," Daniel said. "Remember what I asked you just now? It can't have escaped you that I'm feeling a bit . . . miffed." He stressed the last word, determined to coax this Finnish policeman out of his shell somehow or other, but Joentaa merely nodded and said nothing. The silence began to get on Daniel's nerves. He was just about to tackle him again when he got an answer after all.

"I can well understand why you're puzzled," Joentaa said.

And relapsed into silence.

Just before Daniel could prompt him, Joentaa asked a question of his own. It took Daniel by surprise.

"Did you really promise to visit her?"

"Visit who?"

"Jaana Ilander."

"What do you mean?"

"Jaana Ilander hoped you would visit her."

"How do you know? What are you getting at this time?"

"She must have been very fond of you. There was a photo of you beside her bed."

"What?"

"Do you understand why she left you the apartment?"

Daniel didn't answer.

"She's compelled you to keep your promise after all."

"Really?"

"You did promise to come to Finland, didn't you?"

"I . . ."

"If you promised, why didn't you come?"

"What is all this? What are you after? Why are you poking your nose into my affairs?" Daniel had risen and was looking down at the policeman, who avoided his eyes.

"What is all this?" Daniel repeated.

"I'm sorry," Joentaa said.

"Did you know Jaana Ilander?" Daniel asked.

Joentaa shook his head.

"So what's your angle? Why all this interest in Jaana and my relationship with her?"

There was a long pause.

"My wife died not long ago."

Daniel was taken aback. "I'm sorry," he said uncertainly.

"Earlier I asked what you thought of the weatherman . . ."

"Well?"

"Sanna thought he was funny. She always laughed when she saw him."

Daniel waited for some clue to what the man was trying to say.

"Everything I see has some connection with Sanna. There's always some . . . association of ideas. Do you understand?"

"Not entirely."

"I wanted you to come here. I wanted you to know what happened. I wanted you to confront the situation—it's a similar situation, after all. A person you were fond of is dead. I wanted you not to evade the issue."

Daniel nodded slowly. He did understand. In a way.

He would have to give it some thought, he told himself.

"When I came home earlier, I was glad to see the lights on," the policeman said. "It's nice to have you here."

"Delighted to hear it," Daniel said. He didn't know whether he meant it or was merely being sarcastic. He caught sight of the glass of milk on the table and felt a renewed urge to laugh, although there was nothing to laugh at.

He stifled his laughter.

"Tell me about Jaana Ilander," said Joentaa.

Daniel couldn't help laughing. Why?

"Why are you laughing?" Joentaa asked.

Daniel picked up the glass, drained it at a gulp, and asked for a refill.

To gain time, he thought.

Joentaa got up, took the carton from the refrigerator, and poured him some more. Then he sat down again and looked at Daniel patiently. He had asked a question, after all, and he was still awaiting an answer. Daniel got the impression that he would wait forever if necessary.

"I don't know why I'm laughing," Daniel said. "I just do, sometimes. Hasn't that ever happened to you?"

"Yes, of course," said Joentaa.

Of course. The man evidently knew the simplest answer to any question.

"If I'm laughing at anything, it's myself," said Daniel. "Certainly not at you, never fear, although I do find it funny in a way, drinking milk with my evening meal."

"What's funny about it?" asked Joentaa. Sooner or later, thought Daniel, this man will pull it off—sooner or later he'll drive me insane.

"Forget it," he said.

"Tell me about Jaana Ilander," Joentaa repeated.

"What the hell do you want to know about her, man?" Daniel shouted.

Joentaa remained provocatively calm. "Haven't you ever wondered how she died?" he asked.

No, he hadn't. He really hadn't.

"So how *did* she die?"

"She was suffocated, probably in her sleep."

Daniel felt a dull pain behind the eyes. This afternoon's view of the frozen lake had tired him out. He would have to go to bed before long.

"I very often wondered how Sanna would feel during the moment before her death," Joentaa said. "I couldn't rid myself of the thought."

Yes, he would go to bed soon.

He would take a pill and go to sleep.

"I'm afraid I'm a bit tired after the journey. Would you mind if I . . ."

"Of course not," Joentaa said at once, getting to his feet. "I've made up the bed for you." He hurried out with Daniel at his heels. The bedroom was icy, the window open. Joentaa shut it. Daniel surveyed the room. The double bed had twin mattresses. One was freshly made up, the other bare.

"I'll show you where the bathroom is," Joentaa said. While Daniel was following him, he thought of the bare mattress and of what the man had said. He hadn't really caught on until now: the policeman had told him his wife was dead. He hadn't really registered that sentence, that statement; he'd stored it away in his mind, regarding it as just another absurdity in a situation that had struck him as absurd from the first.

The bathroom was very small. Joentaa, who had laid out a towel for Daniel, was saying that he could heat the sauna, perhaps tomorrow.

"About your wife," said Daniel. "I'm sorry."

Joentaa nodded.

Daniel tried to imagine what it meant—what it would mean to him if someone informed him that Marion was dead.

He didn't know.

He wondered how Jaana Ilander had felt during the last moment of her life.

His fatigue disappeared once he was sitting on the bed by himself, and he found himself missing the policeman's probing questions. He had spent the whole day in a kind of daze—it had run its course like a film, a piece of fiction.

But Jaana Ilander was really and truly dead. He wouldn't visit her when the time came because the time would never come, not now.

He stretched out on his back and closed his eyes. The darkness was disagreeable, and he wasn't tired anymore. He got up, turned on the light, and took the cell phone from his jacket pocket. He dialed.

He was relieved when he heard Marion's voice.

"Sorry not to have called before . . ."

"I was asleep already," she said.

"I'm sorry, I—"

"Any news? Are you in a hotel?"

"No . . . No, this policeman who met me, he's putting me up."

"At his home, you mean?"

"Yes. He's . . . very nice. A bit odd, mind you. Drinks milk with his supper, but very nice in other respects. I still don't know any details about the will. I'll make inquiries tomorrow and—"

"What's odd about it?"

"What?"

"What's so odd about drinking milk with supper?"

Daniel didn't answer. "Nothing," he said after a while. "Nothing at all. Sleep well."

"I'm glad you called," she said.

Daniel meant to say something more, but he didn't know what, and Marion had already hung up.

6

Arto Ojaranta called to his sister to drive with care, but she obviously hadn't heard. She steered the jeep out onto the snow-covered roadway in her usual, determined manner. Little Anna looked through the rear window and waved to him. He waved back and waited until they disappeared from view.

Alone again, he thought. At last.

Anna had spent the whole evening tinkling on the piano—appallingly—and his sister had made it clear to him, in her shrill, penetrating voice, that her life was going swimmingly on all fronts. She was so happy. She'd given her latest partner his marching orders a few weeks ago, and everything was fine now—better than it had been for ages. Yes, she'd been in the best of spirits. All that had irked her from time to time was Anna's piano-playing.

"Anna, that's enough!" she called, but Anna had only grinned and gone on playing.

It surprised him that Anna could afford to take such a liberty. He always felt uneasy when his sister was around. He couldn't remember ever having imposed his will on her. Arto Ojaranta, the senior executive, the shrewd businessman whom everyone in the firm respected and probably feared a little too, knuckled under whenever his sister chose to give him another dressing-down.

Today Raija had gone easy on him. She'd gone easy on him in general ever since "the Laura business," as she now called Laura's death, although she visited him considerably more often. All she'd said about the Laura business today was that the police were being intolerably slack and she doubted that the killer would ever be arrested. As she saw it, he must have been some unfortunate, drug-dependent burglar who had lost his nerve.

Arto Ojaranta refrained from trying to rebut this theory because he hated arguing with Raija. Besides, he himself was still unable to fathom what had happened.

He hadn't the least idea.

If he could imagine any sequence of events at all, it was not far removed from his sister's scenario. A burglar. A stranger, someone who must have made a terrible mistake, because no one could have had any good reason for killing Laura.

What disposed of that line of reasoning was his recollection that the burglar obviously had a key, and that he hadn't taken any money or articles of value.

Arto Ojaranta accepted that it was futile to speculate about Laura's death because Laura's death was inexplicable.

Dismissing things from his mind was something he'd always been good at. He had always been quick to grasp when something was unproductive and quick to act accordingly. When negotiations became bogged down, when they took a wrong turning and there was simply no point in pursuing them further, he knew what to do: break them off.

He didn't think of Laura too often these days, though he missed her. She had been important to him—he had recognized that in the days immediately following the funeral, and the recognition had surprised him. He hadn't noticed it while she was alive.

He missed her, yes, and he still had this vaguely empty feeling, but that too was wearing off. He'd spent the weekend with his girlfriend in Stockholm, and something akin to relief had overcome him as he sank his teeth in the firm flesh of her shoulders.

Arto Ojaranta turned and walked back to the house through the flurries of snow. He had this empty sensation again, but he was thinking less of Laura than of Alisa, his Swedish girlfriend. If only Alisa were lying in the bedroom at this moment, naked and expectant. Perhaps he would pay another visit to Stockholm next weekend. He hoped she would have the time and inclination to see him.

He hoped Alisa would never take it into her head to leave him.

As he walked back through the snow to his blue villa, he had the vague feeling of apprehension that had often assailed him since Laura's death. True, he had changed all the locks. No one could get into the house and no one had any interest in harming him. He knew this perfectly well, but as long as Laura's death remained a mystery he would probably continue to feel this faint sense of uneasiness that always set in when peace returned and darkness fell.

Bracing himself against the wind, he cleared the steps that led to the front door in two long strides.

He shut the door behind him.

The house was agreeably warm, but the silence unnerved him. There had been many times in the last few hours when he wished his sister would make up her mind to go home and take tinkling Anna with her. Now he wished she was still browbeating him while Anna hummed to herself and banged the keys.

He went into the living room and settled down in front of the television. The news was on. That was good—there was something reassuring about the news: the announcer's crisp voice, the sense of being on top of things, of understanding the world. Afterward, sports. Highlights from the ice hockey league. TPS Turku had lost away to Hämeenlinna, but that didn't matter in the preliminary round. Preliminary-round matches were utterly unimportant—he'd never understood why anyone could take it into his head to watch them in the stadium. He had occasionally gone to knockout matches with

Laura. Laura had been very athletic. He himself was rather idle in that respect. You've no need to worry about your figure when you're as tall and slim as you are, Laura had lovingly assured him. She'd been really proud of him for looking so good compared to the pot-bellies of their acquaintance.

If only Laura had known how easy he'd found it to lie to her on the phone . . .

Laura had been an exceptional woman, all things considered. He almost laughed when he recalled the young policeman's theory that she might have had a lover, it was so incredibly wide of the mark—so much so that even the policeman, whose only knowledge of Laura stemmed from witness statements, couldn't seriously have believed in it. If he remembered right, he himself had put the idea into the man's head.

Why?

It reassured him that the television was on. It was comforting to hear voices and see pictures. He'd often fallen asleep in front of the television in recent weeks. He found it easier to fall asleep with the lights on, with something going on around him, and he would do the same tonight. But not until he'd made his rounds.

He had become accustomed to making his rounds—he found that reassuring too.

He went from room to room, checking the windows and locking the doors. As he went down the stairs to the cellar he got that uneasy feeling in the pit of his stomach. He experienced it every night, but nowhere near as badly as he had in the days just after Laura's death.

Everything was gradually getting better.

He locked all the doors and took a bottle of good red wine from the wine cellar. While climbing the stairs he toyed with the idea of putting in another call to Alisa. He yearned to hear her voice. It was a clear, vivacious, youthful voice. He recalled that once, right at the beginning, he'd felt an urge to masturbate while speaking with her.

He itched to call her, but he would have to think about it first. She would probably be asleep by now, and he didn't want to annoy her. He decided to think it over in the armchair with a glass of wine. First, though, he would complete his rounds, which always ended with him double-locking the front door.

Ojaranta made for the door, a snow-white rectangle already visible at the far end of the passage. He could faintly hear shouts and gunshots issuing from the television—a crime series, probably.

He continued on his way to the door.

Out of the corner of his eye he glimpsed something that puzzled him. It didn't sink in at first. It was something unimportant, something quite trivial, but it disconcerted him, so he turned to look.

And screamed.

He screamed and felt his legs give way beneath him. The next moment he was lying on the floor. He cowered against the wall and screamed until the picture before his eyes went blurred: the ugly picture that was back in its niche behind the hall cupboard.

7

D aniel was dreaming.

He was driving along a wide asphalt road in brilliant sunshine. The sandy expanses on either side resembled a desert.

He was driving a convertible with the roof down.

The airstream was forcing his head back. Sand was swirling into his face. He pulled up and rubbed his eyes.

When his vision cleared he turned and looked in all directions. He was alone, but far to his rear he sighted a flickering blue speck. It was coming toward him, growing steadily larger, taking shape.

A police car.

He remembered now.

He had killed someone.

He didn't know who it was. He didn't know exactly what he'd done, or how and where he'd committed the murder, or why. He knew only that he was guilty, and that they would pursue him wherever he went and whatever he said in his defense.

The police car drew nearer. He felt scared—panic-stricken at the prospect of the lies he was about to tell and the policeman's reaction to them.

When the patrol car pulled up in front of his convertible the scene darkened as if a blue transparency had been superimposed on it. It was so dark, he couldn't make out the policeman's face.

The policeman got out and came slowly, patiently toward him.

Daniel sensed that the policeman knew everything. There was absolutely no point in lying to him, but he would lie regardless. He had to, he couldn't do otherwise.

Because he didn't know the truth himself.

The policeman was friendly but firm. His every movement conveyed that he knew the facts, and that Daniel stood no chance at all.

He asked Daniel to open the trunk.

Daniel started talking. He didn't hear what he said, but he'd never talked so much or so fast in his life. He behaved as if they were good friends and tried to laugh the whole thing off, but the policeman wouldn't buy it.

He merely stared at the trunk and waited.

Daniel didn't know if the person he'd killed was in there. He didn't know where that person was or where he'd hidden the body.

He opened the trunk.

He couldn't see a thing, it was too dark, but the policeman seemed satisfied. With a nod, he told Daniel he could close the trunk and drive on.

Daniel did so. The scene changed when he was back in the car, and the desert turned into a dense forest. He was driving into the darkness along a narrow track. He knew that the body was some-where here in this forest. Without actually witnessing the scene—himself, digging—he remembered having buried it here.

He drove on, peering left and right in the hope of discovering some clue, some feature he remembered.

He simply had to find the body before the police did.

Ever further into the darkness he drove, but all at once, just when he could see almost nothing, the track behind him was brilliantly illuminated. Spotlights pinpointed his car and a man shouted something he didn't catch. The man sounded very agitated. He was bellowing, but his words—if they were words at all—were wholly unintelligible.

Still uncomprehending, Daniel woke up.

His panic took several seconds to subside. Then he let his head sink back on the pillows and waited for reality to overhaul his dream completely.

He could still hear the voice uttering unintelligible words. The voice was real—it belonged to the Finnish policeman, Joentaa. Daniel sat up and looked at his watch. Just after midnight. He concentrated on Joentaa's voice. He was on the phone. Daniel got up, walked unsteadily to the door, and opened it. Joentaa was just draping his overcoat round his shoulders.

"What is it?" asked Daniel.

Joentaa effortlessly switched to German. "Nothing. I have to go out."

"Why?"

"Something has happened—something that may be of help to us."

"I'd like to come too."

To his surprise, Joentaa didn't object.

"We must hurry," was all he said.

"Just a moment." Daniel went back into the bedroom and got dressed. He donned his jacket, which was hanging on the chair, and his shoes, which were on the floor beside the bed. "Ready," he said.

Joentaa was already standing beside the front door when he emerged. As Daniel came toward him he saw that the policeman was staring past him, either absently or with total concentration, he couldn't decide which.

"What's happened?" Daniel asked when they were sitting in the car. It was bitterly cold and snowing heavily. In a forest like this they would soon be snowed in, Daniel reflected. Having started the car after several attempts, Joentaa drove off along the forest track.

"What's happened?" Daniel asked again.

"A painting the killer stole is back in its place," said Joentaa.

Daniel gave him a baffled look, but Joentaa seemed to have said all that he considered important. He drove slowly and patiently in spite of his obvious, feverish impatience.

Minutes went by in silence.

Daniel was about to try again when Joentaa braked sharply and lost control of the car. It spun several times on the hard-packed snow. Daniel, who felt sure they were going to turn over, heard himself cry out.

After a few interminable seconds they came to rest on the wrong side of the road.

Daniel looked over at Joentaa, who seemed surprisingly calm. After peering through the windshield for a moment or two, he backed the car until it was facing in the opposite direction.

"Sorry," he said, without looking at Daniel.

Daniel saw that Joentaa's hand was trembling as he engaged first gear and moved off again.

"What is this?" Daniel shouted at him. "Are you crazy, or something?"

"I'm sorry," Joentaa said, "we must go a different way."

"What?"

"We must go a different way."

Joentaa was driving faster now, Daniel noticed.

"Why? I thought . . ."

But Joentaa said no more. After a few minutes he pulled up outside a café, jumped out of the car, and pounded on the door. Daniel got out too. The door was opened by a bleary-eyed woman in a dressing gown. Joentaa pushed past her into the café. Daniel gave the woman a nod and followed him. Joentaa was already running upstairs to the first floor.

The woman called something Daniel couldn't understand.

When he reached the landing he almost bumped into Joentaa, who had paused at the head of the stairs.

The woman went on shouting in Finnish.

Joentaa walked slowly to the door, which was open. Someone had snapped the scene-of-crime tapes.

At the door he paused again.

"*Mitä, mitä!*" the woman shouted, or something of the kind. She was now standing behind Daniel, holding on to the banister.

Joentaa didn't reply.

Daniel was about to go to him, but he stopped short when the policeman turned his head.

Joentaa was weeping.

8

It was only a tableau.

Joentaa realized that.

The tableau he saw wasn't genuine, but it overwhelmed him. Not that he knew why, but he felt he had to make sense of it.

The tableau was authentic and, at the same time, entirely false.

Joentaa had a searing pain behind the eyes. He could see a man and a woman, and the woman was Sanna. She was sitting in the middle of the room. He couldn't see her face, only the outlines of her body. The man, whom he knew to be a murderer, was standing over her.

He knew the woman was Sanna without being able to see her features.

He knew that Sanna didn't belong here—that he should have seen another woman. And, as this realization sank in, the tableau disintegrated and the pain behind his eyes subsided.

The room was deserted. That apart, everything was right. The candles were burning, the wine bottle was standing exactly where it had stood before with the two glasses beside it, one of them half empty. But the room was deserted. It was bereft of the two people who had brought it to life.

Jaana Ilander and the man who had killed her.

Joentaa pictured the man who had created this tableau. He had taken a lot of trouble, spent a great deal of time reconstructing it all. Everything had to be exactly as it had been that night, as authentic as possible. The candles were the same white candles. Joentaa felt sure they were identical, just like the glasses and the wine.

They would have to check, but he felt sure of it.

Everything looked the same, but everything was different.

The original bottle, glasses, and candles had been bagged and re-moved by forensics. The photographs were missing, naturally. Forensics had also removed the photographs lying on the floor.

The missing photos must have presented the man with a problem, Joentaa reflected. He had been compelled to compromise, and he didn't like compromises.

Joentaa walked into the room.

He tried to grasp something, to gain some impression of the man he was after. The man who had been here only a short while ago.

Maybe only minutes before their arrival.

They might have been in time if only he'd caught on quicker.

Moving closer, he saw that there was a photograph on the floor after all.

Jaana Ilander plus parachute.

The man must have found it hard to part with that photo. And with the hazy landscape that was back in its place in the blue villa. Why had he parted with those things which meant so much to him? Why had he run such a risk in order to return them?

Daniel's perturbed, bewildered voice broke in on his thoughts.

"What is this place?" he asked.

Joentaa turned. "It's Jaana Ilander's apartment—*your* apartment. This is how it looked that night . . . the night she was murdered. The killer was here. As far as possible, he's arranged everything the way it was on the night of the murder."

Daniel didn't speak for a moment, at a loss for words. "But what does it mean?" he shouted. "What's the point of this absurdity?"

Joentaa said nothing. He said nothing because he didn't know the answer. But the answer was important, and he felt it was within his reach. He saw Daniel tremble, saw him gradually recover his composure.

"I'm sorry," Daniel said. "I'd like to leave . . . I'll wait for you in the car."

Joentaa gave him the keys.

"Please wait downstairs too," he told the owner of the café, who was standing in the doorway.

"Did you hear what I said?" he demanded.

The woman gave a start. "Of course," she said. "I'll be down in the café if you need me."

"Thank you." Joentaa took out his cell phone and dialed Ketola's number.

"Yes, what is it?" Ketola barked after a moment or two.

"Kimmo here . . ."

"Where are you? We're waiting."

"I'm at Jaana Ilander's place . . . in her apartment."

"What is it now? Haven't you heard what happened here at the Ojaranta place?"

"Yes, Heinonen informed me. He's been here too."

"Who has?"

"The killer. He's returned the missing photograph. Jaana Ilander plus parachute."

Ketola said nothing.

"He's arranged a tableau reminiscent of the night of the murder. It's like he was trying to reconstruct the whole thing."

Ketola still said nothing.

Joentaa waited.

"I'll be right over," said Ketola. The line went dead.

Joentaa left his cell phone on. He hesitated briefly, then walked along the passage to the bedroom. As he approached the door, which was ajar, he had a momentary feeling that Jaana Ilander would be lying on the bed. She would look dead, but really she would be asleep.

This mental image vanished when he pushed the door open. The room was brightly lit. There was no one on the bed, only the striped mattress. Niemi had removed the sheets, pillows, and blankets in the hope of finding some clue to the identity of a killer who left no clues.

Joentaa walked slowly back to the living room. He strove to understand what had prompted the man to create this scenario and return the photograph. Once again, he felt that the answer was almost within his grasp. It was very near, but he couldn't reduce it to a simple form of words.

Why had he wept?

After a few minutes he heard a hubbub downstairs. Ketola's loud, penetrating voice was unmistakable. He must have driven fast in spite of the heavy snowfall. Footsteps could be heard ascending the stairs and Ketola appeared in the doorway, breathing heavily.

"Hello, Kimmo," he said.

Joentaa gave him a nod. "He must have had a key to this place as well," he said. Ketola surveyed the murderer's *mise en scène*. He was looking quite calm and collected again. Behind Ketola stood Niemi, who was a head shorter and had difficulty in seeing past him into the room. He was wearing his technician's outfit of latex gloves and white overalls.

Ketola stood there, motionless save for an almost imperceptible shake of the head. "This is . . ." He broke off and stared at Joentaa, who forced himself to hold his gaze. "This is amazing. Really amazing."

Niemi pushed past Ketola. Niemi, who always seemed in the best of spirits, who winked and seemed amused, although the impression was merely superficial.

"More clues," he said.

"What do you mean?" asked Joentaa.

"The killer has clearly stopped caring whether or not he leaves traces behind. We found some decent prints here in the apartment, on one of the glasses and some of the photographs."

"Surely not?" Joentaa was surprised. It didn't fit his picture of the man.

"Who cares?" Ketola said quietly. Joentaa couldn't think what he was getting at. "Who cares?" he repeated more loudly, laughing. "Who cares? Who cares?" He was shouting the words now. "I don't give a damn! I want to go home, for God's sake. I want to give this shit a rest and take a breather!" His face looked strangely contorted in the candlelight.

Joentaa felt his body tense up. He wanted to say something to alleviate the situation, but he knew he wouldn't. Niemi, who was standing beside Ketola, didn't appear to have heard his outburst. He looked relaxed, impassive.

Joentaa found both men incomprehensible.

He remembered them at the funeral. They had stood silently side by side, Ketola with a black umbrella, Niemi with a colored one. Yes, he could recall those details now. He'd only registered them subconsciously during the ceremony.

He wondered whether Ketola's choice of a black umbrella and Niemi's choice of a colored one had been deliberate. He doubted he would ever raise the subject with either of them.

Ketola was calmer now, outwardly at least. He had blown out the candles and was bending over the photograph. "All right, carry on," he told Niemi and his two colleagues, who were standing hesitantly in the passage. His voice sounded firm and self-controlled, as if he were unaware that he'd been shouting wildly a few moments before.

Niemi was already kneeling on the floor, examining the photograph more closely.

"What gave you the idea to come here?" Ketola asked.

Joentaa sensed his searching gaze and instinctively evaded it. "I don't know. I simply thought he might return some other things as well. What about the youth hostel? Maybe he's taken something back there too."

"I've sent Heinonen to check. I've also set up roadblocks on all the access roads to Naantali in case he's traveling by car. I'd like you to go and see Arto Ojaranta. Have a word with the man—I think you get on better with him than I do. I had to drag every last word out of him, and I still didn't understand what he was trying to tell me."

"I'll go at once," said Joentaa. He was about to leave the room when Ketola stared at him fixedly, as if he had a specific question on the tip of his tongue. Joentaa waited.

"What do you think this means?" Ketola asked at length. "You guessed he was bringing back the things he'd removed, so now tell me why."

Joentaa slowly shook his head. "I don't know."

"You've already surprised us once with your psychic abilities. Surely you must have some idea?"

Joentaa merely shook his head again. He needed to think it over. As he turned away he caught sight of Daniel, who had appeared in the doorway.

"Who are you? What do you want?" Ketola barked at him.

"This is Herr Krohn . . ." Joentaa began.

"What's he doing here?"

"I . . . I brought him with me."

"What the devil for? Tell him to wait downstairs."

Joentaa nodded. He was about to translate what Ketola had said, but Daniel turned and set off along the passage.

"What's he up to?" Ketola demanded.

Joentaa hurried after Daniel and caught him by the shoulder, but Daniel shook him off. He opened all the doors—to the kitchen, the bathroom, the bedroom.

On the threshold of the bedroom he paused.

"I only wanted to know if it's true," he said.

"What?"

"What you said: that there's a picture of me on the bedside table."

Joentaa followed the direction of his gaze. The framed photograph was standing on the bedside table. It showed Daniel grinning at the camera. He seemed to be reaching for it with one hand, as if trying to prevent the photographer, presumably Jaana Ilander, from releasing the shutter.

"Get him out of here, damn it!" Ketola shouted.

Before Joentaa could translate this, Daniel walked out of the apartment with long, purposeful strides.

"Why did you bring him along?" asked Ketola.

"He wanted to come."

"What do you mean, he wanted to come? How did he know about this business in the first place?"

"He's staying with me."

"What?"

"I offered to put him up."

Ketola was about to make some rejoinder, but Joentaa got in first.

"I think I know what's happened," he said.

Ketola stared at him with his eyebrows raised.

"I know why the murderer is returning these things."

He really did know.

And he hadn't consciously thought about it.

It had dawned on him while he was standing behind Daniel Krohn and looking at the photograph: a younger Daniel grinning and reaching for Jaana's camera. A scene from the past: irretrievably past, yet still present in the photograph.

Joentaa knew why he'd wept. It was because he wanted the same thing as the man who had murdered Jaana Ilander.

He wanted to exchange the present for the past.

"I think he regrets what he's done," Joentaa said.

Ketola eyed him intently.

"I think he wants to turn the clock back."

"That's crap," said Ketola, but Joentaa heard him only faintly.

"He wants a second chance," he said, more to himself than to Ketola. "He has visions of returning to a world in which all he's done has never happened."

9

J oentaa asked Daniel Krohn to wait in the car. Daniel raised no
objection, in fact he didn't utter a word.

Joentaa got out and walked up to the blue villa. The front door
was open. Even before he got there he sighted Niemi's assistants in
their white overalls and heard an unfamiliar voice. A brusque, imperi-
ous voice—a woman's voice. She was ordering the forensics team
around, but they were going about their business undeterred. Arto
Ojaranta was standing behind the woman with his shoulders hunched.
Although he topped her by two heads, he was standing there hunched
up and withdrawn.

Someone was banging on the piano in the living room.

"Who are you?" the woman demanded. Her tone implied that she
would kick him out if he gave the wrong answer.

Ojaranta got there before him.

"This gentleman is also with the police," he said hastily. "I'm sorry,
I can't quite recall . . ."

"Joentaa. Kimmo Joentaa." Joentaa shook the woman's hand.

"My sister Raija," Ojaranta mumbled. "You've already met little
Anna, her daughter. Anna's here too, that's her playing the . . . For
God's sake tell her to stop!" The last sentence was directed at his
sister.

"I could hardly leave her at home on her own, not at this hour,"
the woman retorted curtly. "You were the one who asked me to come,
after all." She raised her voice. "Anna, that's enough!"

Anna went on playing.

Joentaa's hand was still aching from the woman's viselike grip. He
recalled that Grönholm had interviewed her soon after the murder.
"A battle-ax," was his casual comment on Ojaranta's sister. Although
Joentaa had been surprised by this drastic description, he hadn't questioned him further.

He also recalled having read the transcript of the interview. The woman's choice of words had been very cold and unemotional, he remembered. They conveyed the impression that she was less distressed by her sister-in-law's death than surprised and puzzled.

"Look," she said, "it's time my brother had some peace and quiet. Can't you go on with this tomorrow?"

"I'm afraid not," Joentaa told her. He felt like adding that little Anna was making far more noise than the forensics team. Arto Ojaranta would certainly get no peace and quiet while Anna was tinkling on the piano.

Joentaa thought he detected that Ojaranta was trembling, forcing himself to remain calm.

"I'd like a quick word with you," he said. "Would you mind?"

Ojaranta gave a resigned shrug. "Of course not." He led the way into the living room, flopped down on the sofa, and limply waved Joentaa into a chair. Joentaa hesitated. Anna's frightful piano-playing was far more audible now.

Anna grinned at him when he looked over at her.

"Perhaps somewhere else would be more . . ." Joentaa began, but Anna's mother cut him short.

"Anna, kindly stop playing!" she called.

Anna broke off and smiled at her wide-eyed. Joentaa wondered whether the girl had noticed that something unusual was going on. She seemed quite unaware of the forensics team and the general commotion.

"Mr. Ojaranta," Joentaa began.

Anna started playing again.

"Mr. Ojaranta, we have to know exactly what happened here today. It's most important to narrow down the time at which . . ."

Anna's tinkling distracted him. She was playing the tune she'd played the last time he came—the familiar tune whose title escaped him.

"Anna!" snapped Raija, who was standing behind her brother, massaging his shoulders.

". . . to narrow down the time at which the picture was . . ."

"I know exactly when," said Ojaranta.

"No, I meant—"

"I know what you meant. You want to know when the picture was returned, and I know when. My sister was here earlier tonight. The picture hadn't been returned when she left just before ten."

"Are you sure?"

"I'm sure because—"

"Because we looked at the empty niche," Ojaranta's sister broke in. "When Arto took my coat out of the cupboard he showed me the niche and said it was where the missing picture used to hang. He asked if I could remember it. I'd never paid it much attention, to be honest."

"Nor had I," Ojaranta muttered to himself. "That's why it was hanging there, because I didn't want to see it."

"Do you know that tune?" Joentaa asked on impulse.

"I'm sorry?"

"The tune Anna's playing."

Ojaranta's sister uttered a scornful laugh. "Anna doesn't play tunes—she can't play, period!"

Joentaa forced himself to dismiss the idea. He felt badly in need of sleep. Why wasn't Anna asleep in bed? "To go back to the picture. You say . . ."

He broke off again because the sudden silence puzzled him. Anna had stopped playing and was glaring at her mother.

"If what you say is true . . ."

An earsplitting din. Anna was pounding the keys in proof of her ability to play perfectly well. Her mother reached her in seconds. She slapped her face twice, yanked her off the piano stool, and hustled her out of the room. Anna burst into tears. Ojaranta continued to loll on the sofa as if he hadn't registered the din or his sister's intervention. "It's quite simple," he said irritably, "the picture wasn't there just before ten, but it was there at eleven."

"You discovered it at eleven?"

Ojaranta nodded.

"But you called us considerably later than that. Around midnight."

"It took me a while to pull myself together, can't you understand that?"

Joentaa understood. Naturally, but he couldn't help reflecting that they might have caught the killer in Jaana Ilander's apartment if the man had got over his shock a bit quicker.

"How are you feeling now?" he asked.

"Peachy, as you can see," Ojaranta retorted.

"You changed all the locks?"

"Of course."

"And there was no sign of a forced—"

"None."

"So how did the murderer—"

"There's nothing he can't do."

"But . . ."

"No, you really must get this straight: he's capable of anything, it's important to grasp that. If he'd wanted to, he could have killed me too. No problem. Maybe he's simply postponed it. Maybe I'll be dead this time tomorrow . . ."

"You've had a shock, I can understand that, but I honestly believe you've nothing more to fear."

"I don't give a damn what you honestly believe."

"Of course, we could always put you up at a hotel . . ."

"No thanks." Ojaranta rose abruptly, as if he'd had enough of talking. He stood there irresolutely for a few seconds, then subsided onto the sofa again.

"Would you do me a favor?"

"Certainly, if I can."

"See to it that my sister leaves."

"We'll station two men outside the house and—"

"Did you hear what I said?"

"Yes, I'll speak to her in a minute."

"No, now!"

"Mr. Ojaranta—"

"Damn it, man!" Ojaranta got up again, purposefully this time, and strode to the door. His sister could clearly be heard outside in the hall, fiercely haranguing her tearful daughter. Halfway there Ojaranta seemed to recover his wits. He came to a halt and his broad shoulders sagged until he once more resembled the hunched figure that had greeted Joentaa on his arrival. He turned back and subsided onto the sofa again.

"I've nothing more to say. I'm going to have a long sleep now," he said, and ostentatiously shut his eyes.

10

He would go and see Tommy tomorrow.

He would give him a nice surprise, bring him some presents and apologize for having been so uncommunicative lately. Tommy would brush his apologies aside with a laugh, challenge him to a sparring match by cuffing him on the shoulder, and all that had happened would be over and done with. It would be in the past— no, not even that.

Tommy's laugh would finally confirm that he had only been dreaming.

Nothing had happened.

He would be an entirely new person.

He was starting afresh.

Tommy would be amazed when he told him about this girl he'd met, this Jaana. Tommy would be bowled over. He would tell Tommy all he knew about Jaana, and he knew a great deal. At some stage he would invite them both to his place, Jaana and Tommy. He must definitely introduce them—they would get on like a house on fire.

He couldn't do so for a while, but do it he would. The very thought of their meeting was wonderful, overwhelmingly so.

With Jaana and Tommy at his side, nothing more could happen to him.

He'd been so calm the whole time, so self-possessed. He'd known he was doing something good, and that had lent him confidence, for who would try to prevent him from doing something good? He'd been careful, of course. He'd realized that no one must see him until it was done. Until he'd done the right thing, no one would be able to see him as a good person.

The key didn't fit. For a moment he'd thought this would spoil everything. It was definitely the right house, the blue house, but the key didn't fit. Although this had made him very nervous for a while, he'd consoled himself with the thought that he was trying to do something good.

He'd slipped quickly into the house while the man, the woman, and the little girl were standing beside the jeep in the driving snow, saying goodbye. It proved to be quite simple in the end, but anyone doing a good deed deserved not to encounter any obstacles.

He'd replaced the picture while the man was watching television in the living room. He would have liked to stand looking at it for a while, but he'd left right away because he had to.

Then he drove down to the beach. It was a struggle, but he convinced himself that all would go well.

He forced himself to believe that Jaana was there.

The key fitted. The place was hushed and in darkness, which reassured him and proved he was doing the right thing.

He took his time, and he was well prepared. He had brought everything with him. He wept as he sat on the floor in the candlelight and looked at the photo of Jaana after her parachute jump.

But Jaana was there.

He definitely sensed her presence.

He sensed that she approved of what he was doing, that she commended him for it. Jaana had forgiven him.

Last of all he drove to the youth hostel. He sat in the car and spent some time looking at the building, which he saw in a new light because he was a new person. He could scarcely remember having been inside. He waited until the memory of it faded completely.

Then he went inside.

The door was unlocked and the faces he passed slid by him. Someone else was asleep in the bed in the big dormitory. The boy the dice cup belonged to wasn't there anymore. He was far away, of course.

He left the building. Once outside, he crushed the dice cup and ripped it apart until nothing remained in his hand but strips of leather and he felt satisfied that it had never existed.

He waited until he was quite calm again.

Then he threw the strips of leather into the river and drove home.

A patrol car had pulled up outside the youth hostel and disgorged two policemen. Four more patrol cars passed him on the road to Turku, traveling in the direction of Naantali. They had nothing to do with him. They sped off into the distance, and he drove through Turku to Maaria without being stopped.

The streets were thronged with people in spite of the cold and the snow. It was the weekend, and they were drinking and celebrating. He thought of getting out and joining in, but he drove on.

He couldn't celebrate with those people.

What he had to celebrate was something quite different, something more momentous.

He drove home.

Now he was looking down from his balcony at the playground. It was entirely covered with snow, and snow was still falling.

He tried to imagine what it would be like if snow went on falling forever, until everything lay buried beneath it. The thought didn't alarm him. He picked some up and felt it cold against his skin, studied the little crystals which he could crush quite easily, just as he too would be crushed when the time came.

He was unperturbed by the prospect.

He thought of Jaana.

Jaana had existed, and from now on she would exist for him whenever he needed her.

11

D aniel Krohn wasn't asleep.

He was sitting on the edge of the bed, trying to collect his thoughts.

He thought back on the trek that had, as he saw it, set the seal on this surreal night. They had been obliged to walk the last mile to the Finnish policeman's house because the forest track was completely snowed over. Daniel had trudged along behind the policeman in his street shoes, frozen to the marrow and wondering if they would ever get there.

He thought of the policeman, Kimmo Joentaa, who was now stretched out on the sofa in the living room. He doubted he was asleep. Ever solicitous, Joentaa had made him some tea as soon as they arrived, brought him a warm woolen blanket, and wished him a cordial goodnight. His manner had conveyed that everything was fine, but he looked as though he might collapse from exhaustion at any moment.

He thought of Joentaa's wife, who was dead. He had forgotten to ask what she died of. She must have been quite young. Jaana had been young too, younger than Marion.

He thought of Marion, who was probably fast asleep and would certainly not take anything in if he called her now—if he recounted all his experiences on this crazy night.

He thought of the candlelit apartment where Jaana had lived. He made a note to ask Joentaa how long she had lived there. He must find out what she had been doing and how she had fared since she stopped writing to him.

He thought of the photo in the bedroom, in Jaana's bedroom, on Jaana's bedside table. A snapshot of himself. Daniel had recalled the occasion as soon as he saw it. He'd tried to knock the camera out of Jaana's hand, but she, of course, had snapped him just in time. Jaana's photography had got on his nerves, he remembered. He hadn't liked being photographed all the time.

Then something else had occurred to him, something quite incredible. He had genuinely forgotten all about it until he entered Jaana's apartment and saw his photo on her bedside table.

He'd even cheated on Jaana.

He'd cheated on Jaana, his holiday acquaintance of only a few days' standing, with another holiday acquaintance, a red-headed German girl. Jaana had been sleeping it off in their tent while he, equally tipsy, had been canoodling with that redhead.

All he could remember of the redhead was her hair, and that he'd successfully avoided her eyes the next morning.

He thought of Jaana's nephew Teemu. She had shown him a picture of the little boy. Teemu would now be around ten years old.

He thought of the candles and the man who had lit those candles, the man who had killed Jaana. He must ask Joentaa what he knew about him. Surely Joentaa would know what sort of man he was and why he had murdered her?

He thought again about the policeman, Kimmo Joentaa, and wondered why he had wept. What had he seen in the apartment other than the burning candles?

He thought of Oliver, who must be absolutely furious with him. If he didn't e-mail at least some of the copy for that election pamphlet tomorrow, Oliver would either make a very poor showing at the presentation or be compelled to write the copy himself, which wasn't exactly his forte.

He heaved himself off the bed and slid his suitcase from under it. At least he'd been composed enough before leaving to bring his laptop along. He resumed his seat on the bed and turned the thing on, then stared at the blank white screen for minutes on end without writing a single word.

He must ask Joentaa about that nephew, Teemu.

He stared at the blank screen and wondered if he was in the process of losing his job. Oliver could be very impulsive, and they'd often clashed in recent weeks.

Ten to one Oliver wouldn't understand a word if he told him about the candlelit apartment.

He looked out of the window. The sky seemed to be growing paler by degrees—almost imperceptibly, but he got that impression. It was nearly seven and he hadn't slept a wink. He couldn't do any work now. If the truth be told, his job had been getting him down for quite a while. Earlier on, in the beginning, he had found it fun, especially the election literature. He'd always lapped up the politicians' compliments, and the less he liked the candidates his agency hyped, the prouder he'd felt when his slogans bore fruit.

He wondered what Jaana had done for a living. Hadn't she mentioned, in one of her letters, that she wanted to become an actress? He must ask Joentaa.

He was feeling dog-tired, needless to say, but he wouldn't be able to sleep. Some thought or other would keep cropping up and nudging him awake.

He contemplated simply catching the morning flight back to Germany. After all, it wasn't certain that the will was valid, and probate would take time in any case.

The apartment . . . Well, he'd seen it now.

For a moment he pictured himself living there.

The thought of that politician, Herr Glanz, surfaced once more. He would call Oliver this morning and tell him everything was okay. He would e-mail him the copy by midday at the latest—he should be able to manage that.

Something had happened when he saw the photograph on the bedside table—what, he didn't exactly know. Perhaps he would tell Marion about it after all. Marion was sometimes far smarter than he imagined.

He tore his eyes away from the blank screen and stood up. He was feeling thirsty. He opened the bedroom door cautiously, so as not to wake Joentaa. He looked over at the sofa as he made for the kitchen. Joentaa wasn't there.

Joentaa was sitting at the kitchen table, drinking a glass of milk. He gave Daniel a weary smile.

"Can't you sleep either?" he asked.

Daniel shook his head. He fetched a glass, poured himself some milk and sat down across the table from Joentaa. Neither of them spoke.

He suddenly felt better.

He gazed at the snowscape outside the kitchen window and reflected that this was merely an interlude in his life. When it was over he would simply take up where he had left off. He had no need to be scared of Oliver, no need to understand all that went on here. No need to understand this policeman, nor Jaana Ilander, nor the man who had killed her. Their importance was confined to this interlude; afterward, it would seem as if they had never existed.

That was a liberating thought.

His fatigue reasserted itself. He felt he should go to bed, but he was so exhausted—too exhausted to make a move. "Jaana . . . had a nephew . . . she told me about him . . . the boy's name was Teemu," he heard himself saying. "Know anything about him?"

Joentaa shook his head.

Daniel nodded. With a vague sense of relief, he subsided into sleep.

12

The heavy snowfall had given way to brilliant sunlight. The sky was a pellucid blue.

Joentaa lingered in the doorway for several seconds, filling his lungs with the mordantly cold air. Then he went outside and closed the door with care so as not to wake his guest. Daniel had been sitting slumped on his chair in the kitchen, twitching occasionally but fast asleep.

Joentaa was feeling tired too. He had been tired for weeks—for months, really, ever since the day he'd sat beside Sanna in Rintanen's consulting room and, in his unvaryingly quiet voice, the doctor had informed them of her condition.

Rintanen . . . He must call him. He must thank him for all he'd done for Sanna and himself.

He waded through the drifts to his car, which was standing at the far end of the snowed-in forest track. His shoes were sodden after a few minutes, and the cold seemed almost unendurable despite the picturesque weather.

The car started after several attempts. Cautiously, he backed it up and turned out onto the main road.

While driving he tried to form a clear picture of last night.

What had happened, exactly?

He still believed what he had told Ketola: that the murderer wanted to be a murderer no longer.

Perhaps he had never wanted it.

If there was no connection between Laura Ojaranta, Johann Berg, and Jaana Ilander—or not, at least, until the murderer had created one—he must have acted beyond the bounds of normality, beyond the bounds of any normal motivation. Perhaps only the man himself was capable of grasping what impelled him.

He thought of the woman who had shot Sami Järvi. He thought of the hours-long interviews he had conducted without getting any closer to what went on in her head.

This man who had skillfully remained hidden for so long—why was he now leaving traces behind? Perhaps because he couldn't remember having been a murderer.

Perhaps he had never truly grasped that.

Perhaps the man didn't understand what had motivated him.

Did the woman who shot the politician understand her own motives?

The murderer had known Jaana Ilander and left traces on her life. He had remained in the background, but her friends and acquaintances had been aware of him. Nothing of the kind applied to Johann Berg and Laura Ojaranta, yet he must have known them too. He must have had some connection with them, some reason for killing them. But if the man himself didn't understand that reason . . .

Joentaa banished the thought because he sensed he was going round in circles. He turned on the radio and tried to concentrate on the road and the meaningless music. Then another idea occurred to him—one that startled him, it was so obvious. If his theory was correct and the killer was genuinely remorseful, if he wanted to turn the clock back, he wouldn't kill again. They need fear him no more and anticipate no more victims. But neither would they turn up any more clues to his identity.

They might never find him.

Perhaps he was already dead. Having tried to turn back the clock, he might have killed himself during the night. All at once, Joentaa found this highly probable.

His ideas were promptly dispelled as soon as he walked into the office and met Ketola's piercing gaze—in fact, he found them singularly inappropriate. What was the point of speculating about the man and pursuing conjectures that were probably quite mistaken? They must find him; that was all.

He thought he read precisely that sentiment in Ketola's eyes.

Ketola was sitting facing a sturdy, gray-haired man and a thin woman, neither of whom looked familiar.

"Kimmo Joentaa, one of my colleagues," Ketola said. "Kimmo, this is Mariella and Antti Ilander, Jaana Ilander's parents."

Joentaa shook hands with them and sat down at his desk, avoiding their gaze. He pretended to be busy while Ketola went on talking to them. He saw in his peripheral vision that the woman's hands were shaking. She was clasping them tightly to her, trying to sit up straight and speak in a quiet, self-possessed voice, but her hands were shaking.

Ketola expressed his condolences, asked a few brief questions, and received answers that got him nowhere—information about Jaana Ilander, what sort of person she had been, what course her life had taken, whom she had known.

Joentaa listened with reluctance. Suddenly angry, he realized that he wanted nothing, absolutely nothing, to do with Jaana Ilander's parents. He'd had his fill of grief-stricken people and had no wish to compare his own sorrow with that of others, for that was precisely what he'd done when momentarily searching the gray-haired man's face for signs of emotion. A hard face with scant room for grief, he'd thought, but what entitled him to think such a thing?

He left the room on the pretext of fetching himself a coffee. Ketola could think what he liked. Perhaps he hadn't noticed over the years that Joentaa never drank coffee.

He really did head in the direction of the canteen, but he bypassed the coffee machine and sat down at a side table in the big empty room that would be thronged at lunchtime with colleagues taking a short break from the everlasting work of detection. He didn't know why, there was no plausible reason, but he suddenly found the whole setup utterly absurd. His efforts to find the killer of Laura Ojaranta, Johann Berg, and Jaana Ilander seemed mistaken and far-fetched.

What did he expect of the man?

What did he expect of Sanna?

Why did he keep thinking of Sanna, who was dead? Why, when she was dead, did he have a guilty conscience for having gone to see a woman in Stockholm? Surely he needn't feel guilty now that she was dead!

Why was he forcing himself to keep Sanna alive?

Why did he think of Sanna and not of Merja and Jussi Sihvonen, whom he hadn't called for ages? Why didn't he think of his mother, who called him from time to time, and whom he summarily brushed off? Why didn't he think of Markku Vatanen, who had offered to visit and was anxious to help him? Why was he focusing his life on a dead woman and on a murderer who might well be totally insane or simply a callous brute?

He wouldn't succeed, he would never succeed, in detaching himself from Sanna. That had been his dearest wish when all was still well. He had wanted to be with her forever, really forever, in death as in life. He had never pursued this idea all the way, sensing that even an attempt to do so might have effaced it altogether.

But that was precisely what he had wanted . . .

Never to lose her.

He knew that he never would. She would be with him for as long as he lived, and the realization tormented him.

At the other end of the canteen a corpulent woman was wiping tabletops. Her apron and the cloth she was using as a swab were pale blue. He wondered if she enjoyed her work—if she liked getting up in the morning to come here.

Ketola appeared. Joentaa caught sight of him through the glass partition, marching briskly along. He was looking irritable and out of sorts, but then Ketola always looked irritable and out of sorts. To his own surprise, Joentaa felt relieved to see him.

Ketola represented the antithesis of futile speculation, whatever that antithesis really consisted of.

"Didn't you hear what I said?" Ketola demanded.

Joentaa didn't understand.

"I called after you as you were going out. I said we were going to see Ojaranta right away, didn't you hear me?"

"Sorry, no."

Ketola accepted this with ill grace. "Niemi found the key as well last night," he said. "The old one that doesn't fit any longer. The killer brought that back too."

"You mean it was hanging on the board as if it had never been removed?" Joentaa said on impulse.

Ketola nodded and gave him a piercing stare. For a moment Joentaa thought he detected a hint of approval in his expression.

During the drive Ketola preserved a lengthy silence and Joentaa relapsed into his own thoughts, which had just reverted to the woman in the pale blue apron when he heard Ketola's voice.

"How are you feeling?"

Joentaa took a moment to absorb the question. He sensed that Ketola was studying his face.

"All right, I guess."

"I hope you're getting over your wife's death," said Ketola. "It must be very hard, given your very special relationship . . ."

What was the man talking about? He scarcely knew him.

He had scarcely known Sanna.

"The Ilander girl's parents seemed calm and composed," Ketola said.

Joentaa shrugged. "The wife was trembling."

"Yes, but they were quite composed nonetheless. They'll resign themselves to the situation sooner or later. So will I, where this business with my son is concerned. One simply accepts the reality of these things, but in your case I'm not so sure . . . I'm not sure you're ready to accept the reality of your wife's death."

Joentaa didn't speak. All that Ketola had said was true, he realized. He concentrated on the road. The blue villa was already visible in the distance when Ketola said: "Incidentally, I know you don't drink coffee."

13

Joentaa's head was buzzing. He was beginning to wonder if he understood anything or anyone anymore. What had come over Ketola? Ketola, who drank hard liquor at the office, who blew a fuse in front of the press, who had scarcely noticed him for years, was talking about him and Sanna as if they were old friends. In a few short sentences, Ketola had got to the heart of what had mystified him since Sanna's death.

Joentaa pulled up beside the jeep that was parked at the foot of the steps leading to the front door. Its silver bodywork stood out sharply against the dark blue of the house.

"That silly cow is here again," said Ketola.

And Anna, thought Joentaa. He could already hear her muffled playing.

Ojaranta's sister answered the door. "You again," she said, and turned away without inviting them in.

Out of the corner of his eye, Joentaa saw Ketola's face darken like a gathering storm. He followed him into the living room, where the woman had already resumed her post and was massaging her brother's shoulders from behind. Ojaranta, sitting huddled up on the sofa, greeted them limply.

Anna, who continued to hammer away at the keys, smiled at Joentaa when their eyes met. He wondered how she could be such a cheerful child with the mother she had. But maybe Raija was a wonderful mother. He knew nothing about her, after all.

"Well," she said, "your people haven't achieved much to date."

"I wouldn't say that," Ketola retorted, sitting down opposite Ojaranta. Joentaa sensed what a supreme effort he was making to ignore the woman. He sat bolt upright and fixed Ojaranta with a piercing stare. "We need an exact reconstruction of last night's events," he said. "I'm sure you appreciate how immensely important that is?"

Ojaranta nodded, but he didn't seem to be listening and evaded Ketola's eye.

"The thing is, the murderer was here in this house. He brought back the picture and the key—he even had time to replace the picture on the wall. That means you may possibly have seen or heard something you still haven't registered. An unfamiliar car, for instance, or noises whose significance may now, with hindsight . . ."

"I'm sorry," Ojaranta mumbled.

Ketola looked up. "What about you?"

Ojaranta's sister shook her head.

"I see."

Anna was playing her tune again, the nagging tune she always played. Joentaa knew it, but the name still escaped him. How many more times would she have to blunder through it before he finally remembered the goddamned title?

"It said in the paper the murderer probably has three people on his conscience," Raija said. "How could that happen?"

Joentaa stared out of the window. The sunlight was dazzling.

Ketola drew a deep breath. "I don't quite understand your question."

"I mean, how can some madman commit three murders without being caught and punished?"

"How indeed?" Ketola forced a smile. Joentaa could tell that he was on the point of exploding, but was managing to control himself. "It is perplexing, I quite agree."

"So we agree," said the woman. "How nice."

Still controlling himself with an effort, Ketola turned to Ojaranta. "What we're wondering, of course, is how the man got into the house."

"You're sure it's a man?" Raija demanded. Her tone conveyed surprise at this successful feat of detection.

"No, quite right, many thanks. I'll rephrase that: How did the person we're after gain access to the premises?"

"I don't care how," Ojaranta said sullenly.

"Ah," said Ketola.

Why didn't someone do something about Anna? How could Ketola endure her incessant playing? He seemed entirely unaware of it, whereas Joentaa was gradually becoming deaf to all else. He had to discover the name of the piece he'd liked as a child, the one of which Anna seemed equally fond. It was probably the only thing she could play.

"You don't care? Of course, I quite understand," Ketola said sarcastically, but he kept a grip on himself.

It was Ojaranta who lost his temper. "You're getting on my nerves, can't you see?" he shouted. "It's time you left me in peace!"

"I know how you must feel," said Ketola.

Why was he being so understanding all of a sudden?

Little Anna was smiling, childlike.

Sanna had wanted three children, which had worried Joentaa a little.

Had he ever been a child himself?

No, he was getting mixed up.

He heard Ketola's voice, which sounded monotonous. Ketola was surprisingly equable today.

He shut his eyes and grasped something, but not in its entirety, only superficially. He saw Ojaranta lounging lethargically on the sofa, as if he would never get up again.

That tune Anna was playing . . .

Joentaa uttered a cry.

He had never shouted so loudly in his life.

He sensed that the cry embodied all his grief.

He saw three startled, unfamiliar faces. Ketola was staring at him, but Ketola was in a completely different world.

The tune had no title, and he had not been a child.

He felt himself get up and go over to Anna. He saw that she was frightened—never before had he seen so much fear in another person's eyes. He himself was the cause of her fear and he regretted it, but he continued to advance on her, heard his cry, and thought of Sanna, knowing now that she would never be close to him again. He also knew that Jaana Ilander would still be alive if only he had grasped what really mattered.

He gripped Anna by the arm and shouted at her. He felt sorry because she couldn't help it, but he shouted at her, shouted the question in her face. Anna burst into tears. He knew she wouldn't answer as long as he went on shouting. He must calm down and ask the question quietly. He asked it again and again, and while doing so he gradually calmed down to the point where he finally released the girl's wrist, sank to the floor, and asked the question in a whisper:

"Where did you hear that tune?"

14

"What do you mean, you know that tune?" said Ketola. "What tune?"

"The one Anna plays."

"Anna can't play," said her mother.

"Leave us alone, for God's sake!" Arto Ojaranta shouted. He put his arms round Anna, who was clinging to his shoulder and sobbing uncontrollably.

They were standing over Joentaa.

He was sitting on the floor, leaning against the piano. It's all over, he thought. He could feel the strength draining from his body.

"I know that tune . . . The murderer played it . . ."

"What?" Ketola was staring down at him with a grotesquely distorted expression. Joentaa almost laughed, although there was nothing to laugh at.

"I heard that tune. I stood beside the man while he played it, and he told me he'd composed it himself."

Ketola went on staring at him, puzzled but attentive.

"He works at the Handicrafts Museum—Johann Berg visited it the day he died. And Anna knows the tune . . ."

"But he was a piano tuner," Anna whispered.

"What?" Ketola turned to face her.

"He came to tune the piano," she whispered.

"When?"

"I don't know . . ."

"When was it?" Ketola barked.

"Stop yelling, damn you!" Ojaranta shouted. "Leave the girl alone!"

"Anna," said her mother, "answer the question!"

"Listen," Ketola said, striving to sound friendly, "I have to know when it was. It's very important to me."

"It was the day before Aunt Laura . . ."

"Yes?"

"The day before she . . ."

"You're tormenting the girl, can't you see?" said Ojaranta.

"Aunt Laura wasn't there the next day," Anna shouted. "Something bad happened to her."

Her words seemed to resonate in the silence.

"This man," said Ketola, "he came to tune the piano and Aunt Laura let him in?"

"Yes, she said it would be a good thing. She said I'd find playing the piano more fun, and Kerttu would be happy too, that's Aunt Laura's sister, because Kerttu can play very well and she's bound to know when a piano doesn't sound right."

"And this man taught you the tune?"

"Yes. He was really only there to look at the piano, but he taught me to play the tune as well. He didn't get impatient like . . ." Anna looked at her mother sheepishly.

"Go on, Anna," Raija told her.

"He stayed until I could play the tune, and it made him very happy, I think . . . although he didn't say much . . ."

"And then he left?"

Anna nodded. "Aunt Laura said he would be coming back the next day to tune the piano some more."

"But you weren't there the next day?"

"No, Mummy came back from her holiday . . ."

Ketola nodded. He rose and gently patted Anna's head. Joentaa particularly noticed this gesture because it was uncharacteristic of him, but then, much of what Ketola was doing today failed to fit Joentaa's mental picture of him.

Ketola had already put on his overcoat and was standing in the doorway. "Kimmo," was all he said.

Joentaa got up off the floor feeling dizzy and weak in the legs. He would have to apologize to Anna later, he told himself.

Ketola drove. Sitting beside him and gazing through the windshield at the dazzling, snowy landscape, Joentaa felt his strength gradually returning. It wasn't over yet. In a way, it was only just beginning.

"What's the man's name?" Ketola asked.

Joentaa searched his memory. It had been an unusual name, he recalled. "Lehmus . . . Vesa Lehmus."

"What's he like? Give me a thumbnail sketch."

"Quiet. Slim, self-effacing. Affable . . ."

Ketola nodded. "He knows you," he said. "It'll be best if we park the car a little way off and I go in on my own. He won't have time to grasp what's happening. What exactly does he do at the museum?"

"A bit of everything, I think. He guided the Swedish tour group round the buildings. He knows a great deal about them. The girl at the desk sounded very impressed by his expertise."

"And he played the piano while you were there?"

Joentaa nodded. "There's an upright in the café. He was playing it then. I . . . envied his ability to play so well . . . Anna played the tune too, over and over . . . I could have prevented Jaana Ilander's murder if I'd placed it sooner . . ."

Ketola made no comment.

"I kept thinking I'd known the tune as a child, but I was wrong. I knew that I knew it, but somehow I didn't put it in the right context."

"Why not look at the whole thing from another angle, Kimmo?" Joentaa sensed Ketola was watching him. "It's remarkable that you recognized the tune at all."

Joentaa said nothing. He suddenly remembered that the man, Vesa Lehmus, had been dressed entirely in black, in a single color, like the man whom Kati Itkonen had seen on the beach. Why hadn't he thought of that before?

He glanced at Ketola, who was driving very fast but seemed in full command of himself. Ketola was being so calm, so self-assured. Perhaps it had something to do with his son—perhaps the boy was improving. Joentaa hoped so.

Ketola parked on the riverbank and got out. "I won't be long," was all he said, but Joentaa could sense his underlying excitement. He stared after him, watched him striding toward the open-air museum's cluster of old wooden buildings in that purposeful, jerky manner of his. He had expected Ketola to ask for backup, but perhaps it was better this way. Vesa Lehmus would be taken by surprise. Joentaa couldn't imagine that the quiet, rather languid-looking young man would try to make a run for it. On the other hand, it had never occurred to him that Lehmus might be the murderer, even though he closely resembled the man they were looking for. Quiet, unobtrusive . . . Why had he never thought of Vesa Lehmus?

He saw Ketola talking to the girl in the little ticket office. He saw her shake her head, then shrug uncomprehendingly.

Joentaa itched to know what she was saying. He itched to get out, but he forced himself to remain calm and stay put. Ketola would wrap things up.

Ketola terminated his conversation with the girl and disappeared behind the buildings. The girl seemed unconcerned. He had obviously pretended it was a routine matter.

He didn't reappear for some time. The girl continued to sit in her hut, motionless. The chill sunlight seemed to have frozen the scene in time.

Joentaa could still feel the numbness, the petrifaction that had gripped him within moments when enlightenment dawned and he'd sunk to the floor at Anna's side.

He must apologize to Anna . . .

He was finding it difficult to think clearly. Somehow he couldn't really grasp that Ketola, a couple of hundred yards away in this idyllic cluster of old buildings, was in the act of arresting the murderer.

But where had Ketola got to?

He had to do something, he couldn't just sit there in the car.

He remembered how afraid he'd felt. Afraid of the murderer's arrest. Afraid because the enigma that was taking his mind off Sanna's death would dissolve into thin air once the murderer acquired a face.

The murderer did have a face now.

A group of cheerful tourists sauntered toward the old buildings and bought tickets from the girl at the desk.

Joentaa felt he had to do something—anything. What if Lehmus had a gun? What if he lost his head?

But the murderer had never used a gun to kill . . .

Armed with brochures and instructions, the tourists disappeared among the buildings.

Joentaa couldn't stand it any longer. He got out, intending to go over to the ticket office, but forced himself not to. Leaning against the car, he craned his neck in the direction of the museum precincts and tried at least to hear something. Ketola's voice, perhaps, calling him . . .

He heard laughter. The tourists, presumably.

Perhaps he should have insisted on calling for backup. Why should Ketola, of all people, be responsible for arresting the man? Ketola had been out of control for weeks. He was calm today, yes, but as unpredictable as the murderer himself.

Joentaa stared at the girl in the ticket office. She was sitting there looking relaxed, but that didn't reassure him. Something was wrong.

He was just about to make for the entrance when Ketola reappeared. Visibly agitated now, he spoke urgently to the girl at the desk. She nodded several times, looking bewildered by what he was saying. He reached into his overcoat pocket and fished out his cell phone. Having issued some brief instructions, he spoke further to the girl, then turned and made for the car at a run.

"He isn't here," he called when he was within earshot.

"Where is he?" asked Joentaa.

"The girl at the desk didn't know. She hasn't seen him today, but she thought he might have got here before her, so I went inside and looked around. Not a sign of him. Then the girl consulted her timetable and was kind enough to inform me that Lehmus has taken the day off. She gave me his address. We must go there immediately. I've told Heinonen to take care of everything else." Ketola gave Joentaa the slip of paper bearing the address. "You take the map, I don't know exactly where it is."

While Ketola was starting the car Joentaa got his bearings with the aid of the street map. "Maaria . . . The first thing to do is to get on the expressway and head in the direction of Tampere . . ."

Joentaa located the street after a brief search. Maaria was a small place, a village a few miles from Turku. He stared at the slip of white paper on which the cashier had written the address in black ink. It was as simple as that. The mystery was reduced to a village, a street, the number of a house.

"Where now?" Ketola growled when they had left Turku behind them.

"Just a minute . . . We turn off right soon, in the direction of Moisio . . ."

There was the signpost already. Ketola swung the wheel just in time to make the exit. "And now?" he asked irritably.

"Maaria should be signposted soon . . ."

It was. The signpost was bent as if someone had tried to swivel it in the opposite direction. Having turned off along the narrow road that led to the village, Ketola slowed down. "Where to now?"

"We're almost there."

"Make sure we don't wind up right outside . . ."

"It's the second . . . no, the third on the left."

Ketola nodded and followed his instructions.

It was one of two blocks of apartments situated in the middle of a wood. Joentaa suspected that buildings like these were unique to Finland. Only Finns would choose to live cheek by jowl with the solitude of the forest outside their front door.

Vesa Lehmus must be living in one of these two long gray slabs which confronted each other like enemies. The apartments themselves, each of which boasted a balcony and two windows, were obviously diminutive. Sandwiched between the two blocks was a playground containing a pair of swings, a climbing frame, and a sandpit almost completely covered with slushy snow. The snowman beside the climbing frame looked as if it might collapse at any moment.

"What's the number?" asked Ketola.

"Just a minute . . . 5B."

Ketola leaned forward and peered at the numbers. "It's over there," he said. "Facing the playground."

Joentaa nodded.

"You wait here," Ketola told him.

"What about Heinonen? Shouldn't he call for some backup?"

"No, we'll wrap this up now," Ketola said, and got out. Joentaa watched him make briskly for the building—and for the man they were after.

Joentaa couldn't help remembering that he had stood right beside their quarry. He had smiled at him and envied his piano-playing.

Ketola was striding resolutely across the playground. Joentaa saw him pat his pocket, presumably to satisfy himself that his gun was where it should be. Joentaa's eyes strayed to the balcony, but there was no one to be seen. He couldn't tell whether anyone was standing at the window, the glass was reflecting the sun. Ketola disappeared inside the building. Joentaa glanced at his watch. He wouldn't wait as long this time.

He decided to give Ketola five minutes.

He stared at the entrance, but nothing happened, no one came out or went in. The two gray buildings made a deserted impression. He felt once again that the scene had frozen, come to a standstill.

He concentrated on the decrepit snowman in the playground until he thought he could see it slowly dissolving in the sun.

He had a sense that everything was going awry. What if he'd been mistaken? If he'd imagined the whole thing? If the tunes had merely been similar? If the piano tuner had simply been a piano tuner quite unconnected with Vesa Lehmus?

But it had been the same tune. It couldn't be a coincidence.

The five minutes were up. Joentaa wrestled with the urge to get out. Another five minutes and he would go in. He told himself that Ketola and Vesa Lehmus would emerge at any moment.

But Ketola didn't appear.

He stared at the entrance, which looked at this distance as if it had been stuck onto the building—as if there was nothing behind it. Then he noticed that someone was on the first-floor balcony. It took him a second or two to grasp who was standing there.

It was Ketola. His face was just a distant blur, but Joentaa could tell he was furious, really furious. For some moments he leaned on the balustrade and stared down at the playground, swaying, fighting off an outburst. Then, with a yell, he swung round and picked something up—a plastic chair. Raising it above his head, he hurled it at the floor with all his might, picked it up, and brought it crashing down again with another ear-splitting bellow.

Joentaa got out of the car and ran toward the building.

15

"Where *is* the bastard?" Ketola roared.

Joentaa tried to catch his breath. "What happened?"

"Nothing, you can see that for yourself! He isn't here!" Ketola made a sweeping gesture. "He's flown the coop, damn it!" He slumped onto a chair beside a wooden table in the middle of the sparsely furnished one-room apartment.

"Are you . . ." Joentaa didn't complete the sentence.

Ketola looked at him sharply. "Am I what?"

"You kicked the door down . . ."

"Oh, so you noticed?"

"But you can't just—"

"Can't just what?"

Mechanically, hoping to evade Ketola's belligerence, Joentaa took out his cell phone but kept an eye on his chief. Ketola seemed to have made him the focus of all his fury.

"Why are you staring at me like that?" Ketola jumped to his feet and came over. Joentaa keyed in a number and forced himself to remain calm. He was relieved to hear Heinonen's ever amiable, unassertive voice.

"Hello, Tuomas, Kimmo here . . ."

Ketola, who was poised to swoop at any moment, stopped short. He seemed to be coming to his senses.

"Hello, Kimmo," said Heinonen. "I know the form, Ketola called me. I'm at the Handicrafts Museum with two colleagues. We're trying to keep everything low-key, so as not to alert the man if he shows up after all."

"Yes, good. We're at his apartment. He isn't here. Ask the girl . . . I can't remember her name . . . the girl at the ticket office . . ."

"Yes?"

"Ask her if she knows of any friends or relations Lehmus could be staying with."

"One moment."

Joentaa heard Heinonen's muffled voice, then the almost inaudible voice of the cashier. After about a minute Heinonen was back again. "She says he has a brother, Tommy Lehmus . . . He lives in Turku . . . 8 Hämenkatu . . . but he works at an old people's home during the day."

"Ask her if she knows where this home is."

"Hang on . . ."

Joentaa saw that Ketola was staring past him with an air of surprise, as if something remarkable was going on behind his back. He swung round abruptly, thinking that Vesa Lehmus had returned and was standing in the doorway, but there was nothing to be seen. Only the shattered door, which was lying on the floor thanks to Ketola's incursion. Ketola walked past him and paused on the threshold, looking quite calm again. His appearance betrayed no hint of his furious outburst or the violence with which he'd kicked the door down.

Joentaa had never seen such a badly maltreated door. Ketola had seemed so calm and self-controlled all morning, as he did now, but what good was that if he blew up so suddenly between times?

Heinonen was back on the line. "The girl knew the name of the home. It's Sinivuori, I've looked up the address . . . Are you there?"

"Yes, sorry. What's the address?"

"It's Kaukvuorenkatu, 42 to 44. Unless I'm mistaken, that's on the outskirts of town."

"Thanks."

"Shall I send a squad car?"

"No, we'll go there ourselves. See you later."

"Check," said Heinonen.

Joentaa terminated the conversation.

"Good idea, excellent," Ketola murmured without taking his eyes off the door, which he'd now propped against the wall. In the passage beyond him were two small children and a man, clearly drunk. The man was sniggering, the children were cautiously trying to steal a look inside the apartment.

Ketola had obviously roused the entire building when he kicked the door down.

"Beat it!" he snapped. "Get lost, there's nothing to see here!" The children ran off, the drunk beat a provocatively leisurely retreat. "You go to this old folk's home," Ketola told Joentaa. "I'll wait here. I can pass the time clearing up the mess I've made." His attempt at a smile was a failure.

Joentaa remembered his plan to have a talk with Ketola, a long talk, but he knew he would never put it into effect.

"I'm sorry," he heard Ketola say when he was already going down the stairs.

16

A s Heinonen had surmised, the old people's home was situated on a grassy knoll on the outskirts of the city. Set in spacious grounds, the long white building seemed to melt into the snowy landscape.

It occurred to Joentaa, as he drove toward it through the grounds, that his mother might feel at home there—many years hence, when the time came. It was a cockeyed idea because Anita would probably never go into a home, nor did he want her to; on the contrary, he would do his utmost to prevent it. He couldn't think why he should be contemplating such a remote and unlikely prospect at that particular moment.

Vesa Lehmus wasn't there—Joentaa suddenly felt quite sure of it. He wasn't in this snow-white building, nor at the Handicrafts Museum, nor at his apartment. Vesa Lehmus had ceased to exist.

He would remain hidden and invisible because he wished to be so . . .

Joentaa's initial impression of the building—the idyllic impression he'd gained from outside—was dispelled as soon as he entered it. He walked down a long, dim corridor without encountering anyone able to assist him. He asked two women for Tommy Lehmus, but they didn't seem to understand. One of them, who was in a wheelchair, was so emaciated that he gave an involuntary start when he caught sight of her.

He nodded to them, forced a smile, and sensed their blank gaze on his back as he walked on.

He climbed a flight of stairs, reflecting how ignorant he was of old age. He had no idea what it entailed and couldn't imagine working in such an institution—couldn't imagine ever being old.

He made his way along another corridor and heard voices. Relieved, he quickened his step. The voices were coming from a big room in which lunch was being prepared. He asked one of the staff for Tommy Lehmus. She knew Tommy Lehmus—she smiled when Joentaa said the name—but she didn't know where he was. She consulted a colleague, who also responded with a shrug.

"You'd better ask the man over there—that's Taneli Pasanen, our director." She pointed to a man deep in conversation at the other end of the room. Joentaa thought he looked very young to be in charge.

"Taneli," the woman called, "this gentleman is looking for Tommy!"

The man turned round and came over to them. He gave Joentaa a look of inquiry. "Yes?" he said.

"I'm looking for a member of your staff, Tommy Lehmus."

"Oh, Tommy . . ." The director's face also broke into a smile. There was something about Tommy Lehmus that seemed to inspire amusement. "I don't know exactly where he is, but we can look for him. What did you want him for?"

"I'm sorry, my name is Joentaa." Joentaa showed his ID.

"Oh," said the director.

"Don't worry, it's only a . . . routine matter."

"I hope so, Tommy isn't the criminal type." The director grinned.

"We're looking for his brother and were hoping he could help us."

"His brother? He certainly isn't here, in fact I don't know if he's ever paid us a visit, but Tommy talks a lot about him. Tommy is . . . well, like a father to him . . . I'm sure he'll be able to help you, come with me."

Joentaa sensed that the man would have liked to pump him. It was only natural that he was curious to know why the CID should be looking for Tommy Lehmus's brother.

"What made you say that Tommy Lehmus is like a father to his brother?" Joentaa asked.

"Well, because both their parents are dead. Tommy was a child when they died—only three years old, I believe. His brother is younger, to the best of my knowledge, so he can't have been more than a baby."

Joentaa made no comment. He sensed the impact of this information. It was irrational of him, he knew, but all his remaining doubts evaporated. He now felt positive that Vesa Lehmus was the man they were after.

He picked out Tommy Lehmus from afar. He didn't know him and had no idea what he looked like, but he instantly grasped why the woman and the director had smiled when asked about him.

Tommy Lehmus was sitting in the midst of a group of old people, who were laughing. While walking along the corridors Joentaa had tried to avoid the eyes that stared at him, possibly with hostility, possibly just with apathy or indifference. He couldn't interpret their gaze, but he sensed that these old folk had ceased to inhabit the world in which he himself lived.

All the more surprised to note the cheerful mood prevailing among Tommy's companions, he grasped that it was Tommy himself who engendered this wholly different atmosphere. Going nearer, he saw that the old people were playing cards. Tommy had just smacked an old lady's wrist. "No cheating!" he cried, and she laughed—they all laughed.

"That's him," said the director.

"Many thanks," Joentaa said. The director, who took the hint, gave him a friendly nod and walked away. Joentaa felt like following suit. He had an urge to turn and walk away too, reluctant to be the disruptive element that wrested Tommy Lehmus away from his charges.

"Excuse me," he said. "Mr. Lehmus?"

Tommy looked up from his cards. "Yes, that's me." He looked into Joentaa's eyes and smiled.

"My name is Joentaa . . . I'd like a quick word with you."

"Of course," said Tommy, getting up. "I'll be right back," he told the others. "Lauri, make sure no one messes with the cards, I've got a first-class hand there."

Lauri, a grizzled little man, promptly cupped his hands protectively over Tommy's cards.

"What can I do for you?" Tommy asked when they were out of earshot.

"I'm a policeman," Joentaa told him. "We're looking for your brother."

"Vesa?" Joentaa saw a flicker of apprehension in his eyes. "What about him?"

"We think he may be able to assist us."

"Has something happened to him?"

"No, no, we simply think he may have some information for us."

"I don't understand. What information?"

"I can't go into details, I'm afraid, but it's essential that we locate your brother."

Tommy stared at Joentaa in silence. He doesn't understand, Joentaa thought. Of course he doesn't, but he suspects something—suspects that something bad has happened.

"Vesa is bound to be at the museum, the Handicrafts Museum. He works there."

"We've already been there. Your brother has taken the day off."

Tommy fell silent. Joentaa could almost see the turmoil in his head.

"Please tell me what it's about."

"As I said . . ."

"Why did you go to the museum, why did you come here? How can Vesa be of help to you?"

"You really mustn't worry."

"Has he . . ."

Joentaa waited.

"You surely aren't looking for Vesa because he's . . . done something?"

"As I said . . ."

"That's quite impossible," Tommy said.

"We simply need to interview him; it'll clarify the whole situation." Joentaa wished it were so. He wished he was wrong, and that Vesa Lehmus had nothing whatever to do with the three murders.

"What gives you the idea that he . . . Surely you must have some reason?"

Joentaa said nothing.

"What's he supposed to have done?"

"I'm sure everything will be sorted out very quickly once we've spoken to him."

"But I want to know what it's about. What's he supposed to have done?"

"I'm afraid I can't say."

"Of course you can! I want to know now!"

"I'd like you to tell me about your brother."

"What?"

"Come with me." Joentaa led the way downstairs. He yearned to go outside, into the open, into the handsome grounds, and breathe some fresh air. It would be easier outside.

"Well, what's it all about?" Tommy called after him.

"I met your brother once . . . at the museum . . . it was a while back," Joentaa said when they were standing outside.

"He never mentioned it."

"It was only a brief conversation. He was playing the piano extremely well."

Tommy nodded. "And he can't read a note, did you know that?"

"Yes, he told me so when I asked about the piece he was playing. He said it was a composition of his own. I got the impression that he's a very private person."

"He certainly is that," Tommy said.

"Do you think it possible that he's hiding something behind that quiet exterior? Phobias or aggressive urges of some kind?"

Tommy looked at him keenly. "I'm not saying another word until you tell me what this is about. Why did you speak to Vesa? Why are you looking for him?"

"We suspect he's killed three people."

Joentaa said it without debating whether he was right to do so. His words took a moment to sink in. Tommy Lehmus came to a halt. He seemed about to say something, but he didn't.

"It's only a suspicion, not a certainty," Joentaa said. "We need to interview him."

Tommy still said nothing. He walked on slowly, heedless of whether or not Joentaa was following him. He went over to a bench and sat down.

"It's only a suspicion, you understand, but we need to interview your brother if we're to resolve matters. That's why it's so important for you to assist us."

"But why?"

"Because you're probably the only person who knows him well."

"Why should you think that Vesa—"

"Can he tune pianos?" Joentaa cut in.

Tommy looked up. He nodded.

"Has he ever worked as a piano tuner? Does he have the relevant equipment?"

"Yes, yes, but what are you getting at?"

"Your brother was playing the piano when I was with him at the museum. One of his own tunes—one that was probably known to him alone."

"Well?"

"One of the victims was at the museum on the day of his death. He belonged to a group of tourists your brother showed around. Your brother must also have met another of the victims, a woman. It seems he tuned her piano the day she died. He must have played that melody."

"That's nonsense, Vesa has worked at the museum for years. Besides, he can't tune pianos properly."

"His expertise is unimportant. If our suspicions are correct, that's how your brother gained access to the first victim's house." Joentaa sensed that he had already said too much, but now that he had started it was a relief to tell Tommy Lehmus everything.

And Tommy Lehmus had to be informed.

"I just don't understand why you . . . It doesn't mean a thing. All right, so Vesa may have tuned this piano, but it still doesn't mean a thing. As for the museum, have you any idea how many people he's shown around the place?"

"It's a strange coincidence that your brother definitely met two of the three victims. We've spent weeks looking for a link, and he seems to be it. I'd like you to tell me where he could be."

"I've no idea. At home? No, of course, you must have looked there . . ."

Joentaa nodded.

"I don't know where he is, nor do I know why he isn't at work today. He hardly ever takes a day off. He's always at the museum—he much prefers it to being at home in his apartment."

"Isn't there any other haunt of his?"

Tommy Lehmus thought for a while, then shook his head. "He's always at the museum or at home in the evenings. He's always at home when I drop in."

"When was the last time you saw him?"

"Quite recently. Three or four days ago."

"Did anything strike you about him? Did he mention a girlfriend, a young woman named Jaana?"

Tommy stared at Joentaa uncomprehendingly. "No, of course not. He's never had a girlfriend."

"How can you be so sure?"

"Because I know all about him—because he tells me everything. If he had a girlfriend he'd tell me at once. He knows how pleased I'd be."

"Why hasn't he ever had a girlfriend?"

Tommy looked at Joentaa keenly. "For one thing, because he's a listener, not a talker, and he keeps quiet when other people are holding forth. Because he prefers his own company."

"I asked you earlier why your brother is so reserved . . . whether his reserve may possibly conceal—"

"Of course he's scared!" Tommy shouted. Joentaa gave a start, and Tommy continued in a quieter voice: "Of course he's scared—he always has been, but he's much better than he used to be. We grew up in an orphanage. Vesa had bad dreams nearly every night."

"Bad dreams about what?"

Tommy thought awhile. "All kinds of things. Some of them were so bizarre, I listened with only half an ear when he told me about them. I do recall one recurrent feature, though: a moon . . . a moon that devoured him."

Joentaa didn't get it, but he nodded. Tommy seemed to be wrestling with some idea, he could tell.

"He did say something odd a little while ago . . ."

Joentaa waited.

"He asked what I would say if he . . . if he was completely different from the way I thought he was—something like that. I didn't know what he meant."

"Look," Joentaa said, "please let me know if your brother turns up." He jotted down his office and private phone numbers on a gas station receipt. "It's vital that we speak to him, understand?"

Tommy nodded, but he didn't appear to have been listening. He was staring past Joentaa at the parking lot and the road beyond it.

Joentaa took his leave. He felt the cold sunlight bite into his face and thought of the moon that had devoured Vesa Lehmus. He thought of Tommy Lehmus, whom he'd taken to on sight—Tommy Lehmus, who had evoked laughter from the old folks he himself had avoided.

While heading back to the city center he remembered Lauri, the grizzled little man whose hands were still, no doubt, protectively cupped over Tommy's cards.

17

It was like a slap in the face, and the slap had numbed him. He looked at Tommy and felt frightened. It was a different kind of fear, far greater and more intense than any he'd felt before.

Why didn't Tommy come over to him? Why didn't he come and tell him that all was well? Why wasn't he laughing, today of all days, when he himself felt like laughing all the time? Tommy was sitting on a bench, staring straight at him, straight at the parking lot, but he hadn't seen him. He was staring past him into space.

The policeman had gone. The policeman hadn't seen him either, although his car was barely twenty yards away. The policeman had looked very sad. Tommy was looking very sad too. Vesa could only guess at his expression from this distance, but he seemed to be crying.

Why was Tommy crying?

He had come equipped with all that was needed to cheer Tommy up. He had brought him some presents: licorice sticks and a bar of nut chocolate, the kind Tommy liked best.

He wanted so much to get out of his car and tell Tommy not to be sad, but he couldn't. He sat there without moving until he grasped that he mustn't on any account get out. He mustn't speak to Tommy, not now. He might never be able to speak to him again, and that thought was so appalling, it buried every other thought beneath it.

The policeman had been talking to Tommy, which meant that something had gone wrong. He must think it over. Only when he grasped what had happened would he know what to do next.

All he knew at the moment was that he mustn't go over to Tommy because Tommy couldn't help him anymore.

He backed the car and drove away from the white building, the home where Tommy worked. He hadn't been there often—it reminded him of the orphanage.

He saw in the rearview mirror that Tommy was still sitting on the bench. He didn't appear to be moving at all, but he grew smaller and smaller.

Tommy would be far away, he thought. Jaana would be far away too. Neither of them would be able to help him, nor would they want to help him until he grasped what he'd done wrong.

18

Daniel Krohn felt that it would always be like this. He would sit on this sofa, staring at a lake through a sheet of glass.

He, Daniel, would always be the same; only the scenery outside would change. It would be white and gray, as now. It would turn green, it would turn orange and dark blue, red and yellow.

And then, sooner or later, it would turn white and gray again.

He would sit motionless on the sofa and watch the scenery change in the same, immutable way.

He sensed that he was smiling. He didn't know how long he'd been smiling or why. He was holding his cell phone, he noticed, but he couldn't recall having taken it out of his pocket. Had he meant to call someone?

Presumably.

Marion, perhaps. Or Oliver.

He had meant to call them ever since his arrival, but he'd spoken to Marion briefly only once and to Oliver not at all. Oliver was probably on the verge of a nervous breakdown because his copy for the politician's pamphlet hadn't arrived.

He hadn't called Oliver, although he'd felt sure he would do so that morning.

He'd slept for hours, leaden-limbed, on the chair in the kitchen. It was almost midday when he awoke, and another tormentingly long spell of inertia had elapsed before he was capable of getting to his feet and debating what to do today.

He wouldn't do anything at all. He wouldn't compose any punchy copy for Oliver and his client, Herr Glanz. He hadn't the least desire to do so, and the thought of Oliver, who made mincemeat of any member of the agency who crossed him, left him cold.

For a while he'd considered doing some research on Jaana Ilander.

The thought appealed to him as it had during the night, when he couldn't sleep—the thought of speaking to people who had known her. People who could tell him what Jaana had been doing with herself, what she was like and whether she had often mentioned him.

Yes, that would really interest him. Perhaps Jaana had spoken of him constantly—perhaps he was a byword with all the people Jaana had been fond of. It would really interest him to know if she'd told her friends about him. It would interest him to know whether she'd spoken of him with affection or detestation.

Still, she'd left him an apartment. Thoroughly odd and absurd though this was, it pleased him in a way. But it was probably invalid anyway, this will he had yet to set eyes on . . .

He flopped onto the sofa.

He thought of Marion. Marion was bound to be worried.

Marion shouted at him over trivialities. She was strident and combative, yet she probably worried about him far more than he chose to believe. He sometimes wished that she would at last do something truly objectionable. If she were unfaithful to him, for instance, he would have an excuse to shout at her himself and threaten divorce. But Marion was insufferably faithful, or so he supposed at least. Insufferable though this was, it was gratifying as well.

He would probably go berserk if Marion cheated on him.

His thoughts turned to Tina, the delectable young theology student he'd omitted to call. He almost felt a trifle proud of this, almost imagined that he'd done Marion a good turn by neglecting Tina. All that faintly disappointed him was that Tina hadn't tried to reach him.

He considered inquiring after Teemu, Jaana's nephew, but was relieved when he realized this was impossible.

Joentaa had taken the car and driven off. He was alone in this house, snowed up in a forest. He had no idea of the direction in which the city lay, and anyway, he would have had to walk for hours. There was simply no point.

Besides, he wouldn't have known where to start. He didn't know anyone who had known Jaana Ilander and he had no idea where to find this Teemu.

He stared at the lake, a broad white expanse of ice, and was relieved to note that exhaustion was gaining the upper hand over nausea.

He had probably got out his cell phone to call Marion. Certainly not Oliver. Oliver he didn't give a shit about, but Marion was entitled to know how he was and what he proposed to do . . . But what was the use of calling Marion simply to tell her that he couldn't supply an answer to either question.

Gazing through the glass at the expanse of ice, he wondered why he hadn't left long ago. What was stopping him? He had absolutely no business here, that was obvious. On the other hand, Marion was waiting for him at home, and if he did something quickly—if he finally succeeded in returning to reality—he might still have a chance of placating Oliver and Herr Glanz and keeping his job.

The light began to fade early in the afternoon.

He thought of the man who had murdered Jaana Ilander. So far, he hadn't grasped the background to the whole affair or the reason why this man had killed her. The policeman, Joentaa, seemed to know something; at least he knew that the murderer was a man. A man who had evidently killed more than once. There must be some connection between his victims, some significance . . . Daniel suddenly understood that this man was prompting him to stay on.

Sooner or later he would speak to this man. He would stay on until they met face-to-face. Then he would ask him why he'd done all these things. The man probably wouldn't understand him because they didn't speak the same language, but he would find some way of surmounting that barrier.

He would question the man, listen to his answer, and understand it.

Then, the affair would be behind him. Then, he would fly home.

Vesa Lehmus had disappeared.

He hadn't shown up either at the Handicrafts Museum or at his apartment, and he had slipped through the dense network of roadblocks.

Joentaa peered at cars' license plates and scanned passersby in the street while driving home, and more than once he thought he caught a momentary glimpse of Vesa Lehmus.

He left the city center behind and concentrated on the road.

It was too late in any case.

He couldn't shake off the thought that Jaana Ilander would still be alive if he'd caught on more quickly, and he now knew that he would never be rid of it.

He had to leave the car on the impassable forest track, as before, and trudge home through the knee-deep snow. He caught sight of Liisa in her kitchen as he passed the Laaksonens' house.

His house, Sanna's house, was in darkness. It looked lifeless, and Joentaa reflected that he didn't want to stay there, couldn't stay there. He knew Sanna would have wanted him to, but it was impossible. He would have to drive or fly away soon, far away, to some place that had absolutely no connection with her.

The night after Sanna's funeral he had taken out his gun and looked at it for a while, but he'd known that he would not act on the idea. He'd sensed that his fear was too great—his fear of the final moment that had overtaken Sanna in her sleep.

Laura Ojaranta, Johann Berg, and Jaana Ilander had also been caught unaware in their sleep.

He wondered why there weren't any lights on.

The notion that Daniel might not be there alarmed him. He'd found it easier to come home since Daniel's arrival on the scene.

He opened the front door and snapped on the hall light.

"Daniel?" he called.

No answer.

Cautiously, he pushed open the living-room door and peered through the gloom at the frozen gray lake lying in the moonlight. His fear of the winter had never been so intense.

He had always been scared of the cold and omnipresent darkness. It had been dark when he cycled to school in the morning and dark when he cycled back at lunchtime, and each time he'd been afraid of freezing to death before he got home.

The first light winter in his life had been the one when he met Sanna.

Daniel was stretched out asleep on the sofa.

Joentaa turned away, quietly closed the door behind him, and went into the kitchen. He turned on the light, ran himself a glass of water, and drank it. Roope, the boy from the house next door, was walking past pulling a toboggan. Joentaa recalled that it was Roope and his friends who had woken him when he was lying on the dock the day after Sanna's death. He wondered if the boy still remembered that day and his curious behavior.

He sat down at the kitchen table and heard the tune Vesa Lehmus had been playing, the one that had haunted him ever since it crystallized out of Anna's seemingly random succession of notes. It was a charming melody. He almost felt that it had some connection with himself, with Sanna's death and his own fear.

He almost felt that this melody could have helped him, had it not been pounding away in his head with such painful insistence.

20

The policeman had been looking unhappy again. He always did. Vesa had noticed this the first time he saw him at the Handicrafts Museum. He had fancied that his own fear was mirrored in the policeman's eyes.

He had thought of the policeman more than once in the last few weeks, and that thought had each time been associated with a wish to ask him what he was afraid of.

Perhaps he could help the policeman.

He had messed things up completely, he realized that now, and this knowledge was eating its way through his body until he could hardly breathe.

He had messed things up completely, but it wasn't too late. He would speak to the policeman and tell him everything, tell him the reason for it all. Then he would feel better.

His legs were aching. It was cold, his shoes and socks were sodden, and the slush came up to his knees.

He had hidden among the trees when the policeman came home. The policeman had very nearly spotted him. Vesa hadn't seen him coming until the last moment. He'd been standing in the front garden, checking to see if the name on the mailbox was correct. *Sanna and Kimmo Joentaa.*

Kimmo Joentaa had a very nice house, the sort of house he himself would have liked to live in. He still didn't know what it looked like inside, but he felt quite sure he would approve of it.

He would ask the policeman why he was so sad.

He straightened up when the kitchen light went on. He saw the policeman staring out of the window in his direction, but he couldn't possibly be seen among the trees. He heard footsteps. A boy walked past pulling a toboggan behind him and singing softly to himself.

He had gone tobogganing with Tommy a few times. Not often. He always found it such an effort to do things. Tommy had sometimes got annoyed and accused him of being lazy, and in the end Tommy had given up asking him.

He must speak to the policeman and explain the whole thing. He wouldn't be able to look Tommy in the eye again until everything was sorted out.

The worst of it was, the policeman mightn't understand. He might be wrong about him.

But he mustn't think like that.

He waited among the trees until the moon grew so big, he couldn't bear the sight of it any longer. Then he emerged and walked toward the house, which was in darkness again. The policeman had turned off the light.

The house ahead of him grew bigger and more real as he approached it. So did his fear of the first words he would have to utter before his conversation with the policeman could begin. He'd always found the first words difficult, in fact many of his conversations had foundered on them. Sometimes they occurred to him later, long after the opportunity had passed—years later, when no one would ever hear them.

He must think out those first words with care. They were important—they were the basis of everything.

He reached the door and touched it with his hands.

Then he turned round, leaned against it, and sank to the ground.

He must work out how to explain everything to the policeman in a single sentence.

He couldn't recall ever having been so cold. The sensation was an agreeable one. It proved he was alive, proved that he would die, created instant clarity, and was so intense that even the moon congealed behind his eyes.

Perhaps he would begin by telling the policeman about his fear.

He would have to explain that this fear was different from other people's. The policeman would understand that. He felt sure he'd detected a fear in the man's eyes that resembled his own.

He would tell him about Jaana and the crucial moment when she'd devoured him.

What mattered most was Jaana's return.

He shut his eyes and fancied that everything would instantly dissolve into a void if he managed to say the right words.

He tried to imagine that void. He'd felt so close to it, but he'd been mistaken.

He was so cold, he could scarcely move anymore.

Only a little colder, and the moon would explode before his eyes. He didn't know when that would be or what lay beyond, but it was bound to be better than all that had gone before.

He felt himself subsiding further, pondering the first words he would say when the policeman opened the door.

What if he fell asleep and this time failed to wake up?

Perhaps he would begin with that.

With his fear of sleep.

With his fear of death.

With his fear of himself.

21

L ife was a depressing, tiring, shitty business.

His mother was getting him down.

"Get a move on!" she called after him.

As if it was his fault he had to live in this shitty forest, cut off from the outside world. He had a longer walk to the bus stop than anyone else in his class. He was dog-tired by the time he got there every morning—so tired he wished the day was over.

The bus was bound to have gone already. He was later than usual today, and he hadn't the least desire to hurry.

Yesterday had been fun, what with the tobogganing and the snowball fight. That was something, at least.

He was nearing the policeman's house. Recently he'd had a funny feeling whenever he passed it. His mother had told him that Mr. Joentaa's wife had died. The news had preyed on his mind for ages. He didn't show it, of course, but it had distressed him and made him feel uneasy.

Mr. Joentaa's wife, Sanna Joentaa, had been a very beautiful woman. Although they'd never exchanged more than a few words, he had always watched her when she was swimming in the lake. He had sometimes thought that the policeman was very lucky, and that he wanted a wife like her, later on—exactly like her.

It had never occurred to him that a woman like her could die.

He felt sorry for the policeman, but lately he'd also felt uneasy when he met him. The man was so . . . so quiet and sad. He didn't seem to be with it at all. On one occasion he'd said good morning to him, but Mr. Joentaa hadn't heard. He'd just walked past with his head down.

He speeded up when he drew level with the house. He was late, and the bus would have left if he didn't hurry. He wanted to get past without looking. Mr. Joentaa must be left in peace, his mother had expressly told him that some time ago, and the house always reminded him of the beautiful woman. He thought of the grave in which she must be lying, and of the fact that her body would sooner or later decay, but he looked across at the house despite himself, he simply couldn't help it.

Someone was sitting there.

Someone was sitting outside the front door, asleep.

He wanted to walk on, wanted nothing to do with it.

Mr. Joentaa must be left in peace, his mother had told him.

He lowered his eyes and forced himself to walk on. He was past the house already.

But how could anyone sleep in this icy cold?

He turned and ran back to the house, approached the sleeping man and hoped he would wake up at once. He spoke to him when he was still a few yards away, but the man didn't stir. He went right up to him and said: "Hey, wake up!" But the man slept on.

He stood there uncertainly for a moment or two, then rang the doorbell. While waiting he reflected that he would miss the bus. He felt ashamed of the thought, but at least he would have something to tell the others tomorrow, when they asked why he hadn't turned up for school.

22

A shrill, recurrent sound.

Midway between dream and reality, Joentaa grasped that this shrill sound was most important. It didn't belong in his dream. It was something new, something that harbored a solution.

He sloughed off the dream and forced himself to get up.

Someone was ringing the doorbell.

He tried to remember the dream as he set off for the front door, but it was gone. He checked the time on the video recorder: half past six.

He hadn't fallen asleep until six, or thereabouts.

He tried to open the door, but it jammed. He pushed it open a crack.

"There's someone lying here," said a voice.

He peered through the crack. "Roope?"

"Someone's lying here," Roope repeated.

The boy's face was pale, white as the snow behind him.

Joentaa threw his weight against the door. He knew what he would see before he had a chance to pursue the thought to its conclusion. He knew who was lying propped against his front door. He squeezed through the narrow opening.

"What's the matter with him?" Roope asked.

Joentaa didn't reply. He was staring down at Vesa Lehmus. He should call an ambulance, he knew, but he knew it was too late.

He saw Daniel squinting blearily through the crack. "What is it?" Daniel asked.

Looking into his eyes, Joentaa sensed that something was dissolving, slipping through his fingers—something he'd clung to very tightly. The paroxysm of weeping took him by surprise. He lost control of himself within seconds, let out a cry, saw Roope flinch and stare at him open-mouthed, saw Daniel, abruptly wide awake, squeeze past the door with his face contorted, felt his legs giving way, felt he was being engulfed by an immense wave containing all that was pent up inside him.

"Who is it?" he heard Daniel shout.

He tried to answer but he couldn't. This is crazy, he thought. He hadn't wept when Sanna died. He hadn't wept when Laura Ojaranta, Johann Berg, and Jaana Ilander died.

He was weeping for Vesa Lehmus, the murderer.

"He was a brilliant pianist," he said.

Daniel stared at him dumbfounded. He didn't know himself what he was saying.

"Is that . . . ?" asked Daniel.

Joentaa nodded. He was trembling, but his sobs were gradually subsiding.

"We must call emergency," he said.

"But . . ."

"Get the phone!"

Daniel disappeared into the house.

Joentaa felt his self-control returning. He was calm now. He could feel himself seething below the surface, but he was calm.

"Roope, go home."

Roope stood rooted to the spot.

Joentaa tried to imagine what effect this must be having on the boy. "Please go home and stay there. I'll come to see you later, we must . . . talk about this. Understand?"

"I don't want to go home," Roope said.

He thought for a moment. "All right, come inside. I'll make you some . . . cocoa?"

Roope nodded.

"We mustn't move this man. Can you get past?"

Roope nodded and squeezed through the opening.

Daniel returned with the phone.

"Thanks," said Joentaa. "Could you make the boy some cocoa?"

"Of course," Daniel said after a momentary pause. He turned and went inside again.

Joentaa called an ambulance. He looked down at the man who was slumped against his front door—who had frozen to death outside his front door. He must have been there for a very long time. All night long. Why?

Why had Vesa Lehmus come to him?

Why hadn't he sensed that he was there?

He dialed Ketola's home number. He knew it by heart, although he'd never called it before.

Ketola answered at once. He sounded as if he'd been awake for hours.

"It's over," Joentaa told him.

No response.

"Vesa Lehmus is lying outside my front door. He's dead."

There was a long pause. "I'll be right over," Ketola said eventually, and hung up.

Joentaa remained standing over the dead man with the phone in his hand. His mind went back to the time he'd been so close to him that day at the museum.

Ketola appeared in due course.

Niemi appeared.

Niemi's team appeared.

So did Heinonen and Grönholm.

Joentaa left them and went into the kitchen. He sat down facing Roope and watched him sipping his cocoa—slowly, with a look of inquiry.

Daniel leaned against the wall and said nothing.

"I won't be going to school today," Roope said.

"No."

"Who is the man?" Roope asked.

Joentaa looked up. "I don't know. I think he wanted to speak to me. It was important to him, I think, but I don't know what he wanted to tell me."

"You knew him, though?"

Joentaa shook his head.

Daniel heaved himself away from the wall and left the room, slamming the door behind him.

Roope gave a jump. "What's the matter with him?" he asked.

"Back in a minute," Joentaa said, and hurried after Daniel, who had just slammed the bedroom door as well.

He hesitated for a second, then gingerly opened the door. For a moment he imagined that Sanna would be behind it, not Daniel; that Sanna was well and Daniel didn't exist—that Daniel was no more alive than the man lying outside his front door.

Daniel turned his back.

"What is it?" Joentaa asked.

"Nothing."

"You know who—"

"Of course I do!" Daniel snapped. He turned and came up to Joentaa. "He's the reason I'm here. I wanted to speak to the man, beat him up, bash his brains out!"

Joentaa retreated a step.

Daniel seemed to quiet gradually. He flopped down on the bed. "What was his name?" he asked.

"Vesa Lehmus."

"Sounds Finnish."

"He was—"

"No, shut up, I don't want to know any more!" Daniel began to laugh.

"But . . ."

"I don't want to know any more. I know enough, it's all quite clear now." Daniel got up and pushed past Joentaa. For some reason, he didn't know why, Joentaa tried to bar his path.

Daniel was looking for something in his jacket pocket. "Damn it," he muttered to himself, "where is the confounded thing?" Successful at last, he produced his cell phone from the pocket and held it out. "Call the airport and book me a seat on the next flight to Frankfurt."

Disconcerted, Joentaa took the cell phone from his hand.

"Mind doing me that little favor?" Daniel said. He was grinning, but Joentaa could sense his suppressed fury.

Joentaa nodded.

"You're one in a million," said Daniel. He slapped Joentaa on the back and left the room, slamming the door behind him again.

Joentaa waited awhile. He was trying to think, trying to put himself in Daniel's place, but he failed.

He thought of Sanna.

He had spent only two periods of any length alone in this room since Sanna's death. Once when making up the bed for her parents and once when doing the same for Daniel. With fresh sheets.

The old ones, which reminded him of Sanna, he'd thrown away. It's over, he thought.

He left the room and went to look up the number of the Finnair office. It occurred to him as he thumbed through the phone book that he must have a word with Roope. He must tell the doctor that Roope had found the man.

Ketola's penetrating voice drifted in from outside. Thoroughly trans- figured and in command of the situation, Ketola was telling Grönholm and Heinonen what to do.

He heard the ringing tone and wondered if the ambulance men had taken Vesa Lehmus away.

A faint, distant female voice recited some departure times. He thanked the woman. She wished him good day and a good flight.

"There's a Finnair flight leaving Helsinki at five-thirty this after- noon. You can book at the airport, there are plenty of seats," Joentaa told Daniel, and handed back his cell phone. Daniel was sitting across the kitchen table from Roope.

"What did you say?" Roope asked.

"He's flying home to Germany," Joentaa told him, indicating Daniel.

"What was that?" asked Daniel.

"He wanted to know what I said and I told him you were flying home to Germany."

Daniel nodded.

"I've been to Germany," Roope said. "I went to Hamburg on the ferry."

"What did he say?" asked Daniel.

"He says he's been to Germany. To Hamburg."

Daniel nodded again. "That man outside," he said after a pause, "what did you say his name was?"

"Vesa Lehmus."

"Why . . . did he do it? Why did he kill Jaana?"

"I don't know," said Joentaa.

"He must have had some reason!"

"I think he liked her," Joentaa said.

Daniel gave a little bark of laughter. "Oh, sure, of course." He drew a deep breath.

Joentaa saw his face slowly crumple.

"Why is the German crying?" Roope asked.

23

Everything was dwindling very rapidly.

Joentaa was somewhere down there, Daniel reflected; smaller than a matchstick man—unimaginably small. Then Finland disappeared and the plane was engulfed in cloud.

The captain, in fractured German, spoke of rain and above-zero temperatures in Frankfurt, of hours and minutes, of arriving on schedule.

Daniel had shaken hands with Joentaa.

Joentaa had insisted on driving him from Turku to Helsinki airport. The drive had taken a good two hours, and neither of them had said a word in all that time.

Daniel had shaken hands with Joentaa. To his own surprise, he hadn't released the policeman's hand for quite a while.

Joentaa was now a little speck somewhere down below the cloud. Everything—the beach café, the house in the forest, the frozen lake, his photograph on the bedside table, and the man outside the door— everything was now so small he would never be able to see it again, however closely he looked. Up here in the air, as one floated along, everything was reduced to zero.

He needn't worry anymore.

He hadn't called Marion.

He would do so as soon as he landed in Frankfurt.

Marion would give him hell for not having called.

Marion would be pleased.

The flight attendant offered him a drink, but he declined it.

The seat beside him was unoccupied. The plane was underbooked.

It was nice not having anyone in the seat next to him. It would give him a chance to think.

He must concentrate on what lay ahead.

Marion.

Oliver, whom he would pacify. It would be quite easy.

He wanted to call Marion and was annoyed with himself for not having done so before takeoff. He wanted to hear her voice, make sure that all was well with her.

Marion would ask how his trip had gone and why he hadn't called.

He wouldn't hold anything back. He would tell her everything, all he knew. He would use the flight to straighten it out in his head.

Marion would be shocked when he told her about the candlelit apartment and the man who had frozen to death.

The flight attendant tried to serve him some food, but he declined it.

Shortly before they parted Joentaa had asked him about the apartment, his inheritance. Daniel had merely looked at him without answering because he didn't know what to say.

"I'll be in touch," he called when the passport officer had checked his passport.

He could sense Joentaa's eyes on his back.

Joentaa had waited until he passed through baggage control and disappeared from view.

He would tell Marion about Kimmo Joentaa. It would interest him to hear her assessment of the man. Marion was a good judge of people.

A surprising idea flashed through his head: perhaps he would visit Joentaa with Marion. He pictured the three of them sitting in the living room and Marion saying how beautiful the lake looked.

He would tell her about that lake.

The flight attendant offered him a drink again, and again he declined.

She frowned, hesitated for a moment, then ventured to ask if everything was all right.

"Absolutely fine," he said.

He called Marion as soon as he landed.

Her response was predictable. She shouted at him, upbraided him, and ended by saying: "I'll come right away."

He could detect a mixture of pleasure and pain behind the anger in her voice.

While waiting for his suitcase in the baggage hall he deleted Tina's phone number from his cell phone.

Marion didn't keep him waiting long.

She hugged him.

When they were sitting in the car she asked how his trip had gone.

He said nothing, just looked at her.

"Did you get the will business sorted out?"

He shook his head. "Not quite. I still don't know if it's valid. I'll keep in touch with the policeman."

"This policeman . . . you stayed at his place?"

He nodded.

"Is . . . Do they know anything about the background . . . I mean, why this woman, what was her name?"

"Jaana Ilander."

"Do they know who murdered her?"

He looked at Marion. Her manner suggested that the dark road ahead was claiming her full attention. She was trying to put her questions casually, but he could tell how much they mattered to her.

He was amazed at how well he knew her—how easily he could read her mind.

"Can I tell you everything later?" he said.

"Why not now?"

"This whole business . . . it took me by surprise. It was bewildering, that's all, and it still is."

Marion nodded. He knew she was finding it hard, but she would be patient. She would wait until he was ready to answer her questions.

"I love you," he said.

He was looking at the road, but out of the corner of his eye he thought he saw her give a little start. He sensed her looking at him, sensed that she was pleased.

"It's a long time since you said that," she said when they pulled up at a red light.

She looked into his eyes.

She smiled, puzzled and disconcerted.

"I know," he said. He would never tell Marion everything, he reflected. He would keep quiet about Tina and the other women, whose names were unimportant now.

"I love you," he repeated. And because Marion was staring at him—because she couldn't take her eyes off him—he added: "They won't get any greener."

24

J oentaa was alone tonight.

He sat on the sofa and stared out at the lake, a gray expanse in the darkness.

He thought of Roope. He pictured the boy in bed, staring at the ceiling, unable to sleep.

He would go to the funeral, he told himself. He resolved to do so come what may.

He would speak to Tommy Lehmus.

He would stand beside him during the funeral.

He pictured the funeral itself. In his mind's eye, only he and Tommy Lehmus were there. And a pastor who was reading something, a text Tommy Lehmus had given him—a text that very accurately defined who Vesa, his brother, had been.

He would understand every word.

He would have a talk with Roope.

And with Ketola.

Ketola had been the last to leave.

"No one must know that the man died here," Ketola had told him. "In the forest, that's what we'll say. I'll see to it."

Joentaa nodded.

"He'll soon be forgotten," Ketola said. "Newspapers don't like unobtrusive deaths. Another few days and they'll be through with him."

Joentaa nodded.

Ketola asked if he could account for the fact that Vesa Lehmus had come to see him in particular.

"Perhaps he thought I was the only person he could talk to."

"Why?" Ketola asked.

Joentaa hadn't been able to answer that question.

When Ketola was already standing outside, Joentaa inquired after his son.

"Better," said Ketola.

He would call Annette Söderström and thank her for that day in Stockholm.

He would call Daniel to make sure he'd got home safely.

He had to do something.

Something important.

He had left it too long.

He got up and went into the bedroom.

He opened the wardrobe, Sanna's wardrobe, which was empty. He had stuffed her clothes into a blue trash bag and taken it down to the cellar. He'd intended to throw it away, but he'd turned back halfway.

The wardrobe was empty save for the plastic bag.

The plastic bag containing Sanna's things from the hospital.

He took out the book she hadn't finished reading.

He went into the living room, turned on the light, sat down, and started to read.

He forced himself to read on, on and on, careful not to skip a single word.

He knew exactly which passages Sanna had laughed at.

When he'd read the last sentence he shut the book and put it on the table in front of him.

It was a nice story, one in which all ended well. Sanna had always liked books with upbeat endings. If she was reading a novel and suspected that it wouldn't end happily, she would give it to him and ask him to read the final chapter. He would then tell her whether it ended happily or unhappily. If it ended unhappily, she wouldn't read on.

He got up and went outside to tell Sanna how the book she hadn't finished ended.

He walked down to the lake. The rickety dock gave under his weight, but he was in no danger of being sucked down into the water, because the water was ice.

He would be able to walk on it.

He did so.

He started to tell Sanna how the book ended.

He went on walking until he'd finished telling her the story.

He turned and saw the house, Sanna's house, in the distance. He was almost at the other side.

He sat down on the ice.

He saw the house, Sanna's house, as a black silhouette.

He felt quite certain that Sanna hadn't heard a word of what he'd just told her.

But that didn't matter.

He would call Anita and tell her she needn't worry about him.

He shouted.

He shouted until he could shout no more.

From now on he would always do that when he couldn't bear it any longer.

He got up and retraced his steps.

As he walked toward the house he suddenly knew he would stay there, go on living there.

His legs were heavy when he reached it.

He turned out the light and lay down on the sofa. He thought he wouldn't be able to sleep, that he would lie awake, but he fell asleep quickly.

Just before sleep engulfed him he thought of Vesa Lehmus, who had been lying outside his door.

Something was over, he thought.

Something was beginning.

He saw Sanna.

She was coming toward him.

She called something to him. A question.

She asked if he could see her riding a red horse.

Yes, he called back.

She was coming toward him, but she came no nearer.

He knew she would come no nearer, she would always be far away, but that didn't matter.

He ran toward her.

Yes, he cried, I can see you!

Sanna was laughing, and he knew why: it was because she detected something new, a new note in his voice.

He ran toward her. He would never reach her, but that didn't matter. What mattered was that he was running.

I can see you! he called.

She laughed. Reproachfully, affectionately.

At last, she cried.

At last.

He ran on.

He would never stop running again.

He would never again have to lie when she asked him that question.

I can see you! he called.

I can see you!

He really could see her.